Creative Collections

SPRINGFIELD WRITERS' GUILD

Cover Photo
Missouri Ozarks

Cover Design
Sharon Kizziah-Holmes

Production Coordinators
Wayne E. Groner and Sharon Kizziah-Holmes

Paperback-Press
an imprint of A & S Publishing
A & S Holmes, Inc.

ISBN: 0692461485
ISBN-13: 978-0692461488

CONTENTS

Acknowledgments

Springfield Writers' Guild is pleased to bring you our first member-submitted anthology. Represented are established authors and freelance writers, and those who were not published before this anthology. It's an awesome experience being published the first time. We applaud the courage and talent of our newbies, who can now affirm their status as published writers.

We are indebted to author Kevin Henderson, Ph.D., assistant professor of English at Drury University and Interim Director of the University Writing Center, who was an early and strong supporter of the anthology. He directed us to Drury instructor Matt Lemmon's Editing and Publishing class for copyediting. Students were enthusiastic about working in a real-world publishing experience. Copyeditors were Danielle Applegate, Debra Course, Meghan Freeman, Haley Jackson, Sarah Lee, Ryan Mitchem, Tanner Roberts, and Dawn Wood.

Guild member Sharon-Kizziah Holmes, founder and owner of Paperback-Press, Inc., guided the publishing process and designed the cover. She is a professional from the get-go and a true friend.

The title, *Creative Collections*, is from Guild member Maggie Brummett, who submitted the winning contest entry from among members.

Our Guild is blessed with an eclectic blend of writers at various points on their journeys to different destinations. Some may decide not to seek publication. All are learners and teachers to whom we give our deepest thanks and appreciation for sharing their talents. Without them, published or not, this anthology would not be possible.

Preface

Springfield Writers' Guild (SWG) was formed as early as 1943, (possibly earlier) and incorporated as a non-profit organization in 1982. We help aspiring and established writers improve their craft, become published, and market their works for payment. SWG, a chapter of Missouri Writers' Guild, is a premier writing group in Southwest Missouri. Our members have won numerous local, state, and national awards.

Today's publishing world offers more opportunities than ever to writers of all genres and, because of the World Wide Web, the dream to become published can be reality. With this in mind, the SWG board of directors decided to nudge our members to a pivotal point in their writing lives–become published. *Creative Collections* gives a singular chance to members who yearned to be published but who were unsure of the process, who shied from being edited, or who lacked confidence in their writing abilities. Everyone who wants to be published should be. That is the purpose of this anthology. We opened submissions to all members, published and unpublished. Thirty-five members responded with eighty-seven submissions of prose, poetry, fiction, and nonfiction. If you enjoy this collection, please tell your friends, and we would love to hear from you. Send your comments to springfieldwritersguild@gmail.com.

If you're looking for a writing home, we invite you to our meetings to see what we do and to rub shoulders with like-minded writers. Our interests include romance, mystery, science fiction, suspense, historical fiction, western, fantasy, inspiration, children's books, poetry, history, biography, and memoir. You're welcome to attend meetings as often as you like, no requirement you join. For information on member benefits and to join online, visit www.springfieldwritersguild.org. We meet the fourth Saturday each month except December. We have an annual writing contest with cash prizes for writers of all genres, and we sponsor activities including book signings and workshops.

Nothing happens until ideas are expressed, and ideas expressed in written words have the power to change our world: from indifference to action, unfamiliarity to knowledge, boredom to fun. We hope you find in this collection something that changes your world for the better.

Springfield Writers' Guild
2015 Board of Directors
Wayne E. Groner, President
Yvonne Erwin, Vice President
Michael Humphrey, Secretary
John Cawlfield, Treasurer
Diane Siracusa, Director at Large

Susie K. Adams

Susie is a freelance writer, author, speaker, storyteller, and active member of Missouri Writers' Guild. The second edition of her book, *My Mother My Child*, includes a discussion guide. She has written a women's ministry manual, devotions, and Bible studies.

A Homeless Dog and the Lives He Changed

Susie K. Adams

"That dog cannot stay here. He has to go! We are taking him back now!"

It was totally out of character for my gentle, patient husband to be yelling at me. His voice echoed a resounding "no" to my pleading eyes as he continued his ranting. "He is not a puppy. He is a full-grown mongrel! In one day, he will tear up your flowers and ruin our yard. He will cost a fortune to feed! Regardless of what you were told, he is NOT a puppy! We cannot keep him. He absolutely has to go today!"

I found myself speechless, as I stood paralyzed in the midst of one of those raging storms that appear without warning on the horizon. I did not know what to suggest. If anything, and he obviously was in no mood for any solution other than getting rid of the dog.

We lived in the desert area of southern California near the church where my husband was pastor. The house and yard were small but well maintained by the church. Beautiful desert plants graced the yard and a native ice plant sprawled across the sand and under the fence. We had neither adequate space nor time to consider a pet.

I recalled my friend's pleading phone call earlier in the week. "We cannot take Zing with us when we move. He's a sweet puppy, so cute and absolutely no trouble. Your nice fenced yard is ideal for him. Could you please take him?" At the time, it seemed like a good idea. I was sure I could find him a suitable home if we did not choose to keep him.

It never occurred to me to ask what breed of dog he was. Thinking only of her description of a sweet puppy, I was looking forward to cuddling up to a cute little ball of fur. I should have realized there were potential problems when my friend had someone else drop him off. The "little puppy" was a very big, nearly grown mixed breed dog; part chow and lab with long, thick black hair and stood nearly as tall as me.

Carefully, I pleaded for time to find Zing a home. "How much damage can he do in a few days? I'll ask around for someone to take him, maybe a nice family with kids. Please trust me on this. It will be okay. He'll be gone soon and I will replant the yard."

As if on cue, Zing bounded toward me, planted his big paws on my shoulders and began "kissing" my face. Perhaps he sensed he needed an advocate and recognized me as a friend. As I wrapped my arms around his neck and stroked his fluffy black fur, I knew this dog was not going to a pound, not today.

We kept Zing a couple of days on a trial basis and he won our hearts over in no time. Together we decided to give life with this puppy a try. Yes, he made a lot of messes in our yard, very big messes! His digging and romping completely crushed the beautiful ice plant around the front fence. My flowerbeds were all but gone within the week.

There was, however, more to this new friendship than met the eye. We could not have envisioned what the Lord had in store for us in the months ahead, and what a life-changing role Zing would play in the lives of others.

A few weeks after Zing arrived, quite unexpectedly, a young woman came to spend the winter in our home. She had been abused and neglected and was in need of a safe place to live. She was a tiny thing, all drawn up into a little ball. We found it difficult to communicate with her, although we tried to build trust and slowly encouraged conversation.

It was our unwanted dog who broke the ice. Each day as our little guest huddled alone on the front steps, Zing quietly stood by her side. Ever so gently, he nuzzled her arm until she finally gave him a few pats. At times he laid his big, furry head on her lap, looked up and stared compassionately into her eyes. Within a few days, we heard her quiet voice sharing her deepest hurts. Zing did not seem to mind her crying into his fur as she talked openly with the one who would not judge, condemn or share her secrets.

Zing wove his way into all our hearts. My husband cheerfully carried in huge bags of dog food as he ignored all the extra work keeping the yard cleaned. Zing thanked him by walking him out to his car each morning and greeting him at the gate when he returned home.

My greatest surprise was in gaining a new friend to play games with and a much-needed walking companion. Game playing began one day when I started around the front of our van and saw Zing at the back end peeking at me. I headed toward him and he went the opposite direction. As I turned to see where he went, he peeked around the other side of the vehicle. Again, I headed for him and he quickly turned back. He was playing hide and seek! From that point on, every day, I spent five or ten minutes playing hide and seek around the van with the newest member of our family.

One lonely, unwanted puppy had provided more exercise for me, a cause to giggle and reason to hope for a hurting young woman and joy to a husband who no longer wondered if we needed a puppy.

Oh, yes. We also had a newly designed yard complete with sandy trails throughout the ground cover and adorned with beautifully potted plants.

Confessions of a Family Caregiver

Susie K. Adams

When I was a young girl, I was sure I would be a nurse someday. I loved caring for others, especially my grandparents.

As young teens, my brother and I spent several summers on our paternal grandparents' farm in southwestern Missouri. It was always a fun time to roam the hills where our dad had grown up. Grandma and Grandpa Kinslow had lots of fascinating tales to tell of rearing a dozen lively boys and girls during hard times.

Grandma was a very large woman with strong features and a firm voice. Her Indian heritage came through loud and clear when she was angry, especially when we disobeyed her in even the smallest matter. However, at the end of the day when all the work was done, the animals tended, and family fed, she seemed to relax.

Grandma Kinslow had a lot of aches and pains and suffered quite a bit more than most folks knew. Often she would lie down on the bed and have me rub medicine on her back. As a young girl, I was always amazed when I could feel her begin to relax. Grandma's voice even tempered a bit as she smiled and thanked me for taking care of her. I could easily picture myself in a crisp white uniform caring for my patients and making them feel better.

Our mother's mother lived in a small house in town. She was a short, prim and proper lady of the house. There was a place for everything and everything in its place at all times. Grandma Doke was a super-sweet, huggable little lady loved by all who knew her. As she aged, I was privileged to help her take her medicines correctly and later to wash her face and help her eat her food. Her sparkling blue eyes and tender pats let me know I was doing a good job caring for her.

After graduation, like many young people, I set out on my own to find my fame and fortune. Nursing or any form of caregiving jobs paled in importance when I considered the wages and benefits of other occupations as well as the inevitable need for more schooling.

One thing I knew for sure, I did not ever want to take care of my own mother should she need it. I loved her dearly but we simply had differing views on almost everything. And her rampages when crossed were worse than my Indian grandmother's had ever been. The very idea of that happening was frightening to me.

Fast-forward my life to 1996. I was married, living in California. Our four children were grown with families of their own. As my pastor husband was nearing retirement, he was called to a church in Missouri. I would finally be a few hours from my mother who was still living in her home and seemed to be doing very well.

It was an exciting time in our lives. Soon after the move, Mother came to spend a week with us. She and I had great plans now that we were closer: small trips, art classes, and projects together.

In reality, Mother was not okay. She apparently had not been eating properly or taking her medicines. Her third day with us was spent in the emergency room of the local hospital. This was followed by a seven week stay and doctors held little hope that she would make it. I prayed. I cried. I repented of my thoughts about taking care of her. I loved her so much and was not ready to let her go.

God was gracious to her and to us and we learned she would recover but could no longer live alone. We immediately prepared a room for her in our home. Since she had only prepared for a short visit, I had to go to her house for more clothing and personal belongings. This was difficult for me; my very private mother would not want anyone to go through her belongings. I felt like an intruder looking through her desk for important documents and such.

Our lives and hers would never be the same. I would now be caregiver to the one I insisted I would never care for. My children were ten years old or older when I became their mother so I did not even have the experience of tending to babies and their needs. I was a long way from feeling prepared.

Mother was with us eight years; she died shortly after her 90th birthday. She was loved, well cared for and pampered. I felt God had given me the opportunity to give her the childhood she never had and I spoiled that "little girl" beyond belief.

In addition to congestive heart failure and kidney problems, Mother was in the early stages of Alzheimer's disease her last three years. Constant changes in her needs made caring for her more difficult. Just as I learned how to care for one particular ailment, she developed a new one. I was fortunate that she never got completely bedfast and was always willing to do what she could.

I was blessed with a husband who understood what we would be facing. His first wife had died after a long battle with cancer. He was patient with all the changes that were brought about by having Mother in our home 24/7. Our freedoms to come and go as we pleased were cut short. Mealtimes and bedtimes became irregular. Our furnishings often had to be moved or replaced to accommodate the ever-changing needs of our family.

Some children cannot take care of their parents due to work, health, or other obstacles. Care often falls to a single sibling, one living closer to the parents, or the one more qualified. Many husbands or wives are caring for their mates or handicapped children in the home. I want to share some lessons I learned in the trenches hoping and praying they will benefit you or your loved ones. I will address each issue with my mother as the one needing care. For you it may be a child, parent, spouse, other relative or friend.

You are not alone.

In the beginning, I was so lonely. I felt no one could understand what I was going through. I had many questions and concerns and seemingly nowhere to turn. My youngest children were 10 and 11 when I became their mother so I didn't even have the experience of caring for infants. Mother had always known what to do for me when I was sick or hurt. Now I was the one she would have to depend upon for care.

Everything I did from sorting her medicines to planning her menu seemed overwhelming. I wondered about each little red place that appeared on her skin, about her bathroom habits, about her comfort. Saying something to other family members and many of my friends always got the same reply, "Don't worry so much. You are doing a good job."

It was a real breakthrough for me to find a host of people who could relate to my feelings. Through blogs, websites and chat rooms set up just for caregivers, I learned I was in the majority, not the minority. Most families either are or will be providing care for a family member. And, many are first-timers, just like me. Three of every four family caregivers work a job in addition to caring for a loved one.

Make sure legal paperwork is up-to-date.

Do you know who would make decisions for you if you were unable to do so? Do your parents have current wills, powers of attorney, and durable healthcare directives? Do you know where they are kept? Who has access to them? Who can pay their bills when they are unable?

A nurse provided us with information about the legal steps needed to protect Mother's rights and her wishes regarding healthcare. Later, when I discovered she needed other legal documents, we consulted a lawyer. Mother's banker worked with us so I could pay her bills. At times, the paperwork seemed overwhelming to me and to Mother.

Often we would have to lay it all aside until she was up to it.

It is important these issues be taken care of early when each person is thinking clearly and has a good understanding of what is taking place. Other siblings or family members should be kept informed. My brother lived out of state and was comfortable allowing me to handle everything needed for Mother's care.

Learn to be an advocate.

In the beginning, I did not worry about her while she was in the hospital or nursing facility. I felt sure their trained staff would be dependable. However, I soon learned I needed to play an active role. It was necessary for me to check her medicine list each time she was moved to a different facility to make sure all medicines were transferred.

This was difficult for me. I realized that Mother could not care for herself and I had to be her voice. I learned to question the doctors and nurses when something didn't seem right. I am thankful for kind health care workers who went the extra mile in helping me make good decisions.

During routine visits to the doctor after her hospital stay, I often wondered at some of Mother's replies to his questions. However, I never interrupted or corrected her. Later, I learned to either speak up then or visit with the nurse or doctor later when I had concerns. It is difficult as roles reverse and your parent becomes more the child and you the parent.

Accept people and circumstances as they are.

I remember well the day when my mother looked me straight in the eye and said, "I don't know who you are, but I am not your mother."

It broke my heart. I had to quickly let go of my feelings and accept the fact that my mother as I knew her was not coming back. This sweet lady would be doing and saying things my mother would never have done or said. She was my mother, but at this point, she was also my child. She was so dependent upon me for everything. I found joy in her smile, her beautiful blue eyes, and in the satisfaction of knowing she was well cared for in her present state.

Learning to accept people and circumstances as they are in the present will make caregiving much easier. We cannot go back to the way things were. For me, keeping Mother safe and happy was more important than her understanding her surroundings.

Be willing to accept help.

You cannot do it all by yourself. Allowing others to help not only lessens your load, it provides your loved one another person to relate to. It was difficult for me to yield to having caregivers come in to help. I reasoned that just as Mother managed to care for her children and work a job. I should be able to care for her without help.

After a few years of struggling on my own, I realized I did need help. When the first caregiver came, I was as nervous as she. I did not know what to expect and I really didn't want someone else doing my work.

As it turned out, in addition to having the extra help I needed, Mother seemed to improve with each caregiver visit. She looked forward to someone else coming in, giving her a bath, and fixing a meal for her.

When friends or family offered to spend a few hours with Mother so we could go out together, I accepted. One neighbor would come spend a night or two so we could attend a conference or simply have a get-away. Again, this was difficult for me at first, but I learned to trust and to enjoy the time away. It was good for us and for Mother.

Take care of yourself.

I felt guilty at first hiring others to help us so I could go play. Then I felt guilty when I splurged on something just for myself. I felt my job was to care for Mother and my family and I would get rest later if I needed it.

You cannot mentally, physically, or emotionally handle caregiving duties 24/7 without caring for yourself. You need time to rest, to refocus, to refuel. Your rest may come in bite-sized pieces, an hour in the sunshine with your feet up and a good book. On one of Mother's short hospital stays, I hired a housekeeper to thoroughly clean our house while my husband and I spent the day away. She even had a pot of stew cooking in the crockpot when we came home. What a welcome we had as we opened the door that evening.

Keep a journal.

Learn to keep a journal. If you do not think you will ever keep a daily journal, at least put one small notebook designated for that purpose on a table or counter and jot down a few things. There are feelings you may never be able to express later and funny happenings you won't want to forget.

It is also a good idea to write down new medicines and the effects they have. Note the things that make your loved one happy, what makes her sad. Which foods does she really eat? What worked this week to help her walk better or sleep better? What was significant about this day? These things will be helpful as you visit with her physicians.

My journals were not so much about cut and dried details of every day as they were about feelings. Each day brings on a new set of trials and victories, and if not written down are soon forgotten. Mother was so precious to me. I wanted to record everything about her sweet expressions as well as her sassy times.

You are making beautiful memories each day that need to be preserved. The time will come all too soon when you are left with only those priceless memories!

It was not my lot to become a nurse, but I have a new appreciation for them. I believe healthcare workers deserve honor and respect. I know firsthand their jobs are often tedious, messy, and tiring. I also know the rewards of a hug and smile from a hurting patient make it all worthwhile.

I believe I was blessed by getting to care for my mother all those years. I hope I can be an influence and help to others along the way as they care for their loved ones.

The Miracle Cottage

Susie K. Adams

Warm, unbidden tears welled in my eyes and trickled down my cold cheeks. Hoping to avoid a deluge of questions, I meandered through the empty house alone, lagging behind my husband, Russell, and the eager young realtor who was showing us the property.

How do I stop this waterfall? Why am I so emotional over a very small, empty house on a bitterly cold and windy December day? What is it about this place that stirred my emotions without warning?

My pastor husband was preparing to retire from the pastorate and our church-provided housing would end. We needed an adequate home for ourselves and my aging mother living with us. Small church salaries had left little savings, yet we agreed apartment living would be considered only if absolutely necessary. We moved forward on faith.

We prepared a list of what we felt were absolute necessities as we considered either renting a home or purchasing one in need of repair. Of major importance were three bedrooms to provide for us and a guest room for family and friends. Two bathrooms were needed to adequately care for Mother without disturbing the family. A third, very important priority was a level entrance into the home. We were getting older, and maneuvering steps with Mother in a wheel chair was out of the question.

With our needs clearly defined, we were confident God would provide. High rent and limited space kept apartment dwelling at the bottom of our list. Checking out several "nice fixer-upper" ads narrowed the field. We had neither the stamina nor funds required for remodeling.

Apartments began to have more appeal as we wearied of the struggle to find the perfect house. Giving our quest one last run, we made an appointment to see several homes listed in the local newspaper. They were not exactly what we desired and locations were not the best, however, each had three bedrooms, two bathrooms and level entrances.

At the realtors, we were greeted with a quick handshake and led to a waiting vehicle.

"Good to meet you, I'm Aaron. The agent you spoke with is running late. Our manager insisted I show you a nice place nearby while you wait for his return." He continued to explain this home was not exactly what we had asked for but well worth the look.

I recall grumbling as he drove down a dusty gravel road filled with potholes. Nearing the house, I saw steps leading up to the porch. He had already told us there were only two bedrooms. Feeling very put out, I pondered the idea of staying in the car while Russell and Aaron walked through a cold house that definitely had nothing to offer us. I knew, however, this was not the best approach. My attitude clearly needed an adjustment!

Miraculously, something changed as we pulled into the driveway. I immediately felt at home. Without warning tears flowed with no shut-off valve. There is no explanation except for the Lord's Spirit at work in my heart. What happens next bears testimony to God's hand at work.

I could barely see the house for the trees. The small, brown dwelling on the hillside was dwarfed by woods; tall oaks and maple trees graced the lawn. Below the hill were a walnut grove and a small, dry creek.

As a troubled child, I had found solace under a huge oak tree in our yard. My family owned twenty acres and I was well acquainted with every sturdy, faithful tree. I knew when they were ready to dress for summer and exactly which shade of orange or red each would choose to wear in fall. They were my friends, sturdy and reliable. They cooled me on a hot summer's day and sheltered me in the storms of life.

Now, under those barren trees in mid-winter, I felt I was at home. Suddenly, it did not matter if the house had the right amount of bedrooms. I knew we could manage if we were to buy this place. But, could we? And, would we? And, should we? If ever there was a time for Godly wisdom, it was now.

I composed myself and managed to smile as I joined the men in the back of the house. I nodded as Aaron continued to describe the merits of each room. I watched for any reaction from Russell. There was none. None! I mean, clearly no reaction. I wondered what he was thinking, but was afraid to ask.

My doubting thoughts were interrupted with a surprising comment. "We could put a daybed here in this large living room for guests. Have you seen your mother's room and bath yet?"

Oh, gee! Now I was really crying! He had us moved in already and we had not seen it all or discussed finances. It was becoming apparent God had arranged the appointment for us to see this home. We would have never considered it an option on paper. It did not even come close to our list of priorities.

"Mother's room" just happened to have extra wide doors to accommodate her bulky wheel chair and a large window overlooking the beautiful woods. In fact there were extra-large windows in each room complete with window blinds and new draperies. Her adjoining bathroom was huge with a walk in closet, an extra wide shower, and plenty of room for three chests of drawers for her supplies.

On a second list of things to look for in a home, I had privately listed seven "wants" but not "needs." How amazing it was to check every single item: large windows, big yard with trees, huge closet for Mom's things, close to town, eat-in kitchen, back porch and a working fireplace.

Yes, that tiny brown house became our beautiful little cottage in the woods!

As we moved in, we continued to discover how God had provided in ways we could not have imagined. For instance, to avoid steps, we simply wheeled Mother out the front door, across the porch and into the attached garage. Mother's bedroom joined the large living room, which made caring for her simple. Windows were large and low, giving her good views from anywhere she sat. A large front porch and covered back deck provided her opportunity to enjoy fresh air and sunshine.

Retirement was short lived and within a few months, Russell was back to work and needing office space. Our roomy bedroom was easily converted into a bedroom/office with a large bay window overlooking the back of our property. Already in place were floor to ceiling bookshelves covering an entire wall. An unused cabinet in the kitchen was absolutely perfect for storing office supplies.

We have lived in that home in the southern Missouri hills over fifteen years. Every single day, without fail, I wake up thanking God for the land, the house and the deer, turkey and other critters that roam freely.

"Trust in the Lord with all your heart, and lean not to your own understanding. In all your ways acknowledge Him, and He will direct your paths." Proverbs 3:5-6.

Ramon Ballard

I was invisible throughout my schooldays (due to my shyness). I had the lonely child's habit of making up stories and holding conversations with imaginary persons. Invisibility has definite advantages, especially when combined with a vivid imagination. I created magical, fantasy worlds, which I told to my imaginary friends.

The Nativity

Ramon Ballard
Illustrations by Ray H.

O ur story begins on a bone-chilling December day not all that long ago.

Penny Pig bustled around her sty, her mind in a flurry. *Christmas is in two days*, she thought, *and I have so much to do. There are trees to decorate, stockings to hang. There is simply not enough time.*

Bert Packrat scrambled past her without as much as a how-do-you–do. Unusual, Bert always stopped by her sty to talk about gossip that affected the farm.

"What's the hurry, Bert?" Penny called after her friend.

Bert skidded to a halt and turned, clearly upset. "Sorry Penny, but there is no time to spare. I must hurry." Bert turned and continued to scamper at top speed without leaving a suitable explanation.

Penny, not a pig to be left in suspense, yelled after her friend. "Hold on just a minute RAT, you can't just run off like that. Spill the beans. What's the gossip?"

"I'm sorry, my news changes Christmas as we know it,

and I would rather not discuss it until after Christmas. Good day, Penny."

"HALT!" the pig grunted. "Tell me everything now."

Bert twisted uncomfortably, doodling squiggly lines in the fresh fallen snow with his paw. "You know I sneak into the farmhouse and take things all the time?"

"Yes, you're a thief. What's new?"

"I'm not a thief, I'm a packrat. It's what we do." Bert continued.

"Okay, you're a packrat thief," Penny said impatiently.

Bert stared at Penny, his eyes showed hurt. "I need to go. Sorry."

"I apologize, Bert. Please forgive me and continue."

"Well, see I never venture into the family room." Bert whispered looking to see if anyone could hear him. "I made a wrong turn."

"Stop yammering Bert and get to the point."

"I'm getting there. I ended up in the family room, by mistake."

"That is life shattering." Penny turned to continue her decorating.

"That's not the news," Bert shouted. "The family was inside the room, I almost got caught."

"Great story, riveting, but it's not quite earth moving." Penny said, unamused.

Bert lowered his head. "You want earth-shattering? Are you sure you're ready for earth-shattering?"

Penny paused, and hung another corn-on-the-cob ornament on the tree. "I'm listening."

"Christmas is NOT all about Santa, Frosty, or Rudolph."

Penny looked surprised, snorted, and whirled around. "Don't be absurd. We all know that Christmas is Santa and Santa is Christmas. Case closed. Merry Christmas, Bert." She returned to her little tree.

"The family stood around some figurines singing songs and praising this," Bert rustled through his backpack and found a small object.

"A porcelain figure of a baby?"

"Yah, I took it when the family left the room." Bert whispered. "Farmer Jones told his family that this baby's birthday is the reason for Christmas."

"Impossible," Penny said in shock. "Impossible."

"It's true. I haven't a clue how I know it." Bert scratched his ear and gently returned the baby to his pack. "It's true."

Penny plopped to the ground with a thud, *"Impossible."*

***

Moon glow reflected from the snowfall. Penny tossed and turned in an attempt to sleep. The evening slop remained untouched. *A human child responsible for Christmas, that can't be,* she thought. What little sleep she was able to get was disturbed by visions of sugarplum fairies exploding.

The more Penny tossed, the angrier she got. The more she turned, the more determined she became. *I'm going to prove to that Rat that Santa is the TRUE meaning of Christmas.* The snow began to fall, first tiny delicate flakes, soon replaced by snow the size of Brussels sprouts.

Penny sighed, *tomorrow; I'll prove it first thing in the morning. I'm determined, not crazy.*

It is not common knowledge, but pigs are stubborn creatures. Storms of epic proportions won't stop a pig once its mind is made up.

Penny tossed one last time, and then turned one more time, snorted, and rushed from her pen into the raging snowstorm. Obviously, she would get no sleep until she proved the rat wrong.

Tomorrow's Christmas Eve, she thought as she trudged against wind and snow, headed for the tree trunk Bert called home. *The Rat needs to be shown his error tonight. No way I'm going to risk a visit from Santa because of Bert.*

***

Bert, sleeping and tucked into a nice ball shape, was awoken by a very loud knock. Startled, he waited for the impending earthquake. When none came, Bert returned to his ball shape and dozed. The tired rat's eyes had barely slammed shut when his slumber was shattered for a second time by another loud knock.

"Rat, I know you're in there," a familiar voice bellowed. "We have some unfinished business."

"Go away pig. It's late and I need my sleep," Bert complained.

Determined, Penny knocked on the tree trunk again. "It's just a little before six. You started this, now I'm going to finish it."

"Fine. If I go with you and prove you right, will you let me sleep until Christmas Day?" Bert grabbed his backpack, headed out the door, and slammed it behind him. "Let's go Pig!"

"Bring it on, Rat," Penny replied.

Not one word was uttered as the two trudged through the snow. Soon the drifts were so high that Penny offered to carry Bert on her back, which he accepted without as much as a thank you. Both seemed to forget they were best friends.

Bert shimmied through a tight fitting opening once they reached the farm's main gate, and laughed at Penny when she temporarily wedged herself in. They continued their quest once the pig freed herself.

Bert ordered Penny to stop and pointed to an object a few yards from where they stood. "That's not good," he remarked.

Penny strained, looking for the 'not good' object ahead. "That's only Harriet Ostrich. She must have escaped her pen."

Sure enough, the ancient ostrich, an old friend, stood in the middle of the yard, shivering, her head buried neck deep in a snowdrift.

"We must help her," Bert said, diving head first into the drift.

"Nonsense, she got herself into the mess, she can certainly find a way out." Penny yelled, too late to have any effect on Bert. "She isn't our problem."

Bert popped his head from the drift. "All creatures are our problem."

Penny's jaw dropped open. She had never heard Bert say anything about caring about creatures before, let alone helping them out. "Okay, who are you? And what have you done with Bert?" Bert, who had reached Harriet, turned to Penny. "It's me, Bert. I can't explain, but I've felt like a new rat, ever since I stole the baby Jesus." He disappeared beneath the snow. A mumbled "Are you going to help or not?" drifted to Penny's ears.

***

Ordinarily the sight of a pig, a packrat, and an ostrich walking through the middle of town would cause a panic or at least a small commotion. However, nobody paid any attention to the odd trio. Most of the townspeople hurried by them, busy with their holiday shopping. A few stopped long enough to wish the trio a Merry Christmas. Bert and Penny ignored the people altogether. Harriet was content pecking at various outside decorations, swallowing ornaments whole.

Penny gloated as they stopped next to a yard decorated with snow covered Santa's reindeer, elves, and bright boxes tied up with string.

"There's your proof Bert," she oinked gleefully. "Notice there's a Santa, and no sign of a baby Jesus. Satisfied? Let's go home now."

A loud hissing sound came from Santa as Harriet pecked at his jolly old belly. Within minutes, the entire display lay flattened.

"I suggest we find someplace else to search," Bert whispered.

"Home! I've proven beyond a shadow of a doubt that this baby Jesus thing is a myth."

"You haven't proven anything Penny. Except that Santa is vulnerable, and maybe allergic to ostriches." Bert motioned for Harriet to follow them. "We'll continue."

"But..." Penny stuttered. The rat would not change his mind, so she finally agreed to continue the quest, sure she had already proven her point.

The questers came to a department store in the middle of town. Penny clapped and danced with joy. "Do you need any more proof Rat? What's in the store window? And who is that, blocking the doorway and ringing the bell?"

Bert's ears drooped. "A mechanical Santa and his elves are in the window display. And Santa is ringing the bell."

"And where is your baby Jesus?" Penny asked, still grinning.

Bert couldn't believe his eyes. Had Farmer Jones been wrong? "There is no baby. I'm sorry I doubted you Penny. Let's go home." Bert's heart fell to his stomach.

Bert's head hung low as he turned toward home. Just then, music drifted through the town.

Oh little town of Bethlehem, how still we see thee lie...

Penny's ears perked up. "Oh, Bert, that's beautiful. It's coming from over there," she pointed in the direction of a crowd. "Let's check it out."

***

"Hey look, there's Dereck Donkey and Mildred Cow," Penny exclaimed, as they got closer to the crowd. "'Sup, Dereck?"

Dereck looked at the pig, "Ssshhh, the program's about to start."

Curious, Penny and Bert nosed their way to the front of the crowd. They were surprised to see Mrs. Jones and all of her children dressed in robes. Some of them wore brown, while two of the oldest children wore white and were standing on ladders. Penny's eyes drifted to the farmer's infant son.

Bert whispered "Penny. That is exactly the scene I saw in the farmer's family room. And the baby is..."

"I know, the baby Jesus you stole."

Farmer Jones stepped out of the crowd, and began reading from a book.

And there were in the same country shepherds abiding in the field, keeping watch over their flock by night. And, lo, the angel of the Lord came upon them, and the glory of the Lord shone round about them: and they were sore afraid. And the angel said unto them, Fear not: for, behold, I bring you good tidings of great joy, which shall be to all people.

For unto you is born this day in the city of David a Savior, which is Christ the Lord. And this shall be a sign unto you; Ye shall find the babe wrapped in swaddling clothes, lying in a manger.

And suddenly there was with the angel a multitude of the heavenly host praising God, and saying, Glory to God in the highest, and on earth peace, good will toward men.

And it came to pass, as the angels were gone away from them into heaven, the shepherds said one to another, Let us now go even unto Bethlehem, and see this thing which is come to pass, which the Lord hath made known unto us.

And they came with haste, and found Mary, and Joseph, and the babe lying in a manger.

Bert stared in wonder, too happy to speak.

Tears of joy fell freely from Penny's eyes. "It's true, Bert. It's true."

Naomi Brandner

I am a Chicago native. I moved to Springfield in spring of 2013 to be near my husband's family. I am an administrative assistant by profession. I enjoy reading and belong to Friends of the Library in Springfield.
My other hobbies are writing and traveling.

A Blaze of Glory

Naomi Brandner

I look forward to it with excitement all year,
That wonderful season called fall.

Long walks amidst colors so bright,
Who could overlook the stunning beauty, a blaze of glory?

The weather is absolutely divine.
I feel the warmth of sun on my face
And breathe deeply of the cool air.

I just finished a Gala apple, crisp and sweet.
Later by the bonfire, I'll have s'mores with my friends.
Mulled wine will keep me warm within.

Squirrels run around with acorns in their cheeks.
Canada geese bask in the warm sun.
People ride their bikes for one last time.

Too often individuals speak of it with dread.
"I hate winter," they say.
They don't celebrate the beauty.
"Live in the moment," I respond, "and look at that blaze of
glory!"

Let's Eat Out!

Naomi Brandner

It's amazing how our social lives revolve around food. Picnics, pot luck dinners, or eating out on special occasions. Most people take these social occasions for granted. When I was a child, our family didn't have a lot. We were always on a budget, but my parents had a few creative ways to allow us to do what other families did.

One thing that we enjoyed was eating out – at a restaurant, of course. But, we rarely got to eat at one. It was for a special treat only, like high school graduation. One Saturday afternoon, I felt like having a special treat. There was no reason other than it was a nice day out, and I wanted to enjoy it.

So, I asked my mother, "Can we eat out for lunch?"

The response, "Absolutely."

My mother didn't elaborate with details. She simply packed a picnic lunch that included fried chicken, potato salad, and homemade cookies. Of course, I don't really remember seeing her pack the picnic, or take it with us.

About a half hour after we left, we arrived at one of our favorite parks near North Avenue Beach. Wait a minute, I thought. This isn't a restaurant; it's our favorite place to visit! The excitement of being at our favorite park overshadowed the fact that we weren't eating at a restaurant. However, we were eating out, just outside at our favorite park.

I carry this tradition out to this day. I don't have any children, and I still have to watch my budget. When we need to get out the house and enjoy the weather, I plan a picnic. I make deli sandwiches, and potato salad, at home. Naturally, we would enjoy a fun beverage (adults only). We go to the Springfield Nature Center, which is just a couple of miles from our house. The weather is perfect, I'm in good company, and the view is spectacular.

Another thing that we looked forward to during the summer was the picnic at our place of worship. It had the same excitement as our family picnics. More importantly, we would get to have foods that we weren't allowed to have at home, because they simply cost too much. My mother would bring something simple, such as homemade potato salad. The whole family enjoyed the gourmet experience. To this day, I still enjoy having picnics with our friends from our church.

My mother had the same idea for treat night. We couldn't afford to each have an ice cream cone at the local ice cream parlor. I can still remember it, Cock Robin, a predecessor to Dairy Queen. It cost too much for each of us to have our own treat, so we bought the whole half gallon. It was a challenge to pick out which flavor we wanted, even with the limited choices. Someone had to be disappointed, but we had enough ice cream for three days. Unfortunately for me, Cock Robin is not in business any more. I still carry on the tradition, however, and bring home a half gallon of our favorite ice cream on Friday nights during the summer. We eat it out in the backyard.

Even candy was considered a special treat in our house. We were allowed to have candy only when my mother actually offered it to us. We could not just help ourselves, it was rationed, only two pieces please! The only reason we had any of it in the house was because of the sales after a holiday. Once again, I carry on the same tradition that I experienced when I was young. I only purchase candy after the holidays, and I limit my husband to just a couple of pieces.

Our family didn't have a lot, but experiencing financial difficulties brought us together. Most of my favorite memories were the times when we actually had very little. I hope to experience the same feelings of warmth and prosperity with my friends, now that I'm an adult.

M.L. Brummett

I believe a good book should be a treasure trove of adoration in the reader's hands. A good novel should cast readers into another era and give them the opportunity to live adventures outside of their own lives. Readers should know each character personally in a good piece of literature, and no matter how often readers open their favorite books, they should find something comforting and familiar that will enrich their lives.

Semper Fidelis

M.L. Brummett

From her forthcoming book, Semper Fidelis

Joe sat in the trenches. He was wet and worried, hot and beaten. Battles pounded one after another. He had been fighting since they arrived on the shores of Bougainville the first of November. All he wanted to do was sleep a full eight hours. It was one bloody engagement after another. Luckily, he was so exhausted that he could fall asleep on command.

For the moment, Joe had time to lay low; he rested for a while. Someone else stood guard over the 3rd. Virginia, his sweetheart, was always on his mind; he missed her terribly. He took one last look at her picture under his helmet before he tried to rest. It was difficult to turn his mind off. There was just enough room in the foxhole for Joe and David. Jessie was a few feet away, sheltered in his trench. Joe's amphibious Jeep sat camouflaged between the trees; it served as additional protection. Their conversations were kept low, their movements minimal.

"Hey Joe, did you hear about that guy that killed all those Japs, seventy of them!" David whispered. "They were 20 yards off the gun, man. That was impressive!"

"Yeah, I heard." Joe responded. "Did you hear what reconnaissance reported this morning? Apparently, a camp of Japs didn't think the war was still going on. They were lounging around and drinking beer when our mortars tore them apart." Joe shrugged his shoulders. "You've gotta stay on top, man. They should know that. This is war."

"Hey, Joe, I hear we get real turkey and dressing tomorrow for thanksgiving." Jesse loudly whispered across foxholes.

"Awe that sounds swell." Joe smiled. His stomach grumbled. "But they're not going to get turkey out here on the front lines. Forget it guys. Not even Roosevelt can make that happen. That turkey is for the uppercut. Still sounds good though." Joe settled deeper in the hole, ready to catch a few winks before the next battle. "You guys better get some real sleep and quit daydreaming about food." Joe suggested.

Jesse smiled. He sunk lower in the ground. His leg was stiff and swollen beneath his pants. He massaged it, but the squishing of the puss and infection made him sick to his stomach. Jesse propped his leg up against the dugout. He tried to get comfortable for the night.

It had been a long day. They were a part of two battalions from the 3rd that worked their way through eight-hundred yards of slimy muck with water to their armpits. Tangles of thorny vines inflicted painful wounds. The marines were exhausted; some fell asleep setting up in the water when time allowed. Their mission was to make sure all available tanks and supporting weapons were moved forward beyond the east fork of the Piva River. Battles enraged through it all. The 3rd Marines bore the brunt of the fighting. The battles were close combat; neck to neck. Bayonet fighting was tough. Joe could see the fear in the enemy's eyes before death.

The night felt thick on November 23. While Joe rested, the Army set up seven battalions of artillery. They lined up 155s and 105s, mortars, and 90mm AAs; cannons were rolled between bushes and forty-four machine guns were ready for battle. When the Japanese retaliated, they didn't stand a chance.

Morning's light beamed through the tops of the coconut trees at 0730. A thick ray of light opened Joe's eyes once again to reality. I did get a little sleep, he thought. He stretched his arms the best he could in close quarters. He heard groaning from Jesse's foxhole. "Jesse, are you okay?" Joe pulled himself level to the ground, stiff from the night.

He surveyed his surroundings.

"Oh shit, Joe." Jesse wailed. "My leg looks like a coconut tree, man. I can't feel it anymore." Jessie moaned in dire pain. Joe could almost feel the pain himself.

Joe slithered over to Jesse's foxhole. "Damn, Jesse. You need to get out from the front line. I'm getting a corpsman." Jesse made no argument. Joe pounded the black pole in the mud on the trenches ridge to signal help. Jesse grabbed Joe's hand. His grip was bone breaking. Joe knew chances were slim that Jesse could get back to camp. They were too deep in the rain forest, and the enemy was pitted around them. The combat medics were search and rescue, basic training. Getting Jesse through the combat zone would be a challenge for the most skilled corpsman. He's not going to make it there, Joe thought, but he had to try to get his friend some help.

The corpsmen encouraged Jesse to remain calm. They placed him in a canvas and lifted him out of the foxhole. Jesse was too tall. He hung over the end. They placed a blanket around his shivering body.

Jesse was at the mercy of his comrades, but the enemy was merciless. Nobody saw it coming. There wasn't time to think. The attack began at 0835 on Thanksgiving Day. A wincing burst of flame and thunder shattered everything around them. The shells splintered shrapnel everywhere; it snapped twigs off bushes and made blades from the coconut leaves. The bombing demolished an 800 square-foot area. It left marines dead, bleeding, and some still drowning in their own blood.

Joe landed twelve feet away; he dropped from a ten-foot blast through the air. His arm caught barbed wire on his way down and ripped away inches of flesh. He knew he was still alive; he couldn't hear anything. The blast was deafening. Through tightly squinted eyes, he tried to focus on what was going on around him. His gut hurt.

Something felt warm on his back. It was unsettling, unnatural. He knew it was not a part of his gear. His body racked with pain as he reached back to get it off. He recognized the corpsman band around the arm, but it was no longer attached to a body. Joe threw the bleeding arm off his back, across the broken land, out of his sight. He screamed, as he never had before. His teeth gnashed as he tried to concede to reality.

All of his training surged back into his brain; he knew the ground was his safe place. He lifted his head over the torn earth enough to survey his surroundings. It was a churned mass of mud and human bodies. Dripping blood and pieces of flesh hung from the trees and bushes.

The powder and smoke was thick. But it wasn't thick enough. He could still see hell. Jesse's torso had been blown over a tree stump; his head was still attached. Joe could see his friend's daunting eyes through the smoke. "Damn it... Oh God..." Muddy tears ran down his face. "Oh! Damn, Jesse." Joe respectfully pulled a broken coconut leaf over Jesse's eyes.

He trembled as he looked around. Joe sat against the tree stump; he could hardly breathe. Blood was running down his arm. He wasn't sure if it was his or not. He tried to wipe the tears from his eyes; his vision was still blurry. Joe couldn't hear movement anywhere around him. He wondered if he was the only one alive.

Enemy artillery roared not too far in the distance. Joe heard a Nambu machine gun stuttering. Japanese battle cries echoed through the forest. It sounded like hand-to-hand and tree-to-tree, killing any remaining life. Joe knew he had to find some place for cover. The Japs liked to loot after their kill; a cigarette here and ration bar there. American souvenirs were valuable. It was their honor to rip the dog tag from a slain American soldier; it was just as common as the nicks that were carved in the butt of an American rifle after each kill. He had to be ready if they came his way. Joe inched through mud and blood to find shelter. The trenches were blown apart. Nothing recognizable around him. He took refuge under some remaining ripped foliage, and camouflaged his face with mud. God I hope this isn't flesh, he thought.

The passing of time was immeasurable. The artillery sounded like the Japs were heading the other way. Joe felt like his surroundings were more secure. He lay on his belly. With a composed sigh, he buried his face in his folded arms. He cried from the depth of his soul. He was alone, but grateful he was alive. "Oh Damn." He cried out loud.

His breathing calmed. It was time to start looking for others. No man left behind. Only the sounds of burning brush crackled around him. Joe crawled out from under the foliage. "Can anybody hear me?" Joe yelled. His hearing was still muffled from the blast. He faintly heard a few pain filled mutterings from souls begging for help. Joe couldn't make out where they were. One suicidal bullet broke the silence. Joe worried the marine couldn't hear his offer for help; maybe the pain was too much to handle.

He heard tanks breaking through the forest; the ground rumbled. Were they U.S. tanks, Joe listened; his hearing was still stifled from the blast. He thought he could hear English being spoken. He knew they were in search of the wounded. "Over here." Joe yelled. "I'm over here!" He inched into an open area where he knew he would be found. The defending cock of the U.S. Rifle sounded wonderful, from what he could hear. Once the marine identified Joe as an American, he was placed in a rescue jeep. He was taken back to camp for medical attention.

Joe rested in the crude temporary infirmary. He could hear the bravery of hero's as they tried to survive; there were more prayers offered than Joe imagined God could ever answer.

After treatment, there weren't enough beds for Joe to stay and heal. He was released from the infirmary, but not back into combat, at least for a few days. His hearing was slowly returning; his vision cleared. He wasn't allowed to do any of his amphibious duties. I can't just lie around here for days, Joe thought. Joe was permitted to help the wounded while he healed. He wasn't trained as a medic, but he knew he could help lift their spirits.

Battles raged. More and more marines were carried back to camp. Some were still alive to share war stories. Others were not so lucky. After a couple of days passed, vivid details about the bombing began to flood back into Joe's memory. He was still working through the trauma. Joe's face furrowed in anguish when the thought about his friend David. Images of David's face flashed repeatedly through his mind's eye. Joe thought David might still be out there. Maybe he was buried in the trenches, Joe agonized. His hands trembled, his lips quivered.

Joe sat at the bedside of a wounded marine; a double amputee. He tried to remain composed for the marine's sake, but his head was spinning. Joe tried to listen to the young man's perils about how he lost his legs, but in middle of the young man's story, anxiety got the best of Joe. He didn't take time to excuse himself. He ran through the tented doorway. Confused and scared, Joe began to beat the coconut tree outside the infirmary until his knuckles were bleeding. It was the only thing he could think to do. His shouting was heard throughout camp.

"Hey. Hey. Hey. Slow it down there, son." A corpsman held Joe's arms back, and restricted him from hurting himself any further. Corpsman Scott had helped Joe when he rolled in from combat; he was familiar with the front line bombing. Joe's exploits were nothing new to the corpsman. He had seen trauma more times than he wanted to speak of. He calmed Joe down and invited him to sit on the rocks with him. He knew Joe to be a strong soul; he just had to work through the suffering.

"Marine. It's okay. Tell me what you're thinking about. I'm here with you, Joe. Tell me." The corpsman's hand was strong and steering on Joe's shoulder. Joe's lips painfully stretched over his tightly clenched teeth. Agony seethed in his eyes. He tried to hold back the tears. He was a marine. Semper Fidelis. There was no place for crybabies in the war,

Joe thought. He tried to fight through the anguish.

"Why has it taken so many days for David to cross my mind? Where is he?" Joe inquired. "He was my friend. I forgot all about him. He was right beside me!" Corpsman Scott noticed Joes trembling hands.

"Who is David?" The corpsman asked.

Joe looked angered. He didn't want to hear that somebody else had forgotten about David, or for God's sake, they didn't even know him at all. Joe wildly glared Corpsman Scott in the eye. "David Anderson. His name is David Shelton Anderson." Joe calmly confirmed; deeply breathing. "He is a solid guy from Ohio. He has a baby boy named after him that he hasn't seen yet. All he wants to do is get back home to his new bride, and his baby boy." Joe punched the tree again, hard. Drops of blood swung back hitting the corpsman. Joe knew the truth in his heart. His voice quivered. Reality painfully penetrated his soul. Joe buried his face in the trunk of the tree. "David didn't even want to be here in the damn war!" He cried. His pounding slowed. His fist rested above his head.

"I understand Joe." Corpsman Scott guided Joe back to sitting position.

"So, do you know him?" Joe's voice was heightened.

"I do, Joe. I know him. He was a quiet guy. He had strong family values." The corpsman was afraid of what Joe's reaction might be when he told him David didn't make it either. "He was a strong man." The corpsman respectfully bowed his head.

"Was?" Joe whispered as he clutched his bleeding knuckles. Only a few survived that bombing, Joe knew it. There could be no other explanation, but he had to hear it. "That word seems to be spoken around here every day, doesn't it?" Joe rhetorically asked. "He *was* a good man. He *was* a brave man. That's what everybody says as they stand over the body of a dead marine." Joe tucked his head; both hands were tightly fisted. "Just say it. David's future is over. He just was..."

Joe sat silently for a few minutes. Corpsman Scott sat quietly at his side. He allowed time for Joe to grieve. The war wasn't stopping; Corpsman Scott had to move on. "I have to get back in there to help the living, Joe. I'm sorry about your friend. Really, I am." He put his hand on Joe's shoulder for encouragement.

B.J. Clausen

B. J.'s award-winning poetry has been published in over thirty anthologies. She has self-published three poetry books: *Musings, Glimpses,* and *Pelican View,* and two historical nonfiction books: *Delnorte Bites,* and *Delnorte Bites: A Second Helping.* Her inspiration comes from the Redwoods of California and the ocean by which she lives.

My Mother

B.J. Clausen

My mother was a dichotomy. She was spoiled by my dad, but she loved to give. She could play piano by ear and loved to play at church, but sometimes felt under-appreciated. She was a wonderful cook and baker, but a terrible housekeeper.

We always laughed about the fact that she loved to invite people over for meals, but always bought the same amount of meat. She would just cut it up smaller. As we got older, we would tell her to buy more. But at the end of every meal, she always had one piece of meat left over. Not recognizing that nobody wanted to take the last piece, she would always say, "See, I told you it was enough."

I never saw her use a recipe, but everything she made was very good. We grew up in farm country, but we were city folk. Cousins often spent the night. Our house always had music. That's the thing I mostly remember about Mom. She would sit and play a while. Get up and do a little housework, sit and play some more.

She loved estate sales and would buy fancy dishes. She loved using these cup and saucer sets for her coffee parties.

The most important thing I learned from Mom was her faith. God was always an important part of our life. I also learned not to be a worrier. This was because, my, she was such a worrier. If she didn't have something to worry about it worried her.

I remember Dad as the calm, loving parent. Just a look from Dad could make us straighten up. I once told my kids I didn't know how he did that. They all laughed and told me I had learned it perfectly.

He worked hard at his gas station 7 a.m. to 7 p.m. every day. But at night he would play games with us: checkers,

Chinese checkers, and ping pong. He knew how to let us win without letting us know he could have won.

He never passed Mom without some little show of affection. Dad was one of those men everyone liked. Women adored him, but he just smiled. We heard stories of his temper when he was younger, but never saw any evidence of that.

I am blessed to have such happy memories of my childhood.

Old Home

B.J. Clausen

Wind whistling whispers
Still empty windowed blue house
Spelled melancholy.

Pioneers

B.J. Clausen

Only several days ago,
the lady and three small children
were city folks, dressed up
for the train trip,
a trip that would transpose them into pioneers.

Now the lady looked wryly
at the crude mud and straw hut,
where she was to bake
and make lovely embroidery
and teach her children to play piano.

Sun throbbed on her back,
through the starched bonnet, to
send tiny sweat rivulets
between her shoulder blades.
She sighed in wonder at
vast expanses of
waves of gold – grass
that swayed to unseen hands
of wind and earth.

She unbuttoned her collar once more,
rolled up her sleeves,
discarded three petticoats,
smiled at her scuffed shoes,
ready to build a place, to sew and cook
and play her piano.

Jim was eight and excited
with huge playgrounds,
no school.
Snakes and horses instead,
with eyes blue with excitement,
he brought the first visitor
to the canvas curtain that was a door.
The Sioux had three scalps on his belt
and Army stripes on his pants.

Too surprised to be afraid
she stuck out her hand to be shaken,
The Indian stared at the piano
that was still waiting to be housed.
He saw the well and bucket,
filled his water bag and watered his horse,
touched the lady's hair and the piano and left.
For half an hour, she trembled and laughed.

Her husband returned home
to find her there, laughing
and playing the piano.
She told him about their first visitor.
He grabbed her shoulders and shook her
for forgetting to use the rifle.

A smoke filled cloud spitting
sparks of red and gold pushed
back the sun.
The arrow-straight wind leveled the
sea of grass.
The Army wagon appeared suddenly.
The Indian and his warriors pushed the piano onto the car
with yells and shouts.

Her husband arrived on a foam-mouthed horse
blackened with smoke, carrying the acrid odor across the
plains,
Saying, "Hurry, we have to run.
There is a prairie fire.
See the flames flashing high."

Tough red hands gently pushing,
the Indians guided the lady and children to the cart, to sit
with her piano.
The man followed, his hand on his hip
and his eyes blinking smoky tears.

Under the rock cliff by the creek
the Indians touched her hair
and held their ears close to the piano,
as she smiled
and played the piano.

War

B.J. Clausen

The lights go out,
a child cried out –
a crooning voice
answers,
"There's nothing to worry about."

The gun fire dies,
a shriek likewise dies –
a choking voice
whispers,
"Don't let my child's rights be denied."

Larry Cunningham

Larry is a retired Marine, a retired science teacher, a retired cattle rancher. He is retired!

Transformation of a Fink

Larry Cunningham

J. Pierpont Finkel, named after the great American financier and philanthropist, John Pierpont Morgan, lived with his mother in a run-down Archie Bunker brownstone on the Lower East Side. I should say, at forty-five, Fink (his nickname from grade school), still lived with his mother until he met Lucy. Lucy provided the impetus for J. Pierpont Finkel's remarkable transformation.

Fink, let's call him Fink for the sake of consistency, never matured beyond the physical stature of an anorexic teen, lost most of his hair before thirty, wore thick glasses and perspired profusely at all times for no apparent reason. Fink never once dated a girl and reminded almost every onlooker of a cowering alley dog, tail between its legs waiting to be abused; he expected to be abused. Fink, however, possessed a brilliant mathematical mind and worked as an accountant for a prestigious company. Unfortunately, due to a lack of people skills, he never received a promotion other than periodic pay raises. The company relied on Fink for its most important accounts; he never let them down. He also diligently saved his own money and invested shrewdly. No one knew, not even his mother, just how prosperous he was–filthy rich, a fortune hidden in camouflaged accounts, interest rolling over, accumulating and swelling. Fink excelled at managing massive amounts of money. A good deal of the capital in his hidden accounts once belonged to unwary and unsuspecting clients. He salted away millions–no one knew–no one had a clue.

Now, enter Lucy Gold (Gold, no kidding). She worked as receptionist for Codel, Inc., a Fortune 500 company Fink audited and pirated annually. Platinum blonde, bubbly, curvaceous, stunningly pretty in a small town cheerleader sort of way, Lucy represented the last woman on earth anyone in their right mind would ever link to Fink. She possessed little education, matching her meager academic abilities, but had plenty of street smarts. Lucy migrated to New York from rural Indiana in pursuit of a stage career, but at thirty quit the quest for stardom. She took Codel's receptionist's position after two degrading, fruitless years of humiliation working as a call girl for a swindling madam. Lucy, quite by accident, sat next to Fink one day in the company cafeteria and became intrigued by his backwardness. She had never known a man so petrified of women.

The relationship failed to flourish at first, but Lucy's interest piqued after he dropped hints of secret prosperity and their connection developed. Fink responded to her cunning methods, methods so subtle he never suspected her intentions. He began looking forward to lunches with her, grinning like a sixteen-year-old. He gave her an expensive bracelet. She had him. Lucy Gold enjoyed one talent–she understood men–and soon knew all she needed about Fink, including the insight that he probably did have money and could be the answer to her quest for a life of ease.

Fink first fell victim to Lucy's friendliness, then her deliciously exposed breasts. The couple's almost comically childish relationship raced into the adolescent stage, giggling and blushing, but lodged there temporarily, unable to progress because Fink didn't have the mental or emotional maturity to take it to the next level. At length, his degree of maturity didn't matter. Lucy wormed her way into Fink's heart and proposed. He accepted. She picked a house. He bought it. They married. He somehow summoned unaccustomed courage and moved out of his mother's home, though the poor woman, after meeting Lucy, became bedridden, frantic with worry, grieving for her confused, beguiled son.

Lucy's new home in the suburbs matched her dream of a lifetime–a maintenance-free Tudor in an expensive, gated neighborhood. She quit work and spent her time at the hairdresser, or shopping, or wheedling Fink to reveal more about his finances. Though ostensibly under her spell, Fink never revealed the extent of his worth, but gave enough cash to satisfy her needs–well, almost. Among other attributes he lacked, Fink featured a teeny weeny peeny and absolutely no jurisdiction over conjugal command.

The home next door to the Finkels sold three months after the wedding and a new neighbor moved in. Life quickly went to hell for Lucy and John. The neighbor built a six-foot high woven wire fence around his yard (leaving the sidewalk open for the mailman) and turned his dogs loose–four dogs: two full-blooded pit bulls and two nondescript mongrels. The dogs barked incessantly.

"John!" Lucy yelled as Fink stepped in from work. "Those dogs have barked all day. You have simply got to do something. I'm going nuts. I called the lazy cops and they say he has the right to keep dogs and they can't do anything. You have got to do something!"

He mumbled something unintelligible and she smoldered. He suffered her spiraling tirades throughout the evening before gaining the courage to call the neighbor, who promptly hung up. Lucy exploded after Fink shrugged off the rejection. "What are you, a man or a wimp? By damn, you either take care of this, or I.... Well, I don't know exactly what I'll do, but you won't like it. Take care of it!"

"Okay, honey. Tomorrow. I'll go over there tomorrow. I will."

They slept in separate beds. He found her waiting at the door when he came home the next day, face red with rage, barring his way.

"Don't you even think about coming in this house until you take care of those dogs! I mean it! They are driving me crazy!" She stood in the door and pointed to the house next door. "Now, dammit! Get your skinny butt over there and act like a man!"

He put his briefcase down, took a deep breath, squared his shoulders and stepped down the walk, his pace less masculine by the moment. When he arrived at the neighbor's porch,

Fink turned and looked back. Lucy was watching, waiting at the door, hands on hips. He took a

deep, resigned breath and rang.

The neighbor, fat, swarthy, a three-day stubble and holding a beer, squinted for a moment, then said, "Ain't you the guy next door? What do you want?"

"Ah, yes, sir. I am he. John Finkel." He held out his hand, offering to shake.

The neighbor ignored him, took a long drag from the beer, turned his head aside and belched, then said, "So, what do you want, Finkel? I ain't got all day."

"Ah, Mr. Smolnik (Lucy told him the name), I...ahh....Well, it's about your dogs."

Smolnik's face turned into a massive frown. "Oh, yeah? What the hell about my dogs?"

Fink fidgeted, looked back to Lucy (hands still on hips), then, unable to look the man in the eye, laughed nervously and said, "Well, um, you know, I hate to complain, but your dogs are bothering my wife."

Smolnik laughed, elbowed past Fink, gave Lucy the finger, then, his face an inch from Fink's, said, "And that goes for you, too, buddy." He stepped inside and slammed the door.

Lucy was livid. She pounced as he sheepishly approached. "Oh, yeah. I watched the whole thing! He flipped me off and you just stood there. What kind of a man are you?"

He tried to placate her, to no avail. Her wrath and loathing gushed over him like a geyser. They slept apart again. Fink, as providence would have it, left town the next day for a week to audit a company in Chicago. The nightly phone call to the still steaming Lucy left him sick to his stomach and sleepless. He dreaded going home. When he arrived, her demands reached the ultimatum level within two minutes. She forced him out the door to confront Smolnik again.

"Finkel? What the hell do you want this time?"

Fink fumbled for words and fidgeted. "Well, I'm sorry to say, my wife–" The concussion of the crashing door blew his eyelids and collar up. He could see Lucy standing in the door.

She yelled, "Be a damned man! Take care of it!"

Fink turned, faced the door again, sighed heavily, held his breath and pushed the button.

Smolnik's face turned motley purple. "That's it, you little jerk. You ever ring my damned bell again, I'm gonna deck your ass! Now, get the hell off my property!" The door slammed.

Lucy raged. She called Fink every name she could think of, belittling, threatening, promising, cajoling, crying. Finally tiring of his indifference, she gave an ultimatum, "You can either fix this mess or get the hell out! Don't even think about coming back until you can act like a man! I need a real man!"

Fink did the only thing he could think to do. He sighed, went next door and rang that bell. Smolnik didn't say anything; he punched Fink so hard Lucy heard the splatting sound all the way

across the yard. Fink fell backward and split his head on the sidewalk. Sixteen stitches and a nose guard later, Fink returned home to his glowering wife. She had called an ambulance but refused to go to the emergency room with him. He had taken a cab home.

He slept alone the next week, listening to Smolnik's dogs all night every night and Lucy all day every day. Then, J. Pierpont Finkel unexpectedly did the most unimaginable thing. He quit his job of twenty years, secretly drove to a nearby lake and rented a cottage. No one knows exactly what he thought about during the next week, but when he returned home, Fink was the owner of the lake cottage and a changed man.

Lucy thundered, "It's about time you got your skinny butt back here! Where have you been? Those damned dogs–"

"Woman, you shut the hell up! I'm tired of your mouth. Not another word!"

She recoiled, disbelieving, mouth open. "How dare you! You left me here to face that slob by myself. I went over there. He called me all kind of names. What are you going to do about that? Oh, I know–nothing! Hell, you wouldn't make a wart on a good man's fanny."

He slapped her, then in a menacing whisper said, "I will take care of it."

She still didn't recognize the change in him and laughed derisively. "Yeah, right. Mr. big guy's gonna take care of it. He'll punch you senseless, deary. You can't do anything."

"I said, I'll take care of it," he growled, his cold glare never wavered from her eyes.

She rubbed her stinging cheek, tears cascading. "Yeah? Well, buddy, you do that, but I'm not waiting around. And, for your information, I filed for divorce while you were out gallivanting around. I'm outta here." She opened the cloakroom door, pulled out a packed rolling suitcase, tossed her head and walked out, flipping her hair. He never saw her again.

Fink didn't move for minutes after her departure, then smiled, satisfied with himself, and called a cab. Later, well after dark, with ingredients from a hardware store, he poisoned Smolnik's dogs. They all died agonizing deaths in the night. Smolnik was waiting on Fink's front steps the next afternoon when he came home. The good neighbor didn't say anything, just grabbed a resigned Fink by the shirt collar and smashed his nose repeatedly until Fink collapsed. The hospital stay lasted eight days–three in intensive care, followed by five more for observation of a severe concussion. Fink remained, as always, impassive about the whole thing, possibly even content.

He put his house up for sale, bought a new car, hired a lawyer to conclude matters with Lucy, then sat by the window, staring, waiting for his deliberately underpriced home to sell; it sold ten days later. He signed the papers that afternoon, rang Smolnik's doorbell just after dark, shot him three times in the heart, then drove to his secret cottage at the lake. After a celebratory toast to a new life, J. P. Finkel settled down for the first satisfying night of sleep in over two months. He felt content, almost wallowing in euphoria. Free at last.

Fink sat bolt upright in bed at midnight, awakened by the sound of the next door neighbor's barking dogs. He screamed until out of breath, the suffering scream of a beaten man. The scream morphed into hysterical laughter. Fink sobered, opened the nightstand drawer, retrieved the pistol he used to silence Smolnik and headed next door.

Gail Denham

For thirty-six years, Gail's short stories, essays, news articles, poetry and photos have appeared in a variety of publications. She belongs to a dozen state poetry societies, wins prizes, and is published in anthologies. Her poetry work eats up her time these days–humor, story, family and faith being the mainstays.

Emil, That's Not Funny

Gail Denham

Emil finally got his walking stick. That's what he called it–a black cane from Walmart. Musta' cost him six bucks at least. All of us down at the coffee place were glad, 'cause we'd all had the privilege of catching Emil when he rounded a bar stool, stepped over the door sill, or tried to sit down while holding a coffee mug and a powdered donut.

When we helped him offen' the floor, Emil would growl like a wounded cougar. "You didn't need to handle me up. I had it covered." Which, of course, he didn't, but don't ever try to out-talk Emil.

Bruises on his shins, elbows, arms, and forehead never stopped the crotchety old fart from lumbering in every gol-durn morning with some cockamamie story he'd dreamed up. After he finally settled, spilling only two cups of coffee, which we had to dab up with napkins, Emil would start in.

One morning, the story was so preposterous, Rusty butted in, "That sure isn't the truth, Emil. You never topped trees. As for leading mules down that mountain tugging a log load – never happened." Rusty was wound up that morning. "I happen to know, you laid linoleum for years after you left the hardware store. No time did you scale trees."

For a miniscule; Emil said nothing, merely gave a ghost of a smile and chewed his donut, powdered sugar blanketing his plaid jacket. "You never knew me when I was young," he said. "I had some mighty adventures. Also had lots of dames that wuz' crazy for me. Even your best girl, Rusty. Me and Carrie Ann were close then, mighty close. Ask her."

Rusty appeared to shrivel a bit, right there in his yellow

vinyl chair. "You never did. Emil, you're a liar and a bumbler."

"Sure did. Look here, I carry this picture of me and Carrie Ann at the Fun House. Remember they used to have that place at the yearly carnival. We sure had fun that night. We wuz' laughing so hard, they near kicked us out. Especially when that air machine flung Carrie Ann's skirt so high..."

"No." At that, Rusty stood up, spilling his coffee and mine, flinging donuts on the floor. "No," Rusty roared. "You're full of manure, Emil. No sir, that's not funny." At that, Rusty grabbed a donut offen' the floor and stomped out the door, kicking Emil's cane way t'other side of the café. Emil only gave that half-smile of his'n and sipped his coffee, dribbling just a little down his sleeve.

I Do What I Do

Gail Denham

I do, always, what I must do because I cannot undo it. There was a young time when change haunted my thoughts. I could jump, wild-minded, into frantic turmoil, roiled adventure, excitement multiplied by twenty, on the edge of a caravan of miscreants who take no hostages, only plummet forward in anticipation of success and more climb.

Still, the strings anchored me to a herd of tender, awkward jewels, promising only long-haul years of wise advice, 24 hour surveillance, watch eyes on every side of the head, care-giving – destination: responsible additions to our world.

Was this enough to forsake personal satisfaction? Or, perhaps this was the ultimate satisfaction for which we could not have known from day one, from which we do not veer or retreat – our meaning of life?

It's as my two-year-old granddaughter sings, skipping room to room, "I do what I do. I do what I do."

Shall we trade for less?

Peddling Gone Wrong

Gail Denham

Saree blew a gasket when she discovered
what Rafe'd been up to. Driving round with
quarts of "shine," right through the red
light zone in his clunky old green pickup.

Saree went and took an axe to the dust-covered
front windows of the tired pickup, let air out
of the thread-bare tires, broke ever' mason jug
hidden behind the tool box in the truck bed.

"Driving through the red light district, at night,
with his lights dim, watchin' for customers!
 Who's he foolin'? Sure, those ladies have
the cash money, but they sure as heck
can't cook neither," Saree muttered.

"Reckon I'll make Rafe's favorite – spaghetti
and meatballs with cheese, and maybe one
of those mix-in-the pan chocolate cakes. He
cain't go nowhere anyway, least not till payday.

"Wonder iffin' there's any that 'shine' left in the shed?
Would make that chocolate cake taste pretty good."

Travelin' with Friends

Gail Denham

We're often reminded that writing is an isolated business. Perhaps that's why I prefer to travel the writing road with friends. What friends? Fellow writers, such as Jack London, Katherine Paterson, and Robert Newton Peck. And whenever I encounter a beginning writer, I urge them to become acquainted with these authors.

In Jack London's fictionalized autobiography, *Martin Eden*, I discover that London believed in his works so much that he just kept writing and submitting manuscripts, even if it meant living in near poverty.

Since I sometimes write for children, I treasure Katherine Paterson's counsel from her book, *The Spying Heart*. Paterson says, "A child's book becomes a best-seller because it is read and loved by hundreds of thousands of children who literally wear out the originally published copies." She encourages me to write stories children will cherish.

Paterson has tackled tough subjects in her books for the young set. She tells me, "Writing is a form of self-judgment, and so, in my books, I must battle the giants I shrink from." Am I willing to face and be honest about my giants when I write?

Best-selling author, Robert Newton Peck, helps me understand the need to write short, exciting, and real. In his book, *Fiction is Folks,* Peck says, "Writers, good ones, don't tell stories. Characters show stories."

Turning to Our Latest Disaster

Gail Denham

Levees collapse, overflow; wind vents anger
on flimsy wood. The old and disenfranchised
cry for water, bread, and milk for their babies.

Rivers leave their beds, surge into houses,
leer at family pictures, cover memory icons,
then toss all into trashy graves.

Subways erupt in fire; people scream, claw
to escape. Soldiers drive through war streets,
murmur frantic prayers. The earth heaves.

Heartsick, the poet gives, prays, struggles for words
of courage or hope which won't be blown up,
broken, or smothered in moldy loss.

Where his pen marks the page, where his knees dent
the prayer carpet, where his thoughts rush to the world,
a tremulous light glows.

Alta Leah Emrick

Alta is a retired office manager and co-pastor with a Doctor of Divinity degree. She has written *Laugh to Live and Live to Laugh* joke book, *Wisdom for Successful Living, Grandma Alta's Fables, Surviving and Thriving with Only God's Love,* and many published articles and poems.

Grace and the Baseball Stadium

Alta Leah Emrick

"**A**re you safe or are you out?"

Let's visualize a sports stadium. On the outside of this sports stadium is a large parking lot. In the parking lot are all those under the Laws of God; but just under the laws only, and not under Grace—in other words, the worldly.

Some people are there for the tailgate party. They are unconcerned about the Laws of God, Grace, or anything else. Maximum pleasure and enjoyment is the name of their game.

Others are there with an Old Testament mind set, while others have many or no gods—that is anyone who searches toward God and finds Him in Nirvana, or the Dance of Shiva, but is without Jesus Christ. To these in the parking lot Jesus is their nice brother, but brother only, or sometimes they elevate Him to a prophet, but prophet only.

These people, then, can only view the door of the stadium, the door of Grace. They are good people and close to Grace, but not interested in buying a ticket, yet.

"The laws came by Moses but Truth and Grace came by Jesus Christ" (John 1:17). The Laws of God are the Ten Commandments. The word Grace in Hebrew means to receive favor. Those under Grace are favored. There was Grace in the Old Testament, but it was given to specific individuals, such as Noah and the Major and Minor Prophets. They were favored because they were singled out for specific assignments.

Then, in the New Testament, God chose to bring Grace to all people through Jesus Christ. To get inside the Stadium of Grace, one must buy a ticket and walk through the door. The ticket is bought by having faith in Jesus as a personal Savior, as told in the four gospels. This faith is the believing and professing that Jesus Christ is Lord and Savior. This is the passageway into the Stadium of Grace. Because there is only one door, there is no other entrance into the stadium. "I am the way, the truth, and the life, no man comes to the Father, but by me" (John 14:6). I repeat "no man" comes to the Father, but by me.

Now, since the people in the stadium are all under God's Grace, all are favored. All are under Grace all the time no matter where they are located because all are in the stadium.

However, there are many places people can sit or stand in this ball field. Even though all are under Grace, there is a responsibility to living the Laws of God. The Laws are outside the stadium in the parking lot with the worldly and inside the stadium under Grace. Remember that Jesus came to fulfill the Laws not to destroy them as in Matthew 5:17. The fulfillment of the laws is that people love God in addition to loving one another and acting lovingly toward each other.

Therefore, while in the ball field all people are to grow in Grace. We also call it growing in loving. Grace expands— it is not flat or one-level. Grace means to be favored and all can grow in being favored and giving favors. In the gospels, Jesus grew in Grace—Jesus grew in favor. Likewise, God anoints us according to our faith and Grace.

Let us consider the different positions in the ball field. Some people are pitchers. They are actively watching their movements intently in order not to be caught off guard. Many times they are persecuted from the stands. In other words, paying close attention to the Laws of God and Love, and being up front with it; proclaiming God's Word; witnessing and letting others see it unashamedly. This position takes the unselfish effort of putting in the time to help others. Many pitchers are in the missionary fields.

Some people are batters. They are up for testing to see how their souls have grown in Grace and what they have learned thus far. Now these people can be graded. At bat one shows how good they can be to keep aim and be direct. Being at bat is being humble enough to let others see if they stumble but being willing to do it anyway—in other words, taking a chance for God.

Some people play the outfield so they can drift around a bit—actively playing, but farther away from the intensity of things. They help "occasionally" when something or someone hits the ball their way.

Some people are on first, second, third, and home plate, depending on when they started to bat, how long they stayed with it, and how they passed the batting test. If they strike out, they must go back to batting—in other words being tested, striking out, and having to relearn the lesson again. However, some people hit homeruns immediately and pass on the first try. It all depends on the person's passion for the Lord and the time they are willing to give Him.

Some people get thrown off of home plate and have to wait to hit the ball again. In other words, they go back through the lessons that they tried to avoid or skip over and did not learn the first time.

There can be sneaking and cheating in the stadium— trying to steal bases within the Laws, but when they get caught, they reap. The Law of sowing and reaping is one of the laws under the Laws of God.

In baseball one can slide and it is okay. In Grace, people can also slide and it is okay, but that is also going to be their reward. They will get an "okay." Okays are okay, but they don't come with heavenly rewards such as greater joy and peaceful lives.

Some people come into the doors of the baseball stadium under Grace proclaiming the Lord and singing the National Anthem at the top of their lungs. It is beautiful, but when they have finished the first song, they are never heard from again.

These are seeds thrown on stony places as mentioned in Matthew 13:5-6. "Some seeds (seeds being the Word of God) fell upon stony places, where they had not much earth: and forthwith they sprung up, because they had no deepness of: and when the sun was up, they were scorched; and because they had no root, they withered away."

It means that those who received the seed into stony places, are the same that hear the Bible teachings of God and receive it with joy. Yet these people have no roots (no courage or depth of character). They continue for a while, but when tribulations or persecutions arise because of God's Word or Christianity, they are offended and walk away.

Some people come into the Stadium of Grace by proclaiming the Lord, yet they are not much at activity. They like to speculate from the bleachers, and they should because these are the ones that usually know how the active ones on the field could have done it better. These are the outspoken judges. Within their viewpoint from such a higher realm, they even see when the outfielders are slack or not attentive enough. For the help they give from the stands, they will also get their place in Grace. For their judging, they will be judged.

"Judge not, that ye be not judged. For with what judgment ye judge, ye shall be judged: and with what measure ye mete, it shall be measured to you again" (Matthew 7:1-2). Which, broken down, means that if we sow unloving judging about others, we will reap unloving judging from others.

In addition, we all know that if these spectators would lay their hotdogs down and come out on the field and play, the Body of Christ would be greatly advanced.

Some people come into Grace and have no particular interest in the game, the Laws, living the Ten Commandments, or even learning the game. They are there for the camaraderie, fellowship, socializing, who they can meet, or to sell their business products. They hang out under the bleachers where it is shaded and cooler—the concession stand area. They spend their time filling the body with treats from the concession stand—things that taste good, such as going to bazars and socials. They like the concession stand area because it is in the shade with a cool breezy air, and they don't have to become under the hot sun, or get the dust from the field on their clothes.

In other words, they don't have to put up with persecutions as the pitcher does, they don't even have to take a position. They don't have to be concerned with playing by the rules of God. They don't even have to learn them. They never fail, never go to bat, and never get humiliated. They never strike out, and their report card is not marred, but it is blank. They ask for little, give little, and receive little.

Some people even walk back out the door—only a few, but some. People get in by their belief and faith in Jesus Christ as Savior, and they can leave by their beliefs. They go back to Egypt into disbelief or another non-Christian religion, sometimes they even take on agnostic or atheistic beliefs. They have the God-given right to leave, but they also lose the favors of Grace and are banned from the Stadium of Grace and the Heavenly Kingdom.

As an example: I went to church with a woman many years ago; let's call her Jeannie Ann. When she came to church she was gravely ill. Through much prayer from the congregation, she was healed. She kept up attendance for two months, and then confided in me that she wasn't going to live for God anymore. She would live for God on her next lifetime here. She left the church.

Let me clarify Jeannie Ann's mistake. Scripture says it is allotted for man to live once and then die. After death, we, then, either pass into Heaven or Hell. No one reincarnates from Heaven to Earth; who would want to? And, no one reincarnates from Hell back to Earth. But, there are people like Jeannie Ann, who walk back out of the Stadium of Grace totally ignorant of the serious mistake their false beliefs will cost them.

Some people find the Stadium too hot, sticky, noisy, or uncomfortable. They didn't meet the right people for their business connections or mating purposes. These people prefer the Old Testament religious views. These are those who did not get free of the material fun, did not like the testing, trials, temptations, or persecutions, and were more interested in worldly ways and money. They would rather be at home in air-conditioning, watching TV and telling themselves that God has a perfect spot in Heaven just for them. And, if I might add, God does have a perfect little garden just for them.

This does not include the frail elderly or shut-ins who can no longer work for the kingdom. They have excused absence cards and anointed blessings.

At the end of the season, people get an emblematic letter, a big "G" to sew on their sweaters. It is a gift from the owner of the stadium. When they put these letters on, it brings different things because it comes in many sizes and colors. Some put it on and can start doing healings. Some can open up and prophesize. Some sweaters wear well with preaching, other sizes are fit for talking in tongues, doing helps, caregiving the sick and frail elderly, organizing hospitality, and so on.

But even if some people don't get a letter for their sweaters, everyone gets a glass of wine as in Galatians 5:22. These character-building wines come in nine flavors of fruit:

1. love
2. joy
3. peace
4. patience
5. gentleness
6. goodness
7. faith
8. meekness
9. self-control

To live the Laws of Grace and love, we must love. To

have Grace, we must have Jesus Christ. How we express love will dictate what position we play in the ball game. Those who direct their love toward themselves will be spectators sitting on the bleachers. Those who direct their love toward others are the active players, who will enjoy warmer sweaters, with prettier letters, and drinking larger glasses of wine.

No One Left Out

Alta Leah Emrick

Every pen has a script with a scene.
Every tongue has a story to tell.
Every note has a song to sing.
Every poet has a rhyme to sell.

Every day has a lesson to learn.
Every lark has a sound to tweet.
Every penny has it moment to earn.
Every candy has its particular sweet.

Every guy has a beauty to date.
Every dog has a family as master.
Every girl has a beau to mate.
Every chair leg has its caster.

Every green tree has a dripping sap.
Every terrain has its form of sod.
Every cat has a loving warm lap.
And every human being has God.

The Contagious Smile

Alta Leah Emrick

Have you ever been angry about everything? Well, I have. I woke up on "the heavy side of the bed," one day and was angry about everything. Things felt out of sorts, and then life proved it so.

On this particular day my zipper grip broke, the shoes were too tight, the pleated skirt sagged unevenly, and the neck scarf had an unraveled thread. The outfit staring back from the mirror looked like stylish attic. I felt like something the cat would not drag in. In addition, the toast burnt, the coffee was bitter, and the toilet paper spool was empty. Most assuredly, Murphy had snuck into this house overnight and wrote all over the walls.

Life consisted of aging parents, a know-it-all teenager, and a boss who was a contender in my daily fight for patience. There was an ongoing civil war at church over policy issues. If I had been living on the sun, a bright corner could not have been found. One morning, like the walls of Jericho, it came "a tumbling down." Unable to rally, I pleaded to Jesus for help. Life, then, took an unexpected but pleasant turn.

Parking close to the office was costly so I parked in the economy lot, a two-block hike to the building. The usual brisk exercise felt like marching across the Mohave Desert carrying a ball and chain. Pushing through the revolving doors, I shuffled to the elevator and hard-pressed the button. With furrowed eyebrows and a bent head, I stepped in and propped my back against the wall. The doors closed.

Suddenly, an eerie feeling came over me. The kind where one feels there are eyes upon them. Like a scared cat, the hairs on the nape of my neck bristled upward. Someone besides me was in the elevator, probably from the street-level floor below. As a municipal building, eccentrics of a potentially harmful nature wandered in and out. The feeling in the pit of my stomach asked, "How safe are you right now?"

We were in the close quarters of a five foot by five foot moving box and I had not noticed another occupant. Slowly, as my body straightened and head lifted to present a confident pose, I glanced up. On the other side was a man. He was tall, lean, and clean-shaven with neatly cut, dark brown hair, and somewhere in his late forties. His well-dressed body leisurely rested against the grab rail. He was intently looking at me.

It was not the stare that grab my attention; it was the smile. His mouth broadly formed an upward, quarter-moon smile. Not laughing at me or snickering, just a genuine smile: warm, kind, caring. It said, "How are you. It is great to be alive." As he was such a contrast from my mood, I was momentarily startled. A challenging stare transfixed my face as if to say, "Do you really mean that smile?" His bright eyes conveyed a "yes." Neither of us spoke.

Motion began as floors whizzed by. The elevator did a minute lurch, doors opened wide, and he stepped out, and disappeared down the hallway. The essence of that smile remained in the air as though someone had doused the elevator with a lingering fragrance. I missed that smile. I wanted it back! My lips parted slowly to form the start of a smile. It became wider and wider—a thick washcloth could not have wiped it away. As I exited the elevator, still donned in the frumpy wardrobe, my spirits had lifted. As my hand turned the office door knob, I was soaring. The day flew by faster than a Concord jet.

All day I thought about the elevator man and his igniting smile. That one-moment smile changed not only my whole day, but also a different way of thinking. Now if I do not initially feel in a good mood, I start with a small grin. Sometimes the starting mark feels phony, like plastic skin that might crack into pieces, but soon I feel happy.

God used a stranger on the elevator to answer my prayer and to find a practical way to think and feel positive on a blue day. I, like the elevator man, have become an unwavering "smiler." I have learned that a smile is the matchstick for a thousand happy thoughts.

The Pushy Sergeant and the Reluctant Lady

Alta Leah Emrick

"**I**'m going to woo you," he said.

Those were my husband's first courting words, a man who waited three decades to find his voice. But who says "wooing" today? Follow along the seven acts of our unique and endearing story.

The Friendship:

Fred was a teenager, and I was thirtyish and married. He lived with his dad's cousin, who was my neighbor. The town's population was a couple thousand and buried deep in the hills of Missouri. Since I had a son, my house was the teen community gathering place, and eventually, Fred visited. Sensing his loneliness, I was an active listener to his detective novels. Enthusiasm oozed from every pore as he related the dastardly deeds. He was cheerful and entertaining. Humor seemed to be a common thread between us, which made the conversations refreshing.

Life took an abrupt turn for both of us. Falling in with the wrong crowd, he decided to enlist in the military and headed for basic training. Goodbyes and good luck were echoed. I divorced and moved back to my hometown. Disillusioned with marriage, all dating ceased. My life was full with a rewarding career, raising a son, active church work, and family and friends.

Years flew by as Fred traveled the globe. If he were stationed close to my hometown, the doorbell would ring. Each furlough brought a visit. Teddy bears were received on holidays. Being blessed with many friends, I assumed we were common garden variety acquaintances.

Eventually, he married in Germany, but it ended in the States. With the stripes of a drill sergeant, he retired after twenty years of service, and became a correctional officer.

The Visit:

"Hi. It's me," a familiar voice came through the phone. He related that his dad had had open-heart surgery, which prompted his returning home. And, by his calculations, it had been 16 years since we'd seen each other, and could he come for a visit?

I stood at the door as a car pulled into the driveway, paused and reversed. I wasn't recognized! Embarrassment pinked my face; a face much older. The car returned and he exited. A stout man stood in front of a gray-haired woman; then, like parting clouds, the years faded. We hugged. He was now 49-years-old and I was 14 years his senior. Like chattering teenage girls, "and let me tell you" melted the years for the next two days. The old spunk was still there.

As the dread of his departure closed in, I surprisingly blurted out, "This has been the best two days of my entire year."

"And for me." His reply was genuine.

I was stunned. It was hard to believe that two days with me were his best in the year. Crossing the room to kiss my forehead, I tilted upward to speak and the kiss landed center on my lips. It tasted sweeter than the nectar of wine itself. Three rapid thoughts came. *That was the sweetest kiss of my entire life, who knew he could kiss like that, and I want another one.*

Sunlight brought the morning; promises to keep in touch were heartily exchanged, and he left.

The Letter:

The words of the letter read that he had loved me all of his life, the love had deepened through the years of absence, and that he was tired of waiting. Would I come out and dance with him? Being old school, I was skeptical. *What exactly does dancing mean in today's language?*

Ring, ring, ring—the phone receiver clattered on the

cradle. "I'm going to woo you," he declared. "I'm not a teenager anymore, and I know exactly how I feel. If you could only feel my heart, you'd know."

The Storm Trooper:

His second visit approached. It was four hours of hefty driving to my home, and the winter weather was treacherous. He started out against my will. If worry had color, my face was pasty-white. Driving all night through a dangerous blizzard, he stormed the door. Resembling a take-the-hill solider, he reached out and enfolded me. No preliminaries—no lead up. Like a stick of hot butter on an Arizona highway, our hearts melted. Dating began, love soared like a tram to its highest peak, and blessings seemed to fall from the sky.

Out of the blue he announced that I was the only person who had ever listened to him, and could the wedding bells ring for us. Like a frightened alley cat, ripples of fear cascaded down my spine—my icy-cold hands quaked. I argued that he was too young. Why don't we just date and say we always had Paris? Furthermore, he needed to be patient. His head reared back as he roared with laughter, "Be patient. I've waited 33 years!"

I spouted there was too much on my plate. Soon a red-rose painted plate hung on my living room wall. It was to "give me more plate space."

Similar to the Cavalry, four take-charge proposals advanced my front. I retreated. He still looked too young. Then suddenly, as if looking through binoculars, I saw his balding head, gray hair, and receding hairline. He *was* an older man. *Where had I been?*

"If I had only two years to live, would you marry me?" I shyly inquired. The "yes" came swiftly. On Leap Year, I took the offense and made the fifth proposal, and we wed.

Matching Differences:

We are totally different and yet as matched as mated geese. He's a gourmet-level cook, I make doorstop biscuits. He's jazz, I'm opera. He's never late, I split the whistle.

However, we now celebrate the differences that irritated us in the beginning. "I love you as you are" has become our successful mantra. We thrive together in the same soil like a beautiful bouquet of wildflowers that bloom in rich profusion.

The Humor Connection:

Laughter is a daily must. There are impromptu comedies, such as our sequestered quiet Christmas day. Bright candles dressed the room; cinnamon incense burned while soft music played in the background. As I exited the kitchen, a man with red velvet shorts, cuffed in a four-inch fuzzy white hem, a Santa's hat, red socks capped in white to the knees, and bells on a wide black belt, jumped in front of me. I doubled over howling.

This might have been payback for my gift to him. Ugly is a Christmastime tradition in my family. Each member tries to out-ugly the other in gift exchange. A chanteuse-checkered stuffed lion, a red-faced woman in a blue frame, and a botched and dented African mask are a few of the artistic atrocities that have been given out. His initiation was complete with my gift of a buggy green-eyed, purple statue with a long red tongue that drooped as it threateningly sang, "I'm going to get you."

Humor also follows at his workplace. His fellow officers keep ribbing, "Now let me get this straight. You married your babysitter?" And, when the nightly news announced an elderly woman had her wheelchair stolen, they inquired, "Fred, was that your wife?"

The Synchronization of Love's Essence:

An invisible finely tuned harmony is ever flowing. It is the rhythm of a couple hearts beating in two-part harmony. If one feels outs of sorts the other feels the break. Perhaps trite, but we make each other's heart sing.

A magnetic pull returns us to each other like being synchronized in time; we want to be in the same room. Our longest goodbyes are work hours, and that is a hardship. Snuggling brings a closeness that transcends worldly awareness, the essence of feelings that become the thinking.

Due to the deepening of our love, blindness to our age difference has occurred. Like cheese on a hamburger patty, we have melted together. If there are degrees in romance, our courtship was a master's and our marriage is a doctorate.

Gibraltar-Solid Love:

We have a very workable bargain. If one is down, the other pulls them up. There is no anger because you said such and such. Instead, there is an invisible "throw me a rope" clue for the other partner.

We redo our vows yearly; this year will be number nine. Kisses, hugs and saying "I love you" ten times a day is our usual ritual. To the delight of my card playing girlfriends, my romantic and bold officer husband will come while the canasta club is in full-swing and give me a teddy bear and a kiss.

As a senior, I had experienced my first appliance, jewelry and child, and was looking toward the golden horizon. Unknown to me, the fat lady hadn't sung my song yet. Now instead, like a flower that turns toward her sun for warmth, my love turns toward my husband's heart. I don't have to die to have heaven. It is right here in my home.

I have learned that love has no age or time limits, there are happy marriages, and life can be great in the senior years.

The Robbery

Alta Leah Emrick

The doctor smiled so very sweetly
Off my feet I was taken back a bit
Concern across his eyebrows shown
He was there for me, *please sit*

It is a shame the world at large
Does not act this wonderful
To all the people they service
Like those taught in med school

Cozy warmth around me flowed
To know someone took note
Listen he did to every word
Prescribing the right antidote

Robbery isn't always done by
A brutally-faced hunky man
With rotted teeth and tattoos
And a beard like dark sand

The doctor's bill soon did arrive
My nerves were quite undone
Doc had a medical degree
Armed with a shotgun

The Rude Awakening

Alta Leah Emrick

A frog I once knew
Was suddenly slew
How deeply I cried
So very sad was I

Then with a whiff
Froggy did a shift
His body ballooned
To a full-grown groom

I'm your new prize
And that's not a lie
Spoke this fine man
In front of me stand

If you're not choosy
Want a little schmoozy
If you're not particular
Climb in my vehicular

Hand in hand we will file
Walking down the aisle
Our lives will be full
Of laughter, our tool

My heart started to beat
My face pink with heat
Oh, golly, oh, gee
Is this happening to me?

Suddenly and with a start
As if hitting hard enough to smart
I was then awfully shaken
When upon my bed I awaken

Yvonne Erwin

Yvonne is a women's fiction author living in Springfield, Missouri. Her first full-length novel, *The Discovery of Joy*, is available on Amazon and Barnes & Noble. She has served the Springfield Writers' Guild as secretary, vice president, and president. She is a member of Ozarks Romance Authors.

Away from Paris

Yvonne Erwin

It was hot in Paris in the summer of 1929. We were drinking, drinking a lot in fact, playing cards upstairs at Pappy's on Rue El Russo when Housley abruptly announced he was going to Spain. Unfortunately for me, I was losing money, and I was fairly drunk. All of us were drunk, except for Harlie, Paul Shepard's wife, who disappeared to the ladies room for a minute because the cigarette smoke made her sick.

Housley folded his cards and stood. "I'm going to Spain," he said. I knew he was goading me. I knew why he was going to Spain.

"The hell you are," I said.

"I am going," he insisted.

"Sit down, Housley, you're not going anywhere," I said. "Quit being an asshole."

"Right, big tough guy, get up in my face, Jack," Housley said, but he didn't move. He stood, hands in pockets. We were a sorry lot, having drunk too much whiskey, too much wine, too much of everything.

I felt Paul's hand on my arm as I started up. He jerked me back down. "Knock it off, Housley. Sit down, Jack."

"Don't be an asshole, Housley," was all I could think to say and I said no more because Harlie was back from the bathroom with new red lipstick on.

Harlie was a beautiful woman but she was not my woman, and in fact she was Paul's woman and he was so much the better for it. Of this, I was certain. I might have been the better for it too, if she was mine that was, but she was not and never would be.

We left then, the game over and my pockets empty. We

walked, Harlie, Paul, and I. Housley disappeared the moment the party broke up.

We were still walking when Harlie said, "Where'd Housley go?"

"He thinks he's going to Spain," Paul said.

She looped her arm through Paul's and she was looking around him at me.

"Why is he going to Spain?"

Neither of us answered.

"You know Housley; he has no thought in his head unless somebody puts it there. Who invited him to go?" She was persistent.

"Alex is there," Paul said. I said nothing.

"Oh," she gave me a look and pulled herself back beside Paul. One thing I admired about Harlie was she didn't hand out judgment on other women. She did not do it and we all knew she could easily judge and execute Alex. We all knew what Alex was, always been, and I, for one, still loved Alex.

We finally found a little café where we had supper and more wine. That was what we did in Paris that year. We watched the parades, held every day it seemed in honor of some dead patron saint. We saluted France's flag as it crossed by and cheered for the gaily dressed participants and then we went to a café and we drank wine to celebrate every single one of the dead saints. It was a matter of respect. So what if we did not believe, and I had no idea what anyone other than I believed, it was a matter of respect. Pay your dues and your dues will be paid.

Housley never did turn up that night. Paul and Harlie eventually wandered off to the hotel and I slumped in the chair a moment longer before following them back.

Housley going to Spain neither bothered nor intimidated me, not much anyway. He would like to have come out and said that Alex invited him, but he did not and I was doubtful she had. In fact, I was rather certain she had not. Housley thought everyone doted on him. I did not.

When I got to the hotel, there was a telegram from my

editor at the newspaper back in Chicago. I was being sent to Italy to report on prostitution and the Italian Mafia in Tuscany. I was to be ready to leave by 8:30 in the morning. It was nearly five already.

I walked to another café not far from the hotel and began scribbling in my journal. Since I couldn't sleep, it was great one could always find an open café in Paris anytime day or night. I was writing the Great American Novel that I could not get published. Crouched over my journal, I no longer felt drunk but I felt low. I kept writing even though it was hard and I lost my enthusiasm for it. I just kept on writing.

A girl sat down by the windows. She was young, blond and her hair was tangled. My immediate thought was she must be in trouble. I wanted to study her without her knowing it. When I looked back up from my journal she was no longer sitting in front of the window and I thought she left until I realized she was sitting next to me.

She was much older than I suspected from across the room and much more worn. I realized where she came from right about then.

"Are you the American journalist?" she asked. Her voice was ethereal. Her eyes were green. "You are, aren't you?"

"I suppose so, yes," I replied. "But who's asking?"

She leaned in close, her chin on her fist.

"I need to tell you something. Your friend, Housley."

"Housley's no friend of mine," I interrupted harshly and while it was true, I waited to hear what she had to say.

"He's in a bad way, mister."

"I have to leave in a few hours. I have an assignment," I began to explain. "Out of the country."

She shrugged. "He said you would say that." The front of her dress gaped open as she got up.

"Wait," I said, neither caring nor being much interested in whatever scrape Housley got into this time. She turned, looking down at me.

"Why? You care nothing about him. You are a scornful man."

There was nothing I could say to that.

"Where is he?"

She told me he was at the Hotel Maison. I knew the name and it was in a less savory section of the city. How Housley got there, I didn't know and didn't ask. She said we could walk to it. Neither one of us spoke much.

When we arrived, I was amazed how shabby the place was, not that it ever had been well kept. Some of the windows were boarded shut. Others had grates welded over them. I wondered if any of the French doors to the balconies opened any longer. The alley was piled with trash and the stench of urine and unwashed bodies was everywhere.

"Do you work here?" I asked her.

"Sometimes," she replied without looking at me.

We went upstairs to a small apartment. It smelled as bad as the street.

Housley lay in bed, naked, tangled in sheets, moaning. His lip was bleeding and a bottle of kirsch lay next to the bed. A dark haired woman was sitting in a chair next to him, wearing a black silk robe with big red flowers on it. She was smoking a cigarette.

"What's he taken?" I asked her.

She rolled her eyes at me. "You name it, mister."

"Help me get him up," I said to both of them. Neither one moved. "Get up and help me!"

My new friend from the café took one of Housley's arms. The other one sighed heavily, stubbed her cigarette out, and came to the side of the bed. "It's his business, mister," she said.

"So you get paid and you can let him go comatose?"

"You're an asshole, mister. Why should I help you?"

"You're not. Help me with him."

I pulled him up. The blond got on the other side and shoved. For no bigger than what he was, Housley was a hell of a haul off that bed. His head lobbed on my shoulder and I smelled his vomit on my jacket. He was mumbling incoherently.

"Walk him," I said. "We're going to walk him around this room, got it?"

The blond put her arm around Housley and nodded. The other one sat back down in the chair and watched.

"Come on Housley, you asshole," I said to him. "Walk now."

"Waaaa," Housley said. "Sonnnnuvabeeesh."

His legs acted like rubber but his feet still worked.

As the blond and I walked Housley around the room, the dark haired woman made coffee and smoked.

We walked for the better part of an hour. When he was lucid enough to realize he was naked, Housley screamed like a girl.

"You've been naked in front of these girls all night, what difference does it make now?" I asked him, throwing the sheet at him. He sat on the edge of the bed, looking as if an apparition approached him and not in a nice way. He gathered the sheets up to his private area.

We made him drink coffee and then water when the coffee ran out.

When I left, the blond girl thanked me before shutting the door. I walked back to my hotel, showered, changed clothes, and barely made my train. Housley was a mess. *He will be worse if he goes to Spain*, I reasoned.

Ten days later, I returned to Paris. The checks from my last few assignments were in and I was flush again. Paul and Harlie were back from the states as well and they brought one of their friends, someone called Robert, with them. Robert was a writer too, they said. Housley was nowhere to be found. We all assumed he was in Spain.

It was still hot and the stench still unbelievable, filling up our pores. The smell and the heat nauseated us, a good reason to continue drinking wine.

"Why do we keep coming back here?" Harlie said. She

was fanning herself with a paper napkin.

"Because we love it," Paul said to her.

That much was true. "It's a city for dogs," I said. We were drinking wine on the plaza of our hotel.

"Oui, oui," Paul said. "And we are dogs."

"We are swine," I reminded him.

"Oh yes, swine. Thank you," he said raising his glass to me.

"Speak for yourselves, gentlemen," Harlie said.

Robert, who said nothing so far, seemed to want to get my attention. Finally, he said, "Can you teach me how to write?"

His hair was slicked back and his glasses were sliding down his nose. He was an earnest young man, although a little silly in my opinion. He wanted my approval.

Instead I said, "No, I can't teach you how to write any more than I can grow grass. Writing comes from inside, it cannot be taught. Improved upon perhaps, but never taught." I was feeling fairly superior by this time, partly because I was half drunk and partly because I had been paid for writing I had done recently, and I felt superior. And because I believed Housley was gone.

Robert sat back in his chair, stunned.

"Oh Jack, now you're being an asshole," said a voice from over my shoulder. She sat down and extended her hand to Robert, who was obviously shaken by her. "I'm Alex," she said.

"Robert," he replied staring.

"Really Jack, you know more about writing than just about anyone. Hello everybody," Alex said. "Coach this young man and don't be such an insufferable boor about it."

She was smoking a cigarette. I poured her a glass of wine.

"Hello Alex," I said. "Where's that Duke of yours?"

"Dead," she replied. "Dead as a door nail. That's why I've been so long in coming. Had to stay for the inquest. Cause of death – being naked with me, I suppose."

She was tanned and beautiful and her hair was darker and sleeker than ever. It reminded me of sealskin, wet, blue, and black, and electric.

"Have you seen Housley?" I asked her. Not because I cared. Only because I was curious.

"Sure," she said.

"Is he with you now? We're a bit worried about him," Harlie said. "The last time we heard, he was in a bad way."

"No, he's not with me. I sent him away days ago. What a bore. Jack, let's go for a walk."

I nodded. The only thing I would have wanted was to go for a walk with Alex. She was wearing a white sundress with a square neckline and sandals. Nothing about her was imperfect. Well, on the surface anyway. We left the table behind, carrying a bottle with us. She leaned heavily against me.

"Oh Jack, I've been so frightened," she said once we were out of earshot of the others.

"Of what?"

"That it would be thought I'd killed the Duke somehow and that I'd never leave that country. Mostly that I'd never see you again, but even if I didn't ever see you again, you know how I feel."

"Yes, and you know how I feel, beautiful Alex."

She took a swig from the bottle without spilling a drop.

"It's a pity. I've two ruined marriages, a dead Duke, and the only man that I've ever really loved, I can't have. The stars are against me, eh?"

I said nothing. We both knew how that was.

"I do love you, Jack. You know I do."

"I do."

"Why are you staring?"

"Because you are so beautiful, Alex. You never change."

She snorted. "What has beauty gotten me? Well, I guess it's made me sickeningly rich, but it didn't bring me love."

"I do love you, Alex," I said.

"I know," she said.

We were close to my hotel and Alex wanted to go upstairs. It didn't matter. Nothing would happen. A high fever during an assignment in the jungle, before coming to Paris and after meeting Alex, robbed me of my love-making prowess. Alex was disappointed in me, I knew it, and I also knew nothing was worse in life than having a disappointed woman. I couldn't keep her at arm's length though.

We slept and then we got up and went out to find a late dinner. We talked of the Duke and his death and our love for one another. It was a good evening and we drank more wine and went back to the hotel and slept some more. August was waning away and I knew I needed to get back to Chicago and take some new assignment. I did not care what really, just so I was making some money.

I needed to see my doctor. The new tickle in my throat gave way to a cough, more or less permanent, and was now congestion and I wanted to see my own doctor in the states. Alex, of course, insisted on coming back to America with me. I, of course, insisted that she not. It was not our way, she and me, to be too domestic together.

The Sister Story

Yvonne Erwin

Quinn

Quinn glanced up from her tablet.

"Knock, please," Quinn said, going back to her tablet.

"Um, look, baby, I have to tell you something." Shelby Graham Harper perched on the edge of the bed, depressing the mattress as her weight settled on it. The dull hue of Quinn's Mickey Mouse lamp turned Shelby's skin yellow. Quinn watched the light quiver.

"What?" Quinn rolled over, holding her stomach. What now? What freaking thing now?

"India's coming back."

"So?"

"And she's moving in here for a while."

Quinn sat up, knocking the tablet to the floor. "Mom, no. I don't like her. She thinks she's better than us, you don't like her either."

She watched Shelby turn the ring that loser, Phillip, gave her around her left ring finger. Throwing up would be good right now. Quinn couldn't stand Phillip; thank God he was gone, but Shelby still wore that cheap Cracker Jack ring.

"I don't want her here."

"Quinn, she's family, she's my sister. Was I supposed to say no?"

Quinn stood up.

"Uh, yeah."

Quinn watched Shelby's face turn downward.

"Why is she coming back?"

"I guess she had a little something happen to her, like

her boyfriend died of cancer. She's taking a leave from the network."

"Why is she coming to our house?"

"Well, it's her house too, I mean, technically. She grew up here."

"No. I don't want her here."

Shelby sat silent, a toad squatting on Quinn's bed.

"Forget it, Mom."

The urge to run hit, it was fight or flight time and Quinn favored flight. She ran out her bedroom door, down the stairs, while Shelby called for her to come back, all the way down to the main hallway, and out the front door, down the walkway to the sidewalk.

Once on the sidewalk, Quinn looked left and right and then crossed the street and began running north.

Her mother's voice sounded in her ears. "Quinn! *Quinn Antonia Demarist! Come back here right now!*"

No way. No way would she share a house with that snob, India. India, the big reporter woman, been all over the world and back, been on TV, India who didn't remember her family so far as Quinn was concerned.

India

What did she look like anyway? The TV anchor Quinn saw on the news looked a little like her, brown hair, angled face, but the eyes and ears were different. Quinn's eyes were brown, her complexion was dark, her ears resembled a taxicab with the doors open. India's eyes were blue, her ears weren't prominent. But still, sometimes when Quinn and Shelby, and sometimes Gwen too, watched India on TV or saw photos of her, Shelby would point out something about India's pose, her stance, her eye movement, and she'd say, "Quinn, you do that too. You're so much like her."

Quinn hated being compared to her aunt. She barely knew India; she had so few memories of her, and didn't know if she liked her or not. All she had to draw from was what her mother said to her about India, and Shelby found every reason in the world to say India thought more of herself than she should; that India left their town and family to be a big star and didn't care about them; that India thought she was better than them. Did Quinn like her aunt? Most likely not.

I don't want her coming here, Quinn thought as she ran. Fear gripped her heart. *She'll change everything.*

"Hey now, slow down lady," a voice came out of nowhere, propelling Quinn to stop and face Gwen. "You're gonna make me trip and fall all over you."

Quinn came to an abrupt halt in front of Shelby's old friend, Gwen.

"Oh, hey, Gwen."

"Where you running to, girl? And why you runnin' when you can stroll, hunh?"

In spite of herself, Quinn grinned, and realized she ran straight to Gwen's block, to her bungalow, in fact. How did that happen?

"You want to come in?" Gwen said. "You look like you all out. Come on, I got Coca-Cola, and I know you like that."

The brick porch with the taupe door opened an invitation. Quinn stood, contemplating about going forward, into this wonderful reality and decided she would.

"Come on, child," Gwen said. "Let's sit on the porch and drink soda and you tell me what it's all about."

Gwen and Quinn ended up sitting at Gwen's Formica table in her kitchen. Quinn gazed around at the apple clock hanging above the sink.

"My aunt India is coming back," Quinn said setting her Coke bottle on the table. "I can't stand it."

"Oh, India, well, I remember her as a girl." Quinn saw Gwen's face light up upon the suggestion of India. "You don't like her?"

Quinn stared into the speckled table top before answering. She had nothing to borrow from as far as India was concerned, when India was a girl or whatever. Quinn wasn't even alive then.

Quinn burrowed her hands in the pocket of her jacket.

"I can't stand her. She thinks she's above us, she's a snob, I don't want her here. She's gonna change everything."

"Change what? Everything's a pretty big word, Quinn." Gwen belched. "Excuse me."

"She's gonna change my mom, she's gonna change me, she doesn't fit in here. My mom says she thinks we're trash. I hate her!"

"But you don't know her, right? You don't know whether or not you like her. You're going with someone else's opinion, I think. What do you think, Quinn?"

"I don't know what I think. But I know my mom is gonna let her come and move in with us whether I like it or not."

"When will she be here?"

"Tomorrow morning, I guess."

"Why do you think she's coming?"

"I don't know, and I don't care."

Quinn stood up, but was instantly conscious of Gwen's hooded stare.

"Maybe, Quinn, just maybe, your aunt needs support right now. Maybe she's not as strong as she portrays, or what you think, and maybe she's not as highbrow as you imagine. Maybe she's a real person. Think about that."

Quinn sat back down on the edge of the chair.

"Uh, no. She's a jerk."

"I doubt she's a jerk. The India I remember wasn't a jerk. Quinn, you only know what you've been told. People hold prejudices, everyone does."

Quinn stood.

"I gotta go."

"Okay. I'll drive you."

"No, I'll run. Thanks."

"Well, in that case, I'll call your mother and let her know you're on your way, right?"

"Sure, thanks." And with those words, Quinn found herself out the door to the sidewalk.

Running back home.

But India was still coming, *tomorrow*, and Quinn didn't quite know how she would deal with that.

Gwen

Gwen Jones saw the green-gray fog, the smoky issue, even before she saw Quinn, enveloped in her aura, running her direction.

Oh boy, here we go, Gwen thought and so she walked to the corner because Quinn was coming that way, and when she saw Quinn, Gwen saw the green-gray aura surrounding her.

Jealously. Fear. Indecision.

Quinn was running, hair flowing behind her ears, eyes wide open. Gwen stepped in front of her, because no one else was going to rescue this girl.

***

Colors, auras, whatever you want to call it, Gwen saw them. Shelby was dark pink, like a spring rose, the color of unconditional acceptance. Normally, Quinn's aura was sea foam green, the color of expectation.

She didn't know why she saw these things, she just did, and over the years Gwen came to accept the strange halos surrounding people she knew and cared for.

The green-gray aura surrounding Quinn was troubling. But perhaps temporary, until she and India settled in together and got used to one another.

Gwen jumped when her cell phone rang. Shelby called and said Quinn was home safe. It was a condition Gwen held with Shelby, to always call and let her know Quinn's status.

Too much confusion, Gwen watched her dark brown hands washing up the last of her dinner dishes. She glanced up to see her reflection in the kitchen window, big eyes, close cropped black hair, chocolate colored woman. How strange to see her own brown hooded eyes bulging in fear. *Too much fear. The girl hasn't had much of a chance. Sad to blame Shelby, but she should have done better. Should have kept those men away from Quinn. Should have protected her from such dark things. But Shelby's got her problems too. Nobody's got a bigger heart, but probably nobody's as short sighted either. That combination's got poor Shelby in trouble more times than once. Oh Shelby, always wanting some man's love. Never getting the real thing.*

Shutting off the lights from the kitchen to her bedroom, Gwen pondered the Quinn question as she often did. *What are Quinn's options in life? She hates school. She hates getting up in the morning. Routine? She bad at that. How's she gonna get a job, how's she gonna live when Shelby and me are dead and gone? Is she gonna have to marry some no account man probably because she's pregnant, and suffer his wrath the rest of her life? Or just be somebody's baby mama and collect welfare and have more babies by more baby daddies, what? The girl don't understand how valuable an education is, she don't understand what work means. Shelby, she don't help it none. She so indulgent and lazy. She ain't shaping that girl right.*

Gwen undressed in the dark and pulled her nightgown on. Easing into bed, the thought came to her.

India will be here soon, and she just might be the answer to all of this.

India

Seriously? India checked the time on her phone, 1:55 pm. And then checked her messages to Shelby, all of the messages confirmed she would need a ride at 12:30 pm and Shelby confirmed she would be there.

India texted her, *"Are you on your way?"*

The text back was baffling, *"Yeah, just left. Been shopping."*

"What the hell?" India said to no one in particular.

India stared around. Airports in general are not pretty

but this one, in St, Louis, Missouri, seemed uber dreary, unclean and depressing. The plastic chairs, the stench of human, all India wanted was to go to a warm bed and quiet, clean surroundings.

"So, are you coming?" India texted back.

No response.

Fifty-five minutes later, India texted again. *"Are you on your way? Been waiting here all afternoon for you."*

Ten minutes later, a text came back.

"Sorry, can't make it. I don't have gas money."

"You're kidding me, right? I'm stranded here."

"Don't know what to tell you. You're the big reporter with the swank life. Sorry."

India clicked the phone off without replying.

You've got to be kidding me. Unbelievable.

India looked left and right. Airport people were teeming about, prospective passengers were chatting together, the operation was a well-oiled machine, everything clicking neatly in place.

Except for her.

Welcome home, India.

David Estes

I'm a former radio and television announcer and news reporter. My father was a Presbyterian minister. I live on the family farm near Bolivar, Missouri. After serving in the U.S. Marines in WWII, I graduated from Drury University in 1949. I have written ten short novels, five on my website, davidaestes.com. Still looking for the big one.

Death, Where Is Thy Poker?

David Estes

"Cassie! What are you doing here at my house?"

"I've come to kill you, Henry."

"Oh. You've come to kill me? Are you going to do it, or are you just thinking about it?"

"I'm gonna do it."

"Such a gorgeous lady... Well, okay then. Let me think. After you do it, uh, let me give you my daughter's phone number. Her name is Lou. She lives in Kansas City. Would you be good enough to call her and explain why I won't be answering the phone? She usually calls about nine o'clock in the morning.

She'll be expecting me to answer, but of course... You understand."

"Uh-huh."

"You're serious about this, aren't you?"

"Uh-huh."

"I thought so. So am I. But we ... we ... have to look ahead to what you'll need to do afterwards. Now then, you'll be sure to call 911 so they'll have someone out here to pick up the body before it gets bloated, or... you know, draws flies. And by the way, there's a city ordinance against dead bodies just lying around, you see. The police have never been here, so in case they decide to enforce the law, I don't think they'd know where to find me."

"Okay."

"I could call 911 for you, if it's a..."

"I know the number."

"And you might want to call my neighbors too. They keep a pretty close watch on what goes on around here, and they like... they don't like finding out about stuff like this second hand. I could call them for you too, except that they might think it strange that I called and said I was dead. They might not believe it, since I've never been dead before. Uh... and then there's... Did I ask you why you're going to kill me?"

"No."

"Cassie, why are you going to kill me?'

"Because you insulted my husband."

"Richard! I insulted Richard? What did I do that insulted Richard?"

"You told him you thought of me as a bed partner."

"And that insulted your husband?"

"Yes."

"Hmmnn. I'll be darned. Where is he now?"

"He's at home watching the Andy Griffith show."

"I thought that went off the air years ago."

"Re-runs."

"And that's why he didn't come to kill me himself?"

"It's the wrong time of day. He never misses Andy."

"Well, I guess that's..."

"There's another reason."

"Oh?"

"Richard doesn't own a gun."

"Richard doesn't own a gun. Aha! Now, let's see, uh, does that mean then that you are the one with the gun?"

"Yes."

"And Richard couldn't borrow your gun to kill me with?"

"No. I don't trust him with a gun."

"You don't trust him. Why... why don't you trust your husband with a gun?"

"I'm afraid he might kill somebody."

"Well now, Cassie, would you be surprised if I told you that I am completely confused by this entire situation?"

"I'm not surprised."

"Now, Richard told you that he was insulted because I told him that I had thought of you as a bed partner, correct?"

"Yes."

"Mmhm. Would it be fair to ask why you were not insulted?"

"I took it as a compliment."

"Well, then... oh-ho!"

"He said if I didn't kill you, he would kill me."

"With your gun. The one you're afraid he'd kill somebody with."

"No. With the fireplace poker."

"Ooo-ooo! That could be painful."

"I'm also allergic to brass."

"It looks to me like we have arrived at an impasse here, I mean..."

"Maybe."

"As I understand it now, you're going to kill me, because if you don't, Richard will kill you with the fireplace poker. Is... is that a true statement?"

"It is."

"And you don't want to die that way because you are allergic to brass?"

"That's correct."

"I see. Well. Hmmnn. Let me think. Uh... Do you have time for a cup of coffee?'

J.C. Fields

J.C. Fields, nom de plume for John Cawlfield, wrote his first short story in high school and published a research paper in an obscure science journal his senior year in college. In 2005, he opened his laptop and started writing again. His debut novel, *The Fugitive's Trail*, was published in 2015. John lives with his wife Connie, in Battlefield, Missouri.

Cause and Affect

J.C. Fields

Captain Lucas Flores appeared next to my desk and handed me a piece of paper. He said, "Get your kit, Powers. We've got a jumper."

I looked up from my computer and stared at him. "My partner's on maternity leave. I can't go after a jumper without a partner—you know that, Captain."

He shook his head. "Not my decision. Tenth floor called, they asked specifically for you."

Tenth floor is where the chief of police resides. He makes the rules and I guess he can ignore the rules.

My name is Ryan Powers and I'm a detective in the Temporal Integrity unit. I looked at the slip of paper with an address scrawled in Flores's handwriting. I looked up and said, "Captain, this is in Silicon Valley, out of our jurisdiction."

Flores shook his head. "Powers, you know you're the only cop in this part of California that understands temporal displacement. You're elected. Now go."

Saying I understand temporal displacement is like saying the pizza-delivery kid understands hybrid engines. I'm comfortable making the jumps, but ask me to explain the physics, forget it. I stared at Flores, grabbed my kit, and headed toward the elevator.

My destination was on the northwestern side of Silicon Valley, south of San Francisco. Timelane, Inc. was one of the new companies located in the old Silicon Valley area and contributing to its resurgence. I'd dealt with Timelane before. Its founder, Reed Manly, had been an experimental physicist at Caltech until fifteen years ago. He supposedly inherited a ton of money, left his position at Caltech, and started Timelane. Now he was making millions sending scientists and historians back in time for the government.

Manly had introduced time travel to the world ten years before and, as was the case with space travel in the earlier part of the century, the rich and famous flocked to his door for test rides. A trip back to watch the first Apollo moon landing mission take off would cost you a cool million dollars. There was talk of going back and preventing Oswald from assassinating JFK. History tampering made politicians apoplectic, predicting universal Armageddon. The government stepped in and heavily regulated time travel.

Men like me were then trained as cops to stop the perpetrators before they made the jump, or go back and arrest them before they could affect a change. I personally agree with a small contingent of scientists who hypothesize that any change made to our past simply creates a separate timeline independent of ours.

I arrived at Timelane just after eleven in the morning. The majestic building looked like a tall mirror, reflecting sunlight off glass panes on all thirty floors. I shook my head at the wasted energy.

The reception desk android scanned my credentials and said in a very sexy female voice, "Thank you, Detective. Please wait for someone to escort you." I nodded and retrieved my ID. Standing with my hands behind my back, I surveyed the reception area. Original Andy Warhols, Picassos, and Franz Marcs were the predominate paintings. I like twentieth-century artists, particularly Marc's. His stuff's colorful.

Before I could finish admiring all the paintings, a short, chubby man in a black Nehru jacket exited the elevator. He said, "Detective Powers, will you accompany me, please."

I nodded and followed him to the elevators. We ascended in silence to the thirtieth floor. The door opened and he gestured for me to exit. I did, he didn't.

Another android was standing outside of the elevator and said in a British accent, "Please follow me, sir." I followed the machine until we reached an office with an open door. Inside the office, Reed Manly stood and came around his massive desk to shake my hand. He was a slender, tall man, dressed in black jeans and a maroon turtleneck. Crystal-blue eyes stared at me from behind square-rim glasses perched at the end of a prominent Roman nose.

He said, "Detective Powers, it's been a long time. I believe there's been a misunderstanding."

I shook his hand, "No, there's no misunderstanding. An unauthorized temporal jump occurred within this building at nine-o-five this morning."

He smiled, cocked his head to the left, "A computer glitch, nothing more."

I remained silent.

"I can supply you with computer readouts confirming the problem."

I smiled grimly, shook my head, and said, "Sorry, we have independent confirmation."

He crossed his arms over his chest and remained silent for a few moments. "I see."

I held up a ten-terabit flash drive, smiled, and said, "I need to examine your jump records. Please have someone download them immediately."

"If I don't?"

I shrugged. "Then I'll pull your Temporal Transition License. You'll effectively be out of business."

"You don't have the authority."

I chuckled and said, "Yeah, I do. Now—"

"It was a necessary jump. I... We couldn't register it."

"Why?"

He was silent as he turned and walked back toward his desk. "The very existence of time travel depends on this jump."

I really couldn't help myself. I laughed.

He turned and stared at me. "I'm being serious."

I nodded, but remained quiet as I suppressed another

chuckle.

"The only way we were able to perfect time travel was the influx of a billion dollars I inherited from a relative."

I continued to stare at Manly, but remained quiet. I had a funny feeling I knew where this was going. I said, "So, how is it related to an unauthorized jump?"

He abruptly turned and glared at me. "It has everything to do with it. Without those funds, we couldn't have completed the research. Without those funds, we couldn't have developed the technology. Without those funds, your current job wouldn't exist."

I stared back at the man. Finally I said, "Who was sent back?"

Manly shook his head. "I can't tell you."

I reached for my phone and punched in a number. He stared at me and said, "What are you doing?"

"Negating your temporal permit."

His eyes grew wide and he yelled, "Stop!" I didn't press the send icon. "I was sent back, or should I say, my thirty-years-younger self was sent back."

I stared at him. Finally, after several moments, I said, "Do you have memories of this event?"

He paused, diverted his eyes to stare at the top of his desk, and then finally nodded. Turning back to the window, he stared out over San Francisco Bay. "Six months ago, I made a registered jump to my college graduation. I brought my younger self back and versed him on the future. At first, he refused to help us. But eventually he agreed to our plan?"

"Our plan?"

"Figure of speech, it's an odd sensation spending substantial time with a younger version of oneself."

I frowned; *odd* was not the word I would have used.

He nodded. "I... We spent several months devising a strategy on when to buy a company's stock and when to sell it. The timing was key. Once I sent my younger self back, it took fifteen years for our plan to amass the funds we needed. He... I was successful. Timelane received the funding on the appointed date."

I stared at the man without saying a word. I pressed the send icon.

***

My jump was made from the Federal Temporal Law Enforcement Center in Oakland two days later. I was to arrive eight hours ahead of Reed's younger self. The early arrival would give me sufficient time to find my way to the other end of the gate Timelane used. Gates are funny. They are fixed, yet time travel is not. I could go back a hundred years using the Fed Center, but I would always exit at the end of their gate located in a storage room at the San Francisco Opera House. The same was true for Timelane; their gate was a closet next to the gift shop in Coit Tower, up on Telegraph Hill near Chinatown.

An hour before the younger Reed Manly was to emerge, I was in place, ready to arrest him. This was the part of being a time cop that bothered me. If I made the arrest, would I be changing the past? And if I did, would I be aware of those changes? So far, my own timeline had remained the same, I think, even after fifty temporal interventions.

I showed my police credentials to the two elderly women operating the gift shop, explaining to them I was on a stakeout and to ignore me. Once I had everything ready, I stood outside of the closet, leaned against the door. My chronograph indicated I had forty minutes to wait. During these final moments before an arrest, my mind always starts to wander. I'm not a philosophical person, but I often wonder if I'm the one breaking the chain of events that were supposed to occur.

The paradox of temporal law enforcement is discussed at length during our training. There really aren't that many of us across the country, but we meet on a regular basis. The consensus of the discussions during those meetings: If the Laws of Temporal Displacement allowed us to stop someone from changing the past, then we are part of the natural flow of events. I find this argument weak at best. How do we know if the Laws of Temporal Displacement even exist? We don't. These so-called laws were hypothesized in the early years of time travel. To me, they seem more like assumptions than laws. But the scientists and politicians who postulated them insist they are unbreakable.

The kit on my belt started to vibrate. The so-called kit is a device with two functions. First it can put a damper on a temporal displacement field and prevent someone from jumping back or forward in time. Its second function is detecting the imminent arrival of a time jumper. The younger Manly was about to arrive.

The device on my belt stopped vibrating and the closet door slowly opened. I stood off to the side as a young Reed Manly emerged. I grabbed his left wrist and snapped one side of my handcuffs around it. He stared at me without understanding as I grabbed his right wrist and completed securing his wrists in the old, but still efficient, handcuffs. Once he was secured, I flipped a switch on my kit. The dampening field would prevent any residual temporal waves from returning him thirty years back to the future.

His wild expression continued. I smiled as he stammered, "Wha—Wha—What are you doing?"

"Placing you under arrest."

He continued to stare at me for several moments. Finally he said, "Why? I haven't done anything?"

I shook my head, gave him a slight grin, and said, "Conspiracy to commit temporal adjustment. It's a federal crime where you just came from."

He wasn't able to speak. Sweat popped out on his forehead and his eyes darted around the hallway. "How... Why are... What—For god's sake, I haven't done anything yet."

"Doesn't matter, a charge of conspiracy to commit is more about intent, not actually preforming the act. The older Reed Manly explained your plan to me."

His shoulders slumped. He nodded and said, "I didn't really like the person I became in the future. I'm not surprised he sold me out." He raised his head and said, "It's kind of sad how money can corrupt, particularly your dreams."

I stared at him, but remained quiet.

He chuckled slightly. "I wasn't even sure time travel was possible. My research in college suggested it was. It's kind of like when they developed the nuclear bomb over a hundred years ago; they knew it was possible, but what would be the consequences of actually building it?" He was quiet for a few moments as he stared at the floor. "I wonder why he told you about our plan."

I shrugged. "Probably thought I'd agree with him. I didn't."

He shook his head slowly. "I didn't like the future I saw for myself." He sighed. "I wonder what would happen if I don't invest the money. Would the money still be there, but from a different source? Or would somebody else invent the damn thing?" He paused and stared at me. "The whole issue gives me a headache."

"It can do that." I reached down and turned off the damping field. I figured by now the temporal wave had disbursed. "Since you're going back with me, it doesn't matter; the timeline has already been brok—"

***

Captain Lucas Flores appeared next to my desk and handed me a piece of paper. He said, "Your up, Powers. We've got a jumper."

I looked up from my computer and stared at him. "My partner's on maternity leave and I'm not in rotation—you know that, Captain."

He shook his head. "Not my decision. Tenth floor called, they asked specifically for you."

The tenth floor is where the chief of police resides. She makes the rules; I guess she can ignore the rules. I looked at the slip of paper with an address scrawled in Flores's handwriting. I looked up and said, "Is this...?"

Flores nodded. "Yeah it is."

I arrived at Timelane just after eleven in the morning. The majestic building looked like a tall mirror, reflecting sunlight off glass panes on all thirty floors. I shook my head at the wasted energy.

Several black-and-white units, their light bars rotating, were parked in front of the building. A crowd was standing outside of an area secluded by yellow crime scene tape. I walked over to one of the uniforms and said, "I'm Detective Ryan Powers. I was told we have a jumper."

The young uniformed woman nodded at an object on the sidewalk covered with a blue tarp. She said, "The body's been identified as Reed Manly, the founder of Timelane, Incorporated. His assistant said he was despondent this morning, something about funds drying up for his research. Apparently while the assistant was getting coffee, Manly broke out a window on his thirtieth floor office and..." She pointed to the body. "That's all I know, detective."

I nodded. "I've met Reed Manly. He's the lunatic on TV who's always talking about the need to raise money for time travel research. Where's the assistant?"

The officer pointed to another group of officers surrounding a young man. I walked over to the group and saw the man they were questioning. He bore a remarkable resemblance to Manly, except he was thirty or more years younger. I said, "What's your name?"

"Reed Manly."

"Are you his son?"

The guy just stared at me. A sudden wave of déjà vu swept over me and I frowned. "Have we met before?"

He smiled and nodded.

The Nowhere to Hide Affair

J.C. Fields

A cold north wind bit hard at his exposed skin, stinging the eyes but not distracting his concentration on the vacant field diagonally across the intersection.

The man standing next to him said, "The trajectory of the bullet places the shooter's location toward the middle of that field." He pointed in the direction of FBI Agent Sean Kruger's stare. "Plus there was a slight downward angle to the bullet."

Kruger blinked several times, frowned, and said, "Was the victim leaning forward?"

Fellow FBI Agent Thomas Shark shook his head. "No, the guy had just finished filling his tank. Surveillance video shows him walking upright toward the driver-side door of his SUV when he was shot." Three inches taller than Kruger's six-foot frame, Shark, a recent graduate of the FBI Academy, was high-school skinny with an Ivy League haircut on top of an angular face.

Looking down, Kruger saw the spot next to the gas pump where the body had fallen. The chalk outline was still faintly visible amongst the numerous oil stains on the concrete. "If the shooter was hiding in the grass, there would be an upward trajectory to the bullet. There's nowhere to hide over there that gives a shooter an elevation."

Shark smiled grimly. "The local police chief is ex-FBI. He asked my boss to have you brought in. He said you're the best profiler the bureau has and that you'd figure it out."

Kruger ignored the compliment. "The report I read declared all four victims were random. The only connection is the chain of convenience stores. Correct?"

Shark nodded. "All four victims had just completed filling their vehicles with gas and were walking back to the driver's seat. Each victim was upright and shot center mass. The bullet paths angled high to low. Three males and one female, with their ages varied. None of the victims were acquainted with each other, according to their families."

Kruger nodded. Looking back at the convenience store entrance, he said, "Who owns these stores?"

"A corporation located in Tulsa, Oklahoma."

"Any disgruntled employees?"

Shark chuckled. "Lots, they have a high turnover."

"Figures. Okay, I want a look at the surveillance videos."

***

It took several hours for Kruger to review the disks at the local FBI office. When finished, he sat in front of the computer and rubbed his eyes. He stood to get a refill of his now ice-cold coffee. As he was pouring, Shark walked into the break room, and said, "Find anything?"

Shaking his head, Kruger said, "No." He stood there staring at the steaming, dark liquid. "Are there any surveillance videos from surrounding businesses?"

"What are you looking for?"

"The camera angles at each of the convenience stores only show the pumps. We need a shot of the street or in the case of the last victim, the intersection."

"That could be a problem."

"Why's that?"

Scowling, Shark said, "All of the shooting locations are in residential areas. We couldn't find any surveillance cameras around, except for the convenience stores. The last location we visited had a possibility. The church across the street to the east has security cameras, but they're all trained on the parking lot, not the street."

"Did anybody bother to look at those videos?"

Shark was quiet for a long time, then slowly shook his head.

Taking a sip of his coffee, Kruger grinned, and said, "Well, I think I'll go look at them."

***

The church cameras revealed nothing out of the ordinary. One showed the south parking lot and very little of the street next to it. The other viewed the east lot, but it had a clear view of the road north of the church. Kruger looked closer at the east camera angle. The west parking lot of an elementary school was visible in the top left corner of the grainy, black-and-white video. He concentrated on the video recording for the hour prior to the four p.m. shooting and for an hour afterward.

Normal traffic was visible prior to the shot being fired, just cars and school buses picking up students. After the time stamp indicated the shot had been fired, Kruger observed nothing out of the ordinary until police cars entered the picture speeding down the road. Frustrated with not seeing anything unusual on the video, he asked the church's secretary to make a copy of the disk.

It was late afternoon when he was sitting at a stoplight a mile north of the church. A school bus approached the intersection from the east and turned right. Kruger watched the bus and noticed the window directly behind the driver was open. It was open at the top. The red light turned green, and he accelerated his Ford Mustang to catch the bus. The road going north had two lanes so he pulled up next to the bus and looked closer at the windows. He grinned, slowed the Mustang, and let the bus pass. Pulling the car in behind, he followed.

Ten minutes later, he was parked in front of the bus barn's office. He entered and found a couple of drivers checking a schedule. One of them turned toward him, frowned, and said, "Can I help you?"

Kruger produced his FBI credentials and said, "I need to speak to a supervisor."

The driver who had spoken stared at his badge. "Uh…"

The other driver, a middle-aged woman, said, "I'll get her. What's this about?"

"I have a few questions for her, that's all."

The woman nodded and left the room while the other driver continued to stare. Kruger turned toward him and said, "Nice day."

The other driver, an older, gray-haired gentleman, never took his gaze off of Kruger until a middle-aged woman came out of a back office. She tapped the older man on the shoulder and said, "You can stop staring, Jerry." The older man changed his attention to the woman and walked off. She stuck her hand out and said, "I'm Margie Stewart. You're with the FBI?"

He showed her his ID. "Yes, Agent Sean Kruger, I have some questions. Is there somewhere private we can talk?"

"Follow me." She led him back to an office in the rear of the building and motioned him to a chair in front of her desk while she sat behind it. "What's this about?"

"School bus windows open from the top down, correct?"

She nodded.

"How high off the ground is the top window?"

She jerked her head back and stared at him. "Uh, I don't know. Why?"

"I just need to know."

"Well, Agent Kruger, let's go measure one."

Ten minutes later, Kruger was looking out the window behind the driver's seat on one of the thirty buses in the lot. Margie Stewart was outside with a tape measure. She yelled up to him, "Exactly nine and a half feet to the middle of the window." With a crisp nod, he walked down the three steps to exit the bus. She stood with her hands on her hips and said, "Okay, what's this about?"

"Have you heard about the four individuals shot and

killed at local convenience stores?"

"Of course. Who hasn't?"

"I think they were shot from inside one of your busses."

***

The following morning found the school districts students with an unexpected day off. Kruger had made three phone calls the previous afternoon: the first to agent Tom Shark, the second to the superintendent of the local school district, and the third to Teri Monroe, head of the forensic division at FBI headquarters. Agent Shark locked down the center city bus barn, and Kruger isolated the south side one. Teri Monroe and eight forensic technicians arrived later that night.

Monroe stood next to Kruger and said, "You think the shots were fired from inside one of these buses?"

"I do." He watched the four forensic technicians organize their search. "Last night the supervisor isolated the buses that run routes close to the shooting locations. You can start there. If you don't find anything, you can broaden the number we check."

Monroe nodded. "If a rifle was fired inside one of those busses, we'll find it."

Chuckling, Kruger said, "I know; that's why I called you." She smiled broadly at the compliment and walked toward the search teams.

An hour later, Kruger was working with Margie Stewart reviewing personnel records when Monroe entered the office, she said, "I believe you'd better come with me. They found something."

Looking up from the computer, Kruger stood and followed her out.

As they approached a bus, yellow crime-scene tape was already stretched around it and a local uniformed police officer stood guarding the door. Monroe and Kruger passed under the tape and climbed the three steps to the seat platform. Two technicians were already there—one Kruger knew, the other he didn't. Charlie Craft was a young apprentice of Monroe's. Kruger had met him on a previous case and was impressed with the young man's work. As they entered, Charlie turned and said, "We have gunshot residue on the inside of a window, second row, driver side."

Kruger said, "What type of a pattern?"

Charlie grinned and said, "Like someone stood in the aisle and fired a rifle through the open window." He pointed to a chalk circle drawn around the window. "Inside the circle there is residue, outside none."

Kruger looked at Monroe, who was beaming with pride for her young apprentice. He said, "Call the center city location and see if they're finding the same results."

Monroe turned and left the bus. Kruger grinned at Craft and said, "Nice work, Charlie."

The young man's face turned red. He looked at the floor, nodded, and said, "Thanks, Agent Kruger."

Kruger was about to say something else, when Monroe stuck her head back in the door and said, "The other team just found residue in another bus and one of the teams downtown found one."

***

By noon a total of five buses were located; three in the south side location and two in the center city facility. Kruger had a list of drivers who had driven those particular buses for the past year. He looked at Margie Stewart and said, "Why so many?"

She shrugged. "We don't have a lot of turnover, but we have substitute drivers who work at both facilities."

Nodding, Kruger said, "I'm not finding a common name on any of the lists. Who else would have access to drive one of these buses?"

Stewart shook her head. "No one..." She paused and bumped her forehead with the palm of her hand. "I should have thought of it before, maybe one of the mechanics or safety inspectors."

***

Kruger and Agent Shark sat in an agency Chevy Malibu and watched as a SWAT team from the local police department surrounded the mechanic's small, rundown house on the city's north side.

Shark said, "Doesn't look like anyone's at home."

Kruger concentrated on the house and said nothing.

As the team of officers in full protective gear got into position to storm the house, Kruger said, "Drive around to the back alley."

Shark looked at him, started the car, and said, "What's wrong?"

Kruger shook his head, "Just a feeling—probably nothing."

As the car eased away from the curb, Shark navigated it to a cross street and turned toward the small alley that ran behind the houses in this section of town. As they approached, a middle-aged man, dressed in sweat pants and a dirty tee shirt walked rapidly across the street in front of them. Shark pointed to the picture taken from a school district ID taped to the cars dashboard, "That's him, the mechanic," and accelerated.

As the car reeled toward him, the man stared at it wide eyed. Now at a full run, he quickly crossed the road. Shark slammed on the brakes, before the car came to a screeching halt, Kruger was out running after the fleeing man.

Now in his late forties, Kruger was still in top shape. He caught the slower man within fifty yards and tackled him to the ground. After restraining the man's arms behind him with handcuffs, Kruger yanked him to his feet and pushed him back toward the agency car. Shark was now standing next to the Malibu. Kruger frowned at him, pushed the suspect past, and in a low voice growled, "Thanks for the backup." Shark opened his mouth to say something, but quickly thought better of it.

Kruger led the man back to the small house, now occupied by the SWAT team. As he entered through the back door, he yelled. "FBI. I have the suspect." The stench of sour milk and overflowing ashtrays assaulted Kruger's nostrils. Two SWAT team members appeared in the kitchen just as Kruger sat the man down at a small table. The chair creaked with the added weight. Floyd Vaughn was read his Miranda rights and placed under arrest.

Beads of sweat glistened on top of the suspect's bald head, running down into the ring of gray hair just above his ears. Thick glasses adorned a bulbous, blue-veined nose, and his glazed eyes stared at the table.

One of the SWAT members walked up to Kruger and said, "We found a rifle, suppressor, and a tripod in his closet. They're processing it now. I think we're good on this one."

Kruger nodded, stood over the man, and said, "Why did you shoot those people?"

Vaughn's slumped shoulders shrugged. "I got my reasons."

"Two of them were fathers with small kids. Those kids are going to grow up now without a dad."

Brown eyes flashed anger as Vaughn looked up, he yelled, "They took everything from me... Everything!"

Kruger knelt down until he was eye level with Vaughn. In a calm voice he said, "Tell me Floyd, who took what from you?"

Tears formed in the corners of the man's eyes. "Everything. I had plans, big plans see..." He looked away. "But those convenience stores..." He looked back at Kruger. "They stole all my money."

Kruger pulled a chair closer, sat, leaned forward, stared at Vaughn, and said, "How did they steal your money, Floyd?"

Vaughn returned the stare. His eyes grew dark and

narrow. "That damn lottery. Those people never let me win the big prize. They just took my money. Then, when it was all gone, they laughed at me."

"Why did they laugh at you, Floyd?"

Looking at the floor, Vaughn sighed and said, "Because I lost."

Kruger sat back in the chair. His eyes narrowed, he shook his head, stood, and walked out of the room.

Jane Shewmaker Hale

Jane was vice president of Springfield Writers' Guild in 1997. She is a charter member of Ozark Writers, Inc. and was president in 2010-15. She is a member of Springfield Writers' Guild, Ozarks Writers League and Missouri Writers' Guild. For MWG, she has been president, vice president, and conference chair. She is a newspaper columnist and has published a children's book series, gift book series, and short story mysteries.

Richest Old Woman in Town

Jane Shewmaker Hale

Big girls walk to school by themselves. They are not accompanied by a parent, a brother, or a grown-up. What was so important about walking those few blocks along Locust Street by myself? It was freedom. It was independence. It was growing up!

As was common in her generation, Mom's career was her home and family. She took her job seriously. She would send my brother Rex and I to school, scrubbed, primped and polished. Standing on the front porch, she'd wave until we were out of sight, then she'd return to her job; cleaning, cooking, washing, ironing, shopping. Her husband, home and children were the shining results of her perfection.

Up Locust Street we walked, Rex gathered boys to walk ahead, my friends lagged behind. Standing like royalty on the corner, across from school, was the grand old two-story house belonging to the richest old woman in town, Mrs. Mary Owensby.

Mrs. Owensby would magically appear in the spring as kids picked cherry's from her tree shadowing the sidewalk or in the summer as they picked her flowers. You would see her in the fall if kids dared "trick or treat" and in the winter when snowballs landed too close to her house.

For some reason, I found myself walking home alone one spring afternoon. I stopped to enjoy a cherry and left my books. Arriving home with a full stomach and empty arms was a dead give-a-way,

Mom sent me to retrace my path in search of the books. MY BOOKS WERE GONE! The street was deserted. It was getting dark. I sat down beneath the cherry tree and cried.

"You're little Janie, aren't you? Your mother won't be

happy if you get your skirt dirty."

I jumped up and looked around. There stood Old Mrs. Owensby. My books were gone and the old lady had reminded me of my dirty skirt. Yes! Mom would be mad. I cried some more.

Mrs. Owensby took my hand. I reluctantly followed her up the steps to her back door. In her kitchen, she cleaned my skirt and magically produced my books. She offered me a cookie, which I declined. She smiled and told me I'd have to stop for a piece of cherry pie someday. I could hardly deny liking cherries.

I remembered to say "Thank you" and was ready to leave when a paper fell from my book. She picked it up. It was a story I'd written. She told me she liked to read, and asked me to share my story. That's how Mrs. Owensby and I became friends. She encouraged me to bring my writing efforts to her.

I did.

During the war years, there was a shortage on staples. The school carnival had a raffle on five pounds of sugar. To the amazement of everyone, I sold Mrs. Owensby a ticket. She won! I had the privilege of delivering the sugar. People told me she would probably donate it to the school. She didn't. She kept it and made cherry pies.

Dad said, "She's tight with her money. That's why she has so much. She never gives anything away."

Years later, I attended the estate sale of Mrs. Mary Owensby. I tromped through the familiar rooms and bought a keepsake.

A woman stopped me. "I bet you would like to have this. It has your name on it, Jane."

She handed me a sheaf of yellowed tablet paper. It was one of my stories!

The lady said. "What in the world is it?"

"It's a long story." I hugged my treasure as I walked beneath the cherry tree on the lawn of my friend, Mrs. Mary Owensby.

Thank you, Mrs. Owensby, for never throwing anything away. And, thank you for encouraging a little girl to write.

Without a Trace

Jane Shewmaker Hale

E ach year as graduation time rolls around, I find myself thinking of the three missing women from Springfield, Missouri: Sherrill Levitt; her nineteen-year-old daughter, Susie Streeter; and Susie's classmate, Stacy McCall.

June 6, 1992, was graduation day at Kickapoo high school, a happy time of pictures, special cakes, presents, parties and plans for tomorrow.

What happened?

Graduation night celebrations spawned parties. Some parties continued through the night and into the early dawn of June 7. During this time, a mysterious connection of the lives of the three women occurred that would plague Springfield until it is unraveled.

Susie and Stacy reportedly attended a sleepover that became crowded and resulted in the serious decision for Suzie Streeter to return home for the night. Was she ill as reported? Did she receive a phone call before she left? Why did Stacy McCall go home with Suzie who was a casual friend?

Friends say Stacy decided to spend the night with Suzie and travel to Branson, Missouri the next day with their friends. Did Suzie have a problem that Stacy felt she could help with? Was she just being a caring friend? Who knows what happened after they left their friend's home? Did they go directly to 1717 E. Delmar or did they stop at a local Steak house where they were reportedly seen with Sherill Levitt and others? Were they at a fast stop store as reported? Why?

Authorities say the cars of the three women were at the

Levitt home on Delmar Street.

Likewise, the woman's purses, medicine and other necessities that they would not have left without were left there. A T-shirt worn by Stacy McCall was there. A porch light was broken. The glass had not yet been cleaned up. When did this happen?

The front door was left open and the TV was still on. Several persons entered the house before police were notified. Nothing seemed to be extremely out of place except the three women, Sherill, Suzie and Stacy were missing and Suzie's small dog had sought safety at a neighbor's home.

Friends and family reported no one answered the phone at 1717 E. Delmar in summons to calls from Stacy's mother, or friends who were planning to go to Branson with the girls that day. When friends went to the house it was silent, open and mysteriously empty.

Was it a frightened Suzie Streeter who was reportedly seen driving a 1964 metallic green Dodge van in the early morning hours of June 7? Did the witness really hear a man's voice giving her instructions? If so, where were Sherrill Levitt and Stacy McCall? Why did the witness wait precious days to report this incident?

The Springfield police department exhausted thousands of leads called in by the curious, frightened, caring community. Billboards with the three women's pictures and an 800 number were displayed around the city. CBS aired a prime time segment "48 hours-Have you seen them?" featuring the case. The hot line started ringing again with possibilities, then nothing.

Fall classes at SMSU started without Stacy although her mother reportedly held onto her schedule and dorm room until the last minute possible.

Cars held as evidence at the 1717 E. Delmar home were released to relatives.

The owner of the house that was being bought by Sherrill Levitt extended time for her to make the payments.

Where, when, why, are questions that remain unanswered in the Springfield Missing Women case?

And, each year at graduation time, I find myself thinking of the missing women who vanished without a trace. I'm sure a lot of others remember, too.

I'm thankful for all the people who are in charge of Project Graduation groups. I hope that graduates will be safe one more night because of this extension of graduation. Remember graduation time, the three Springfield missing women and please be safe!

If by chance, you should see, hear, or find, a clue that might help find the three missing women, report it. It might help solve the case and give closure to a lot of people.

Robert Mitchell Hale

Mitch's short stories are widely published. He graduated from the University of Missouri Columbia in 1980, with a bachelor's degree in animal science. He is an owner of Hale Fireworks, L.L.C. and other businesses. He lives in Buffalo, Missouri and has three children, Nick, Chayla, and A. J.

A Walk in the Park

Mitch Hale

The warmth of your hand in mine, along with the sun on our shoulders, gives me a relaxing feeling of tranquility on this October afternoon. The sound of a small waterfall flowing into a lake mingles with the call of ducks and geese swimming, their reflection doubling their beauty.

We walk the trails in the park and you put your other hand in my back pocket. The sound of your laughter soothes my soul as a feisty red squirrel scampers underfoot chattering his annoyance at our intrusion.

I smell the aroma of hamburgers on a BBQ grill and remember the lunch you packed.

The taste of crisp lettuce, juicy tomatoes, and grilled chicken, halts the growling of my stomach.

You, suddenly, kiss me and chuckle, "You had some ranch dressing on your lips. It's gone now."

The sound of children laughing lures us to a playground. You squeeze my hand while we watch a little girl slide down the slide, her sneakers squeak as they rub the slide.

You set in a swing as I slowly push you. The years of life fade as your laughter mingles with the sound of the children, and you glance over your shoulder, your long brown hair flowing, and a beautiful smile on your lips. The sparkle in your green eyes, white shorts, on tan skin, stirs feelings of euphoria for this perfect day.

We sit with your head on my shoulder admiring the changing colors of the fall. A bright red leaf lands in your hair. Our eyes meet as I twirl the leaf in my fingers. I kiss you again and realize everyday with you is a walk in the park.

Michelle Renee Hermans

Michelle is a Christian author and nature photographer. Originally from New Mexico, she studied government and law and is completing a master's in international policy. She resides in Willard, Missouri with her husband and three grown sons. Her works include books, calendars, photography, and a greeting card line.

My Exercise Prayer

Michelle Renee Hermans

Dear Lord, I know this vessel is Your temple and, with that in mind, I've decided to do a little sprucing up. A major overhaul is more than what's needed, but I thought sprucing up would be a good place to start. After several weeks at the gym, it's become increasingly obvious that I'm going to need Your help in ways that weren't initially apparent to me. For instance, could You please help me recall which locker I have chosen each day, so I don't have to try my combo in every one of the 50 plus locks. Not only does this require an inordinate amount of time, but I'm pretty sure I'm now under routine surveillance by the staff after multiple complaints from fellow locker patrons.

I'd also like Your assistance in keeping the snickers, giggles and full-out guffaws to a minimum when I trip and fall off the stair-stepping machine. Yes, this is an ongoing problem.

Perhaps more importantly, would You please alert me when I haven't plugged my headphones into my MP3 player properly. It causes me, with my ear buds securely fitted in my ears, to jack the volume up as high as it goes while I ponder why the music sounds so muffled. Meanwhile, completely unbeknownst to me, *All Shook Up* is being sent through my speakers to the entire third floor of the health club. With great horror and humiliation, I did finally discover my faux pas, but it was only after several minutes of checking my hair and outfit trying to figure out why everyone was looking at me and waving back to several people who gave me some very strange hand gestures (which I chalked up to a generational trend that I didn't "get"). Next time, and there will probably be a next time, a little heads up would be greatly appreciated. Additionally, for the safety of the entire running community, will you kindly remind me to check which direction on the track I am supposed to be jogging that day? It could prevent another mid-track collision and potentially save an innocent runner.

Finally, Lord, please protect me from the millions of germs that I know lurk behind every weight and under every mat. Don't let me notice the judgmental looks as I drench every apparatus with disinfectant spray from top to bottom, sometimes twice, and please, please, please, never allow there to be a shortage of hand sanitizer or antibacterial soap. I just don't think I could handle that.

Thank you in advance, God, for the physical and emotional protection as I risk it all by braving the fearsome, perilous and ever-intimidating world of health and fitness.

Peace on Earth

Michelle Renee Hermans

The sound of his footsteps on the cobblestone path repeated off the tall brick walls that surrounded the cemetery. The heavy, wet snow covered his old stovepipe hat and soaked through his worn coat. He hardly noticed. His grief numbed him so that every step required great effort and concentration. It was grimly quiet when he reached the bench that he'd come to know so well. He read the engraving on the dark ebony marble bench. "I have told you these things, so that in me you may have peace. In this world you will have trouble. But take heart! I have overcome the world. John 16:33." He sighed and sat down heavily. Peace seemed not only elusive but entirely unthinkable, given the current state of affairs. The war had seethed on for almost three years now and, in that short amount of time, it had robbed him of his entire family.

He stared blankly at the graves that lay before him. His eyes moved from the tombstone of his only son to that of his wife's. The ground on his wife's grave was fresh and he contemplated the upturned earth. Soon it would become indistinguishable from the hundreds of others. Time would pass, the earth would continue to revolve and the seasons would come and go, but life for him would never be the same.

In the distance, he heard the familiar sound of field artillery. Slowly lifting his head, he noticed for the first time he was not alone. The scene wrenched his heart. Mourners of all descriptions had gathered here. A short distance away a woman wept silently as her husband steadied her. Beyond them, he could see a young woman sobbing, sprawled out upon a grave. It was fresh, like his wife's. A fiancée or maybe a newlywed claimed by the war, he suspected. He turned his attention to a mother with two small children. She appeared tired and weary. Their clothes were tattered and unkempt. A struggling widow. He closed his eyes. Where are you, God of peace?

It was then, as he listened to the intermittent weeping and gun shots, that he heard the church bells. Even as the country was being torn in two and its very future uncertain, the church bells would not be silenced on this Christmas Day. They were deep and strong. The sound reverberated through the graveyard. He could feel the percussion through his body. He was reminded of the hope and peace this day promised. He considered the engraved verse next to him, "...in me you may have peace." His consuming grief had blinded him to that truth. Man had sought to destroy peace, but peace is not from man. It is from God.

He bowed his head and prayed for the strength to endure without his family. He prayed for a war-torn nation, the soldiers, both fighting and fallen, and the families they left behind. Finally, he asked for true peace. A peace that surpasses all understanding. A peace that perseveres even in the midst of great grief and chaos. The pain in his heart did not cease, but a sense of resoluteness and conviction overcame him.

He left the cemetery that Christmas day a different man. His footsteps were somehow lighter as he made his way back to town. The day that had begun with total despair and hopelessness now held renewed promise. The church bells' chorus pronounced a glorious eternal truth he now felt deep within his heart: God is not dead nor does He sleep!

Michael Humphrey

Michael has written more than 200 skits that have been
performed on three continents. When asked his favorite
genre, he answers, "Whatever strikes me at the time." He is
married with three children and four grandchildren and is a
native of Missouri. In his free time, he loves to karaoke.

Dad Comes Home

Michael J. Humphrey

Rise and shine, Son. It's time to get up.
Dad? Is that you? What's going on?
Time to go to work!
But it's...
Time to go to work!
Are you sure?
Why wouldn't I be?
Where have you been?
Away.
But, Dad...
Just believe.
Yeah. I will. It's good to see you. I've missed you.
And I've missed you.
So, what's up?
Why don't you make some coffee and let's talk.
About?
It's that talk I didn't have with you.
Birds and the bees?
I think we've passed that point. No, this is about life
lessons.
Coffee on the way!
Can you use our old percolator?
Anything for you, Dad.
I miss the sound. And the smell.
Nothing like it, right?
Better than when you burned the bacon!
You still gonna harp on that?
Nah. Just wanted to say it so you know it's me.
Who else would it be?
Exactly.
While the coffee brews, ya wanna sit?

No, I think I'd rather pace.

Okay. Guess it's your turn.

Let's start with the basics. I know how much you miss me. Yes. I hear you every night.

I'm glad. Some days really weigh on me.

I know. That's why I'm here.

I'm listening.

That's the first thing I want to talk to you about. Listening.

What about it?

You tend to turn your ears off if you don't hear what you want.

Uh, I guess.

No "I guess" about it. You do. I know it's hard, but you need to learn to listen. It's what's going to help you.

But sometimes.

I know. I know. Sometimes it just isn't possible. But make it part of you.

I can try.

Don't try. Do.

Yes, sir.

Second, your mom and I didn't do a good job with you when it comes to money.

Probably.

No probably about it. Take frugality over spontaneity.

Yeah. I'm sorry, Dad.

It's not totally your fault. Now, do something. Make some changes.

I will.

Third, you have four wonderful grandkids. I can't believe how well you've done.

Thanks.

You keep asking, "Am I a good father?" I'm here to say you are.

Really?

You've done what you can when you can. You give them love. You give them direction.

I try.

I watch them every day grow and blossom. Now, do something I didn't.

What's that?

Spoil them, but not to their detriment. Show them that love is more important than any toy.

Okay.

Something else.

Yes?

Do the stuff that we used to do. Show them things that make life fun. Fishing. Hunting. Grilling. Cards.

We played a lot of cards, didn't we?

Yes, I miss those times.

So do I. So do I.

Here's the last part. You're lonely. I know it bugs you. Just know I'm around. That mockingbird you hear outside?

Talk about a pest! Wait? Are you saying...that's you?

Yeah. My way of saying "Focus."

I'm trying.

I've read some of the stuff you've written. You are talented. You have potential. I hope it takes off for you.

Thanks. Coffee's done.

Great. Pour it up and let's deal the cards.

Cribbage?

How'd you guess?

Hey, I'm your son.

Do you have any questions for me?

Yeah. Could I have helped...?

Save the business? I don't know. I really don't. I made some mistakes and that didn't help.

I thought I could've made it better.

Looking at the situation now, I don't think it would've lasted a lot longer. I know. It has bugged you seriously. You have the fire now, but did you then? I just don't see that the family business would have survived much longer.

It hurt to watch it just go away.

You did what you could under the circumstances.

Still.

Still?

Why did you leave?

I made choices prior to that day. It was inevitable.

I don't think so. You gave up smoking. You were doing all the right things. Life was good.

Yes, but it was what I did before that. The smoking. The drinking. I know you don't think so and that's your opinion and you're welcome to it. If anything, the time schedule was moved up. I was weak and, truly, I was a burden to your mom. I wish I hadn't just lain there for so long.

So much to ask.

And my time is so short.

But, you just got here. You can't leave.

It's not my choice. I want to stay and play cards and fish and...

I know. Do all those things we did.

Yes. Just know I'm watching you.

Thanks. Dad, one more thing.

Yes?

I love you so much.

I know. I love you, too. Sorry I didn't say it more often.

I knew.

I'm glad.

How about a hug?

You know it.

A soft kiss touches my face, and I awaken to my wife rubbing my brow.

What's wrong?

Nothing dear. Just a moment in time.

You sure were chattering for a moment in time.

I pause and take a deep breath. Did you start coffee?

No, silly. You know I don't make coffee. I hate it.

A smile comes across my face. Then, the sound of the mockingbird. I burst out laughing.

Why are you laughing?

Cuz he's here.

He who?

My dad.

How do you know that?

Suffice it to say I know. He's leaving hints.

I'm not going to argue. Just going to accept what you say. With prejudice.

Thank you. So, how about some breakfast? I'm cookin'. I feel biscuits and gravy comin' on. Any objections?

Like I'd object?

I take another deep breath. Life is what you make it, and yes, angels do watch over us. Been there, done that, have the tee shirt. Her kiss tells me how right the world can be when the right person is in your corner.

Jerry-Mac Johnston

Jerry-Mac, the fourth generation of a theatrical family, has performed in nearly 200 plays, films, and commercials. He is a prize winning, internationally published poet, playwright, and children's book author. He loves a minor league baseball game, then curling up with a good book, or somebody who's read one.

A Beautiful Specimen

Jerry-Mac Johnston

I f it could be stuffed and mounted, Harry Hepplein was your man. In the relatively small world of trophy taxidermy, his name was among the most mentioned. He'd learned the taxidermy trade from his daddy, who learned it from his daddy. However, it was his love of the live small animals that gave him that extra edge in their preservation after death.

Of course, some thought his stuffing and display of household pets somewhat distasteful. He passed no judgment on people who wanted to save their cat, dog, bird, or other beloved pet as a silent companion for the remainder of their days. He didn't shun the larger game trophy jobs, even though they were a bit more time consuming. It was also the big jobs, which made it possible for him to take on the smaller, more personal endeavors. One big job could pay the utilities for several months and buy many supplies.

To pay the utilities was Harry's main concern. The clapboard shack of his ancestors had seen a great many upgrades and renovations over the years. Sitting in a protected area of the swamp, to which his home had been grandfathered in, it now looked more like a secluded lodge for the rich Floridians and tourists rather than a private home and workplace.

The home's remoteness and rural beauty had been the initial appeal to, besides Harry, the well-known and talented artist and writer Beverly Griswald. She painted, wrote, and talked about what remained of rural Florida and she could certainly talk. As Beverly took up more than the weekend residencies with Harry, they began talk of the creation of another generation to take over the home. They talked about a lot of things. Harry often thought Beverly would talk to herself if there were no one else around. Soon Harry stopped listening.

It was with much concern and media attention that Harry reported Beverly missing. The obvious was feared as Beverly often hiked or canoed the swamps alone taking photos for later inspiration. The concern grew as more time passed, so it came with some sense of relief, despite the gruesome conclusion, when a body was found. Headlines, as usual, loved the gory details of swamp decomposition and alligator attack, which they reported would make it impossible to tell if the victim was attacked by the gator pre- or post-mortem.

Confirmation of Beverly's identity laid any suspicions to rest about her unfortunate accident. Harry's grief was visible, heartfelt, and completely masked his private thoughts. He was very pleased when the media frenzy also began to die down. Beverly had been a local celebrity and his secluded workplace had seen more people in the past few weeks than it had in years. Harry did not need or appreciate the scrutiny his little haven was generating. The illegal shooting of the gator, which he had not done, and the mounting of the illegal trophy, which he had done, would not, could not become known.

It would take more than a Columbo, or the whole cast of CSI to match the bite marks Harry had viciously rendered with the gator he had so carefully mounted. Besides, that gator was now carefully cleaned of its gory complicity and resting in splendid repose near Elko, Nevada. Its new owner, multi-millionaire hunter and recluse, could no more tout this trophy, which now resided in a secret trophy room in his remote mountain lodge, than Harry could.

Though a bit lonelier, life was much quieter in the Florida swamp now. If there was any regret, it was that there wasn't enough left of Beverly for Harry to mount. When quiet, lounging on the rattan deck chair, she had been a beautiful specimen.

Death Base

Jerry-Mac Johnston

L ittle Frankie Cannon played second, as he had been born just east of the base. Little Frankie stood six-feet-three and packed 192 pounds of solid, ball-stopping power. Had he played for the Cubs it would have been Tinker to Cannon to Chance.

He was Mr. Baseball and loved the game, with the exception of the lights. It was the lights that did him in; a high pop-up, lost in the unfamiliar glare, the ball came down like a lead goose and hit him dead-on between the eyes.

After the funeral, they began to say second base carried a curse. On the road, the double plays always worked and the stand-up doubles flowed. It was a different story at home. Easy double-play balls took an odd hop, batters tried to stretch doubles to triples to avoid being caught on second base.

John Mitchell broke his collarbone on a routine headfirst slide. That took ten miles-per-hour off his fastball and his career ended in Single-A El Paso when his car slid into a flooded arroyo.

Billy Bend ell tripped on second during a home-run trot. Two broken ribs punctured his lung. At least he had an education and got a job coaching at a college in Nebraska, but it didn't take long for the booze to catch up to him. Another funeral.

Opening day, Eddie Leasers brought down a line drive and dove for the bag to double up Buddy Wilson diving back. They met head–to-head, both missed the remainder of the season.

So it went. Veteran players might torment the rookies

with practical jokes each new season, but when it came to the dead base, the vets were very serious. Every player, both home and visitor, was nervous around second. They all knew the tales of injuries caused by the cursed base. Finally, finances took their toll and the franchise was sold and moved to a larger city with more baseball money.

The field stood vacant until the city developed it as a park. The city never could figure why there were so many lawsuits concerning kids falling out of the swings or being spun off the merry-go-round, but old-timers knew why. The park went to ruin and was soon just a field again.

Years later, thanks to the new Interstate highway, the town grew and prospered. Soon, one of the national chains opened a superstore on the land. As construction began, one of the senior members of the crew talked about the field, remembering how he and his dad used to attend the games. Someone at city planning caught wind of the ballpark talk, records and photos were researched, and it was determined that home plate was just outside the entry doors. As a small town without a lot of history, it was decided that a brass home plate should commemorate the spot. Nobody gave any thought to, or even remembered, the curse, but at the end of Row G in the parking lot, exactly 127-feet, three-and-three-eighths inches from the brass home plate, was a dead tree in a triangle of dirt where nothing ever grew, shopping carts left by the triangle's curb rolled across the flat parking lot, denting and scratching parked cars, and people who never considered themselves accident prone consistently banged their head on the door frames of the cars if parked near the triangle.

The store prospered, but it didn't take long for people to learn not to park at the end of Row G, and they never even knew why.

Frosty, Fricassee, Foul: Or, Three Strikes You're Out

Jerry-Mac Johnston

Chapter One

I t was a hot, muggy, Ozarks afternoon and Frosty, the snowman, was missing. Frosty wasn't his real name and I doubt any of the guys on our minimal drug enforcement task force even knew his name.

Frosty had a big coke habit, yet somehow it hadn't rendered him totally useless as an informant. Everybody on the task force had used him at some time, but we had sort of a bond and I became his regular go-to guy. He didn't always want money and was happy if I could hook him up with a ticket for our minor league ball club occasionally.

They called him Cokehead for the longest time and the street life and the drugs took a toll on him. His hair and beard turning a premature dirty white. Staying with a reference to his drug of choice, someone labeled him Frosty the snowman and it stuck.

I wasn't worried, although I was supposed to meet Frosty last week. He was as dependable as a druggie could be, so this had happened before. Frosty kept to himself. He didn't show at any of the shelters with enough regularity for anybody to worry about him. A little bit of blow, or in Frosty's case, a lot of blow, slipped under our radar in a town where the processing of methamphetamine was our major industry. You didn't learn that from the Chamber of Commerce.

Somehow Frosty stayed away from the meth, but he still had contacts connecting him to what went on in the streets. I assumed when he came down from his current high he'd get in touch with me again. So I wasn't concerned when Jennifer's number flashed up on my cell phone screen. She was probably calling for lunch, or if I was lucky, maybe a nooner.

It wasn't against regulations, but there was an unspoken recommendation that we didn't fraternize with uniforms. Jenn had actually passed up a chance to go plain clothes. She enjoyed and was a great beat cop. She had a tremendous empathy for victims, but could take down a perp quicker than you could say Jackie Robinson. Plus, she knew who Jackie was and I liked that in a woman.

I took the phone out of the office and into the stairwell where I punched the button to return her call. She answered on the first ring. I spoke before she could say, hello.

"I can get the surveillance van today and I love a woman in uniform."

"Keep it zippered, stud muffin. I'm standing at the creek on the old Trafficway by the limo service and I've got something you need to see right now."

"On my way," I flipped the phone shut and headed to my car. It probably didn't take two minutes and I pulled into the limo lot and parked between two squad cars.

The field beside the limo service had once been a ballpark, but the neighborhood had disappeared and now it was flanked by Stone Valley Creek, the limo service and a small industrial park. An ambulance was parked near what used to be third base.

I didn't know what was going on yet, but I knew the industrial park would be of no use, not a single window the length of the back of the building. That left the limo place and the antique mall across the street as potential witness sites.

Jenn was talking to another beat cop who I recognized, but couldn't put a name to. He turned to me as I approached.

"Looks like we've got a bum fricassee here ."

"You wouldn't know a fricassee from a stir-fry," I said as I looked down at the white haired body lodged between a rock and low hanging tree limb. The recent rains, which had come down torrentially the past few days, had created currents, which probably buffeted the body against that rock unmercifully.

He was right though. The standing puddle containing the body looked like a stew. There was a foul smell emanating from this pot and I turned away for a moment. It didn't take CSI to see it was Frosty and that a single bullet had entered the back of his head, execution style. Rare for our small town.

Jenn didn't say anything as I looked back at the body, but it was she who finally broke the silence, "Guess they won't put too much energy into solving this one."

I nodded. She was probably right, but I knew Frosty's real name. We'd gone to high school together and I'd caught Frosty's perfect game. Only the second in state conference history. I knew who Frosty wanted to be and I would find out who killed him.

Chapter Two

The seemingly unrelenting Ozarks heat wave finally broke. Some thunderstorms, a couple of tornado warnings and flash flooding were all it took. The past couple of days the mid-eighty temps seemed almost subarctic, except for the humidity.

The downside was that my crime scene had been desiccated by the heat and then washed clean by the flash floods. It didn't matter, I had combed the area and came up with nothing except my own sweat soaked shirt and a farmer's sunburn on my neck.

I began thinking the case didn't matter since nobody seemed concerned about the death of Henry Hatcher, small-time dealer, big time-user, AKA Frosty the Snowman,

AKA Henry the Hatchet.

It's probably not what you think unless you had been there and there probably weren't many who remembered Henry the Hatchet. High school baseball didn't have a huge following even when Henry's pitching took us to state.

The Hatchet was a nickname from our senior year in high school. Henry already had a major league splitter. It began at eye level and I was lucky if I could trap it in the dirt, much less catch it. Someone thought the arc of the ball followed the swing of a hatchet. Add in the whole alliterative name thing and it stuck. It made for good press.

Henry always liked what I told him I'd overheard as I chased one of those splitters to the backstop. One scout leaned over to the guy beside him and said, "That ball starts in Missouri and drops straight down to Arkansas."

Despite the splitter, no colleges came calling. Henry could bring the heat like a pro, but he had trouble with "reading, 'riting and 'rithmatic." He still managed to be a twenty-third round draft pick, but even that didn't cheer him up. The drugs seemed to help and he took a different path.

A week ago I was called to fish him out of a dried up midtown creek. It was strike three for Henry. Someone had done a number on him with the proverbial blunt object. I seemed to be the only one who cared and after a week, I still had nothing to go on and fewer clues.

I hoped lunch with Jennifer would brighten my mood. She was on patrol by our favorite oriental buffet and texted me to meet her. She was aware of my frustration. Cases like this were cold when we got them and quickly went to freezing. Maybe some sushi would get my brain working.

I slid the plastic indicator by my name to "out" and headed for my car. (Yes, I have a beeper, but it's just another bulky thing weighing down my pocket. I just want people to know I wasn't a complete Neanderthal.) Before I could get in the car, my cell rang. It was Mick Logan from the State Patrol crime lab. I don't know how we lucked out having the lab here, but I was glad we did. The lab was open for use by small community forces and fortunately was only a couple of blocks from our precinct. How I'd become friends with a transplanted New Yorker and a Yankee fan was beyond me. Could have been the tickets he always seemed to have and shared to the local minor league games. Those state boys got all the perks.

Mick began speaking almost before my 'hello' evaporated into the hot summer breeze. "Got the info on Hatcher. Death from the proverbial blunt object." I smiled to myself. "Deterioration due to approximately five days to a week in the water, lots of post mortem bruising, each bruise looks like it came from a different source."

"As if the body were in a storm drain and washed out and over a lot of rocks, before it lodged in the tree?" I suggested.

"I'll buy that," Mick replied, "especially since there was only the one indication of extreme force."

"Let's not forget the bullet to the back of the head." I was trying desperately to contribute to the conversation.

"Post. I think someone wanted to take you in a different direction on this one."

"So we know that someone has a gun, it's not much, everybody in the Ozarks has a gun and I'm still stumped."

"I ain't done here, hillbilly." I don't know how he managed to say that with affection but he did. "You're gonna love this, found a little chunk of wood imbedded in the flesh of the skull. Tried to clean what I initially thought was blood and it turned out to be propanol, butanol, diacetone and resin."

"And that should impress me because?"

"Because those are the ingredients of the ink in Sharpies and to find it on a piece of Northern Ash could mean...?"

It took me a few seconds and as Mick began whistling "Take Me Out to the Ballgame," I got it. "...an autographed baseball bat."

"You got it buddy."

I didn't sound as enthused as Mick, "So what do I do? Get a task force, stake out all three gates to the park and ask everyone who comes in if they collect memorabilia?"

"You'll probably have to ask the staff too," Mick replied with a helpful tone.

As I drove to the restaurant, I tried to think positively. I had a clue, but some voice in my head kept asking, "What are you gonna do with it?" I didn't have an answer.

Lunch cheered me–Jenn had a way of doing that–but by the time I got back to the office I was feeling like the ace starter who had been benched in the first inning for giving up five runs. I had interesting information, but I still had a dead friend, who nobody really cared about. I thought about tonight's game. Jenn and I were going to meet Mick and all I could think was the guy sitting beside me might be a killer. I decided to sit between Mick and Jenn, but I didn't think that would help. It was going to take more than an ink-stained piece of wood to solve this case.

New Orleans, Nov. 2013

Jerry-Mac Johnston

Bourbon Street is quiet
this cold
    rainy
November night

So I had to admire
the one
    intrepid
        well-endowed
young lady
    who struggled
        using only one hand
    lifting a coat
    two sweaters
        and a T-shirt
    to expose a breast
        while a drink
    filled her other hand

I thought
    what happened to good manners
Why doesn't
one of her male friends
come to her aid
    and offer to hold her glass

Chivalry is obviously
    dead

The Dog Ate My Homework

Jerry-Mac Johnston

When I was younger
    I thought
        I should be able
        to make music
    I had no illusions
        of Carnegie Hall
        just to do it
        for myself
    So I got an old piano
    and a young teacher
    and I practiced
    diligently
Mainly because the teacher
    was also cute
    and I thought I might
    impress her
I never got very good
    at the piano
        and she began
        dating an accountant
    At the next lesson
    I came in and played
    she said
    That's the worst
    you've ever played
So I said
    The dog ate my piano
She didn't think
    that was funny
    and it was understandable
    It's possible to lose

your sense of humor
when you
date an accountant
But I thought it was funny
and I decided
to become a comedian

I embellished and told
the piano story
but nobody thought
it was funny

So one night
I went onstage
and didn't say anything
for an interminably long minute

Then someone in the audience
yelled out
You're not funny
So I said
The dog ate all my jokes
Nobody thought that was funny
but I thought it was funny
and decided to write it down
So I did
and you're reading it now
and eventually
the dog died
of indigestion

To My Ex-wife (I Forgot Which One) *XXIII*

Jerry-Mac Johnston

There's a lot to like
about this town

We liked the variety
of restaurants
    especially the
    All-You-Can-Eat
    Mexican at the mall
      of all places

We liked the bike trails
especially the one
which went past the winery
    and the little
    French bistro

We liked the opportunity
to see the opera
    and the theatre
    and the ballet
      and the coffee house
      in the historic district

We liked the proximity
to the mountains
    and the desert
    and the ocean
      and the river

Unfortunately
    it turned out
we didn't like each other

Sharon Kizziah-Holmes

Sharon has been writing since 1992. She is a member of Springfield Writer's Guild and other local writing groups. Her latest book, *The Will and the Wisp*, is a historical fiction novel based on a true story. She owns her own indie-assist publishing company, Paperback-Press and loves helping others hone their writing skills.

Revenge

Sharon Kizziah-Holmes

The pounding sound of horses' hoofs reached his ears, then the riders came into sight. Four men pointed their guns toward the sky. Jack Waters recognized each and every one of them, and next time he was in town, he would be sure to tell the sheriff of their shenanigans... again. It wasn't the first time Luther Wilcox's men tormented him and Lilly.

"Get off my land, you sons-a-bitches!" He started toward the house to get his weapon; but before he could move, shots echoed against the hills as the men shot into the air; the hooligans' laughter, whoops and hollers rang out as they rode away.

A soft whimper was barely audible through the fading noise. He glanced to where his wife stood. "No!" Jack's heart sank to the pits of hell as he watched the woman he loved fall to the ground. "Lilly!" He ran to her and sank to his knees. One of the bullets had fallen from the heavens and struck her.

Blood stained the ground beneath the woman he loved. She was limp when he pulled her into his arms. "Lilly. Lilly!" She didn't move. He needed to do something, but helplessness threatened to tear him apart. "You're going to be okay, my love. I'm gonna go get the doc."

He picked her up, took her inside, then laid her flaccid body on their bed. "I'll hurry." Her tortured moan tore at his soul. She stirred and he reached for her hand. She was alive. "Lilly?" When her eyes fluttered open, they were filled with pain. Her voice was just a whisper and he leaned down to hear her words.

"Don't... leave... me. It's... too... late."

Tears spilled freely down his face. What would he do without her? "You're not going to die." He heard an unnatural pleading in his own voice when his statement changed to a request and he sobbed. "Don't die, Lilly, please."

Blood trickled from her mouth. The sticky red substance marked her pillow. Why did this have to happen? Thoughts of the men who did this rushed through his mind. If his beloved died, his life would mean nothing. He vowed to get revenge by law or by his own hand. Lilly's whisper tugged at his breaking heart.

"I... love... you... Jack."

"My God!" He wiped his tear stained face with his sleeve. "I love you, too, Lil." He knelt by the bed, took her in his arms realizing he had only said those words a few times.

Heat ebbed from her body, her life was fading away. He couldn't leave her to go and get the doctor. Not when she was on her way to heaven. With his darling in his embrace, he took a seat on the bed, leaned back onto the rough wood headboard and held her until she took her last breath.

Alone, the only sound was his own breathing. She was gone. His heart shattered into a million pieces and the scream that ripped from his chest was its own entity. When he caught his breath, he laid Lilly's lifeless body onto the mattress and covered her with a quilt she'd made with her own hands. "I'll join you soon, Lil."

Nothing in life had prepared him for the emotions he felt at that moment. He took his wife's well-worn bible from the table beside the bed, then left the small room and made his way to the hearth. The shotgun was cool to the touch when he pulled it from the mantel.

Even if he died today, justice would be served. Those men would pay, one way or the other. However, he couldn't bear the thought of his sweet wife not getting a proper burial. He placed the Holy Book, shotgun, and some extra cartridges on the kitchen table, then made his way to the barn for the shovel.

***

It was time to ride. Jack made sure the Bible was in the saddlebag and the shotgun in its sheath before he mounted. He felt in his shirt pocket, several shells were there. Satisfied that everything was in place, he took one last look around his little farm.

"Nothing." He patted his horse on the neck. "This place means nothing to me now."

His heart hurt. It felt like a stone, heavy in his chest as he glanced at the makeshift cross he'd placed on his Lilly's grave. One of her favorite things to do was going onto the knoll beneath the trees to have a picnic. He'd always acted like he didn't want any part of it, but she always saw right through him and they'd end up sitting on the ground enjoying the time together.

Things that happened on that hill, at their special spot, would remain cherished memories. Now the mound would be her forever-resting place. God, how he missed her laughter, her loving smile and her soft hands touching his skin.

"Bastards!" He heeled his horse into a gallop. Once he explained to Sheriff Mansel what had happened, the killers would get what they had coming to them. He hoped to see them strung up and swinging from the tallest tree in town.

His spurs jingled with each step as he made his way along the wooden sidewalk to the sheriff's office. He opened the door, then stepped inside. Cigar smoke was thick and the potbellied Wayne Mansel sat behind his desk.

"What can I do for you, Waters?"

"Wilcox's men came to the ranch this morning."

The sheriff sat back in his chair. "And?"

"They killed my Lilly. I want you to put 'em behind bars."

Mansel sat forward once again. "How'd it happen, Jack?"

"There were four of them. They came up toward the

house and before I could get my gun they started shooting into the air. One of the bullets came down and hit my wife." He took off his hat and, trying to calm himself, he turned it in his hands. He looked the other man in the eye. "They're killers, Wayne. Plain and simple. They need to pay."

Shaking his head Mansel said, "Now I can't go off half-cocked and arrest four men. Especially when none of them actually pointed their gun at Lilly and pulled the trigger. I'm sorry she's gone, I know you loved her; but, Jack, it was an accident."

Jack put his hat on and noticed his hands trembled. His blood boiled and his heart pained as it pumped the hot liquid through his veins at an accelerated rate. "It's not right! I'll have no more of it!" He turned his back to the sorry excuse of a lawman and started toward the door.

"Stop right there, Waters. If you go after them, you'll be the murderer and *I'll* have to come after *you*."

He paused, straightened his back then opened the door. "I'll be seein' you, Mansel." He slammed the door behind him, got on his horse and rode west, toward the Wilcox ranch.

All he could see was the crimson fluid of his Lilly's life seeping from her body. Red, that's the color that shrouded his soul. Red for anger, red for the torment his heart was in, but most of all, red for the hatred he felt toward the bastards that turned his world upside down and sent Lilly to meet her maker way too soon.

He reached into his saddlebag and pulled out the Good Book Lilly had held in her sweet hands so many times. Raising it to his lips, he prayed, "Heavenly Father, I'm gonna ask Your forgiveness for what I'm about to do. I reckon You already know what it is, so I don't have to tell Ya. If I don't get to heaven because of my sins, I ask that You take good care of my Lilly. Thank You, Sir." He kissed the book and put it back in its place.

Smoke? He smelled smoke. He glanced up and saw the beginnings of a plume rise above the trees in the west. It was Wilcox's place. "Damn, is the place on fire?"

Urging his horse into a gallop, he hastened toward the growing cloud of black. Then the crackling sound of the flames came to his ears along with a woman's cry. What the hell was going on?

He rounded the corner to see what was on fire. It was the bunkhouse. The woman was Mrs. Wilcox. She was trying to go inside. Jack reined his horse to a stop, jumped off, then ran toward her and the burning building. Tears fell onto her cheeks and her voice was strained when she spoke.

"Help me, please!"

From the looks of the flames, it was too late to save the building. If anyone was inside, it was probably too late for them, too. "Back away, ma'am. There's nothing we can do."

She grabbed Jack's arm. "But Bob's in there. He went in to wake up the hands and never came out. We need to save him."

He thought of the drunken men that had killed Lilly. They must have come back here and passed out. No telling how the fire started. Mrs. Wilcox's face showed her fear when she spoke to him. His heart went out to her.

"My husband's all I have."

Her husband? His Lilly was all he'd had and he knew what this lady was going through. As if the hand of God propelled him forward, he ran through the black smoke that billowed out the doorway, then fell to the floor and began to crawl. His heart pounded hard in his chest. "Hello, can you hear me?!" He listened, nothing. "Is anyone here?!"

"Over here."

The voice was strong, yet weak at the same time. He couldn't really tell where it had come from. The heat was so intense it felt like the flames licked at his back. He started to turn back then thought of the grieving woman outside. "Say again!"

"Over here!"

This time he got a fix on the voice and crawled toward it. The noise was deafening and a crash sounded as one of the walls collapsed. One side of the ceiling fell, barely missing him. Pain riddled his chest and back. Had he been hit by something? No matter, he had to hurry or the inferno would be the death of both of them.

His lungs burned and for the second time that day the smell of death reached his nostrils. He hoped the ceiling hadn't crashed on top of the man. "Wilcox, you still with me?"

"Yes, here."

The voice was close. Jack reached out his hand and felt the man's leg. He was sitting on the floor leaned against the sidewall of the building. Fire was fast engulfing everything and the pain in Jack's chest wouldn't let up. Squeezing, it felt like it was pushing the air right out of his lungs, then he realized it was all of the smoke he was breathing in. "Can you walk?"

"No. I stumbled running in and I think I broke my leg."

It took all of Jack's strength to stand, but he managed to grab the older man under the arms. Everything moved in slow motion as he desperately made his way to the door. The hands of time seemed to stand still, but finally he saw the light of day as he pulled Wilcox out and away from the blazing ruins.

Mrs. Wilcox fell to her knees beside her husband. "Oh, Bob, I was so scared. Are you okay?"

"Broke my leg, Mary, but I'm fine."

Jack lay on the ground. He couldn't breathe and the pain in his back and chest was worse than ever. What was happening to him? He heard the sound of horses approach.

Mr. Wilcox spoke. "It's the sheriff."

Mansel dismounted. "Did Waters do this?"

"No, I don't even know what he's doing here."

"Lilly was killed this morning by a stray bullet one of your hands fired."

"Aw, hell."

Mrs. Wilcox said, "He saved Bob's life. If he hadn't shown up when he did, I'd be a widow, Sheriff.

Mansel pointed to Jack. "What's wrong with him? Was he burned in the fire or something?"

"I don't know. The ceiling collapsed. Maybe something hit him."

The sheriff knelt down. "Don't see no blood. He sure has a funny grey color about him, though."

Their voices faded and Jack tried to focus on what was in front of him. What was it? Who was it? Lilly? The most beautiful sight met Jack's gaze. Lilly stood in front of a rainbow of bright light. Colors he'd never seen before illuminated behind her. They encircled her and she was more radiant than she'd ever been. She glowed with happiness and love.

The cold he'd felt only moments ago disappeared and warmth overtook him. The most beautiful music seemed to lift him up. It sounded like angels singing. His pain was gone and he stood to meet his wife's gaze. "Is this –" Though she didn't speak, somehow her voice rang clear.

"Heaven." Lilly smiled joyfully and held out her hand. He knew eternity waited.

Geraldine Kolb

Gerrie has a bachelor's degree in English and a master's degree in art. For fifty years she taught elementary grades and supervised art teachers. She has travelled extensively in Europe and is author of *Finding Europe in America, a Travelers' Guide*.

Stallion

Geraldine Kolb

The taste of steel is in your mouth,
And leather straps caress your neck,
The cinch tight-binds the saddle weight,
And Martingale restrains your head.

Onto your hooves, shoes have been nailed,
Your flowing mane is in a plait,
A curry comb has sheened your hide.
And now you stand and now you wait.

To help forget your lawless ways,
Your flank has taken crop and heel;
You've learned to dance to mankind's song,
To jump and turn, to bow and wheel.

Into a battle you have forged,
Stepped victory marches, borne the king,
But Pegasus is in your blood,
And in your soul, wilderness sings.

God grant you strength for many years,
Sweet grasses, playmates staunch and true,
And a quick and painless passing,
High on a sun-drenched, clovered hill.

Penny Kubitschek

Penny began writing poems and letters to God when
hospitalized at age eight for rheumatic fever. She is a
Certified Professional Secretary and a lifelong learner.
Besides writing, she enjoys taking college classes, reading,
playing word games, and watching movies.

Breaking the Curse

Penny Kubitschek

"I figure if a girl wants to be a legend, she should go ahead and be one." Calamity Jane's quote shows through the glass top of the desk in my daughter Kristin's home office. The display is appropriate, since from my perspective Kristin is a legend. My love for and pride in her are no greater than any other mother's love and pride, but there's more psychology between us than she realizes or anyone else would guess, due to my own life and circumstances. Each of us is unique, but no one is special. However, I am the only person in the world who can tell this story.

I am the product of two black sheep. My half-sister and I were raised by our maternal grandparents, which was embarrassing in our small town in the 1950s. All my life, I tried to be a better person than either of my parents by making better choices than theirs and seeing that Kristin had a more stable upbringing than mine. Kristin turned out to be much better than I did in every way. Because of her education, achievements, and personality, I feel a curse has been broken. My autobiography, *Breaking the Curse*, explains why.

My story's complexity made it difficult to relate sensibly, so I thank Wayne Groner, memoir-writing coach, for suggesting Linda Spence's *Legacy*, whose extensive questionnaire extracted memories and feelings that led to *Breaking the Curse*. My love and gratitude go to my lovely Kristin for providing our story with a happy ending.

I acknowledge the roles of my mother, Beulah Marks Ayres, and my former husband, Dr. William C. Kubitschek, both deceased, in Kristin's and my lives. This project has been helpful in the process of understanding, and extending and seeking compassion and forgiveness.

Chapter 1

The beginning of my story is impossible to identify. Was it in 1971, when Kristin Anele Kubitschek entered the world in the Mansfield, Missouri, hospital? Maybe it was in 1942, when I was born in my Grandma and Grandpa Marks' house on Bland Street in Canton, Missouri. Perhaps it was in 1917, when my mother was born in her parents' rural home near Williamstown, Missouri. Then again, there might have been an unknown ancestor whose genes of rebellion and poor judgment trickled down through the bloodline, into the woman who became my mother. All those possible beginnings were parts of the backdrop of Kristin's and my personal drama.

My first realization there was a story at all was when my Aunt Grace, my father's sister in Iowa, sent me my first book as a Christmas gift when I was four or five. I recall the immediate feeling my world and life had just expanded and brightened. I also remember thinking, "Something's wrong here. Someone should have given me a book a long time ago. I wonder why they didn't. What about my family isn't right?"

* * *

Writing *Breaking the Curse* is an ongoing process. I have keyed into my computer more than four-hundred questions from Linda Spence's *Legacy*, which covers nine stages of life. The answers I provide, together with stories I have written, will comprise the final book.

Joe Levanti

Joe performs magical, motivational, entertaining illusions for schools, libraries, churches, conventions, businesses, and other groups. He is a professional actor, character dancer, and props stage technician. He has worked many television game shows, sitcoms and soap operas.

How I Found My Perfect Mate
(and You May Find Yours)

Joe Levanti

Rather than hang out dirty laundry, let's just say my first marriage was not a success.

About five years after the divorce, I was thinking whatever bad times there were, there were also a few good times sprinkled throughout and if I could find the perfect woman for me and our marriage had more good times, it would be worth the journey.

One Wednesday night, I heard Dr. William Hornaday in Los Angeles, California, talk about a woman who came to him and said she wanted to get married and wanted him to pray with her.

He said, "That's wonderful. Describe your perfect husband."

"I want him to be tall, dark, handsome, suave, sophisticated, rich and famous."

"And what do you have to offer this man?

"Why, just me," she said.

"The man you just described might be a foreign diplomat traveling around the world and when dignitaries from foreign countries came to visit at your home, you would not have to do the cooking but you would have to direct the staff on what to cook and how to serve it."

"Oh my no," she responded.

Dr. Hornaday then suggested she revise her list and actually make two lists. One describing her perfect husband in detail and the second list on what she had to offer this man.

"You both don't have to be active in sports or have the same interests, but there has to be some balance in your relationship."

She went home, revised her list and nine months later he performed their wedding ceremony. One of the key ingredients is the action she took of writing on paper her dream, wish list, goal, affirmation, taking the time to read it several times a day and to visualize it.

Go into any large book store to the self-improvement section, close your eyes, pick any book at random and someplace in there the author will tell you to get a goal, write it down and read it a dozen times or more a day to help you get your subconscious mind focused.

Armed with this information, I made my two lists.

List number one described my perfect wife. Not just her height, weight, age, face shape, taste in clothes, and so forth, but what kind of a family she grew up in, the kind of friends she associates with, foods she enjoys, hobbies or interests, any grown children, her personality, plus we will love each other and enjoy being together.

The second list was what I had to offer her. To love and honor her, earn enough income for both of us if she chose not to work, and a good health plan to take care of her.

On another occasion, Dr. Hornaday suggested writing goals in the form of a prayer.

For those of you who may be spiritual but not religious, atheists or agnostics, these steps to finding your perfect mate will still work for you even if you choose not to pray about it, because just like scientists work with the laws of science, there are also the laws of success.

Gravity works according to the law of gravity. It doesn't care who or what you are on Planet Earth. If you understand the law of gravity, it can work for you instead of against you, because it works according to its nature whether you understand it or not.

Since this is my story, I will be referring to God, because it's comfortable for me. But I will also give you the secular versions.

Here is Dr. Hornaday's prayer formula.

Thank You God

Or, Heavenly Father, Jesus, Lord, Rabbi, Subconscious Mind, or whatever is comfortable for you. By saying *thank you* first, it's a sign of faith. In my seminars and workshops I say to the audience, "If I'm visiting in your home and getting ready to leave, and you say, 'Joe I don't plan to leave the house today, would you please mail this letter for me?' I say, 'Sure.' What do you say?"

The audience in unison responds, "Thank you." I haven't mailed it yet, but they are thanking me in advance because they trust me or have faith in me to do what they asked.

For

Fill in the details of your goal. Use only all positive words and phrases. Do not mention things you wish to avoid or get rid of because then you are focused on the negative.

Pretend you are talking to a magic genie that came out of the bottle and will grant you any wishes. Be careful what you ask, because the genie or Laws of Success will give you what you ask for, not necessarily what you mean.

This or Better

This is your legal loophole.

You will probably receive something even better than you asked for but have you ever wished for something, received it and said, "What was I thinking when I asked for this?" NOT getting what you asked for might be better in some cases.

Thy Will Is Done

This doesn't mean whether you're going to get it or not. It means God (or Law) works in wonderful, mysterious and sometimes very strange ways to our way of thinking. When it seems like things are going in the opposite direction we think they should, here is where we need our faith again.

Amen

And so it is.

I had my Affirmative Prayer for my perfect wife typed on paper and held by magnets on my file cabinet where I could see it often and repeat it aloud several times a day.

In addition to working props on the nighttime turnaround crew for the soap opera *General Hospital*, where we set up the sets and props for the next day's taping, I was a professional motivational speaker and goal-setting workshop leader. I came in one night a little early. They were done taping and the stage was empty. No one to talk to, nothing interesting on television, and the only reading material in the crew area was a copy of *Glamour* magazine. Being bored, I flipped through the pages where I came across a makeover on a woman. They scrubbed her down to the pores on her face, did a light make up and styled her hair. There in the middle of the magazine were the before and after pictures. I said to myself, "That's an attractive woman." I proceeded to cut out the after photo and put it on my file cabinet next to my Affirmative Prayer.

As I mentioned, I also conducted goal-setting workshops for businesses, churches and organizations. I was a member of the National Speakers Association, where I became friends with Dottie Walters, a speaker, publisher, and consultant who taught speakers how to promote themselves. More and more people were interested in becoming professional speakers, but the NSA only met once a month and people wanted more.

Dottie started a weekly series called Dinner with Dottie, where we met in a nice restaurant and for twenty-five dollars enjoyed dinner and a guest speaker on the different aspects of the speaking profession. Dottie asked me to be the master of ceremonies at the meetings. I warmed up the audience and then introduced the guest speakers.

After the meeting of the third week, a woman named Terry came up to me after the meeting and asked what I did besides the master of ceremonies thing. I explained I conducted goal-setting seminars and workshops and helped people storyboard their business plans. She got excited and said that's just what she needed but didn't have any money and would like to barter her service in exchange for my help. I like to help people, so I asked what kind of business she had. She said she had a match-making service with two fees: $400 just to be on her books, which is the part she wants to barter, but if I married someone she introduced me to, the fee was $2,000. A thousand from each of us, or however it worked out, the total was $2,000. I'm thinking I don't need any of this, but I said I would help her, so I did.

We met at her office and I showed her how to set up her storyboard and then we went to lunch where she asked me a series of questions. Computers were just coming on the scene but she bragged that she did not use computers. She had her own questions on a few sheets of paper and a column on the right side of the pages where in her own hieroglyphics she would comment on how a person responded even if it was a simple yes or no answer.

She asked her questions and I answered honestly to all of them. Her comment was "You sure are particular." I said, "Why should I tell you something would not bother me when it does?"

It may seem like some of the things are trivial to others but it would just end up wasting time for the women I meet and me. Besides, I was just being polite. I had no intentions of meeting my perfect woman through a match-making service, so the thought of a $2,000 fee was not of any concern for me. In my mind, I would be giving a seminar, she would be sitting in the front row, our eyes would meet, violins would play, the romance would be on, and our lives together will be perfect. That's not exactly how it happened.

Three months pass and I get a call from her. She announces she has a match for me. "Who am I speaking to?" I asked. Terry reminded me of our meeting and gave me the work number of a woman I was to call and meet at a public place like a restaurant. On paper it was a match, but not in real life. Another three months go by and she contacts me with another phone number to call. I was busy working on a new seminar so I never called that woman.

Let me explain. Most of her clients were getting one to three possible dates a week. She was sincere about her business. She really only wanted people who were serious about getting married, but because I was so particular, she was having a tough time finding matches for me. I wasn't concerned because I believed this match-making service idea was a waste of time for me. I'm going to meet my new wife in one of my seminars.

Three months go by again and I call the number. I met a woman out in the Valley at a restaurant and the first words out of her mouth were that she's a Communist, her parents are Communists, they've always been Communists, and she is a schoolteacher. Holy mackerel, God, what are you getting me into here? I'm basically conservative, but I made myself extremely conservative to her in our conversation.

"This will never do," she said, and I politely agreed.

Another three months pass and Terry gives me the contact number for Phyllis. I'm debating in my mind do I really want another unpleasant lunch?

I almost didn't call her, but something like a little Jiminy Cricket voice on my shoulder said, "Yes, it might be another unpleasant lunch, but what if? Isn't it worth taking the risk?

I called Phyllis and met her at her place of employment. She was gorgeous. We shook hands and I felt something electric flow through my body. We went to lunch within walking distance of her job and I answered everything she asked. I told her I really liked her and would like to see her again. What did she like to do on an evening out on the town? She said dinner and a movie.

I got her home phone number and address. Six months later, we were married and we gladly paid the $2,000 fee. We did not want to create any bad Karma or negative cause/effect or action/reaction or sowing and reaping bad results.

If you saw the picture I cut out of the magazine and saw a picture of Phyllis, they weren't twins, but if you were casting a movie, they would both be up for the part. We had eighteen wonderful years together, fourteen of them after her heart transplant. She died of breast cancer.

I still have a fantastic daughter and son-in-law, two terrific grandsons, and a wonderful granddaughter. Phyllis passed away ten years ago. At the time of this writing, I'm setting a new goal for my new perfect wife. It all started with writing my clearly defined goal on paper, reading it a dozen or more times a day and visualizing a happy marriage scenario. God (Law or Nature) orchestrated the events. I would never have voluntarily sought out a match-making service.

When do you start your plan? What are you waiting for?

Two Fun Facts

Most of the dates Phyllis and I had were dinner and a movie. She liked to go to the large theaters in Brentwood, California, with the big screens and excellent sound systems. We often had to stand in line for the next showing of a new movie. I had been on a local television interview program, *There Is a Way*, seven times as a motivational speaker. People would recognize me in line and come up to tell me how much they enjoyed hearing my ideas and seeing me. She confessed after we were married that she thought I hired those people to come up to us and say nice things about me to impress her.

The first time I met her, we were leaving her office building to go to a restaurant. Her office was on the top floor of a tall building. It was lunchtime, so we had to wait for the elevator. There were quite a few people already waiting for the elevator. A year later Phyllis said those people at the elevator were not going to lunch. They were going to be eyewitnesses if she didn't come back from lunch.

Magic Engineer Joe and Eddie the Engine

Joe Levanti

Hi Boys and Girls,

My name is Magic Engineer Joe and I want you to meet my friend, Eddie the Engine. I call him Eddie the Ethical and Energetic Engine. Eddie asked me why I call him Ethical. I explained to him it's because he is always on time for work, has a good attitude, and does his very best even when he thinks no one is watching. Eddie does his best because he knows it's the right thing to do.

There is always someone watching you. Sometimes it's a parent, a friend, a teacher, a neighbor or a boss. Bosses are always looking for good workers. Not just how well they do their jobs, but how well they get along with other workers and whether they are a good example for others. Do they avoid gossip? Those are the workers who get promotions and a better pay check.

Do you do your homework properly or do you make excuses why you did not? You won't be fooling anyone if you always have an excuse. Doing it well and on time is always a good thing and a good habit to develop.

Eddie is also a part of the magical illusion act I do for libraries, schools, churches, parties and groups. Eddie and I like to perform entertaining magical illusion shows for our passengers and their family members while they are waiting at the stations.

It's not real magic. It's just a show to have fun. Libraries have books explaining how to do some easy magic tricks if you would like to entertain and amaze your friends. There may be a magic store or a magic club in your area. Be sure to discover what fun it can be.

Eddie the Engine and I travel all over the country bringing passengers, freight, and mail to their destinations. Trains don't carry as much mail as they used to, but years ago they carried almost all of it.

Most of you probably have a smart phone with you all the time. When you send a text message, Tweet, Facebook,* or e-mail, you receive a reply almost immediately. About 150 years ago it took a letter or package anywhere from three months to a year to go from New York to California. The United States of America did not have the roads, Interstate highways and turnpikes we have today.

Usually a letter was put into a sack that went on a wagon train heading west to the gold-rush camps. If someone changed camps, someone would put the letter on a bulletin board until someone else recognized the name and said that person went "north to the such-and-such camp." The next wagon train or person heading that way might bring it to them. They didn't have house numbers, street names or a post office yet.

After a while, the Pony Express was started and riders rode horses with a mail pouch full of letters and small packages through dangerous territories where there were wild animals, rocky lands and robbers hoping to find money in the envelopes or packages. The Pony Express only lasted eighteen months, from April 3, 1860, to October 26, 1861.

Then the railroads were built heading west and east. Railroads eventually built a mail car called an RPO which stood for Railway Post Office. They could pick up the mail in small towns without stopping. A pole was invented that would hold a special mailbag way up high to the level of the doors on the RPO mail car. The stationmaster had a signal sign down the track that told the engineer whether someone bought a ticket to travel or not. If no passengers were traveling that day, the train did not even have to slow down but could actually grab the mailbag without stopping. The mail clerks simply opened the door and put a mechanical arm out. When the mechanical arm hit the special mailbag, it was so powerful it would throw the bag into the mail car. The clerks would then close the door, open the mailbag and sort the mail while they traveled. They also had bags they would throw out of the mail car onto the station platform with mail for that town, or even an empty bag to be filled with mail the next time the train came through.

As time moved on, the post office added airmail that was carried by airplanes over long distances and other countries. When better roads and highways were built, the trucks started to carry most of the mail. In the near future, with e-mail, Facebook,* all the social media sites and e-books, hardly any mail will be sent on paper.

Eddie also pulls tank cars that carry gas, oil or other liquids, boxcars that carry cattle or merchandise, and flat cars that carry large shipping containers or equipment to repair the tracks.

If you have been lucky enough to visit some amusement parks, you may have had the opportunity to ride on a monorail train. Mono means one. One rail? That's amazing.

Maybe you have a model train set, in your home that you put around the Christmas tree once a year or you may have a really nice model train set up in a special room, basement or garage. I belong to a club called Garden Railroading. It has special G-gauge railroad engines and cars that are made to run in the rain, sleet, snow or sunshine. It can be a hobby for the whole family. Families can build large outdoor layouts.

Mine is twenty feet by forty feet in my back yard. It has two different train tracks running at the same time. The plants and bushes are trimmed to the scale of the buildings, bridges and train cars. It also has a waterfall where the train runs behind the falling water.

If you would like to know more about the garden railroad hobby you can start with the magazine called *Garden Railways*. You can find it at most large book stores or look at the end of this story for our website with more information on garden railroading clubs around the world and other indoor model railroads and clubs.

There are conventions every year in different states where you can see outdoor garden railroad layouts in many yards. A club near you may also have garden railroad tours open to the public every year. Eventually you may have your garden railroad on the tour.

You might be interested about railroads in other parts of the world. Their trains look different than the ones in the United States of America. Go to your local library and ask for books about trains in other parts of the world, and be sure to visit Eddie the Engine and me on our website.

If you prefer the smaller-detailed indoor model trains like O, HO, S, N or Z gauge, there are other magazines and clubs to help you. Model railroading can be a great history lesson, a lot of fun and a learning experience for the whole family.

President Harry Truman had his own private railroad car he traveled in and gave speeches from the back platform of the car at the end of the train.

You may also learn creative thinking, how to set goals, problem solving, model making, designing track layouts, and you will have fun meeting with other people who enjoy the same hobby.

Train rides are like traveling through life. We plan destinations we would like to achieve, but have detours along the way due to weather, construction, or natural disasters out of our control. We can still reach our destinations or life's goals as long as we stay focused, have patience, persistence, have a positive attitude and learn from those lessons along the way.

Remember to always do the best you can with anything you do in life. You will also have the satisfaction of knowing you did the very best you could and you will be respected by others for your efforts to accomplish a job well done.

If you have a model railroad or you are working on one, we would enjoy seeing what you and your family are doing. To send your photos, or to find a garden railroading club near you, go to our website, magicengineerjoe.com.

*Facebook is a registered trademark.

Nancy Lewis-Shelton

Nancy is a retired Missouri educator who now works part time as a pet sitter. She enjoys writing, bridge, theater, music, and storytelling. She also reviews children's books, coordinates a storytelling group and participates in many church activities. Published work includes devotionals, nonfiction senior pieces, and educational articles.

The Summer of 1954

Nancy Lewis-Shelton

There have been many drought years in the mid-west but none compared to the sweltering summer of my twelfth year. The month started with temperatures above ninety degrees with each day hotter than the one before.

Mom, Dad and I lived in a rental property on Kansas Avenue in Springfield, Missouri. Few houses in our low-income neighborhood had air conditioning, including ours. In addition to struggling with intense heat, dust drifted in and covered all of the furniture. If we closed the windows, we didn't have the dirt, but the heat seemed worse.

Each day Dad increased our mess by dragging two enormous blocks of ice into the house. He'd put them in tubs positioned in front of large fans in the living room and my parents' bedroom. When Mom complained she didn't receive any benefit from the ice but had to mop up all the water puddles, my father bought tubs and fans for the kitchen and the dining room. However, he wouldn't let her turn on the cook stove because he claimed it created too much heat. Most of the month we ate sandwiches and cold food.

One morning, in early July, my mother appeared dressed in skimpy shorts and a halter top. Then my father entered the living room stripped down to his boxers. Mom remained in the house, but he wandered outdoors in his limited attire. I considered leaving my family but didn't have anywhere else to go. The final embarrassment occurred the next morning when Dad walked by the open front door, naked.

When Mom noticed him, she screamed. "Ed, get some clothes on. What will the neighbors think?'

He complained, "I don't care. I'm hot."

I fell over one of the ice tubs as I rushed into my bedroom. Before anyone called the police, Dad had located his shorts.

On workdays, my parents left the house early in the morning. Mom cleaned rooms at the Colonial Motel, and Dad worked for a hide company. Most days, I was left alone to entertain myself. When it was too hot to stay home, I rode the Number Five bus to Grant Beach Park to splash in the pool with what seemed like hundreds of kids. Other days, I traveled to the public library or wandered around the downtown square. In the air-conditioned Heer's department store, I ogled all the items I'd buy when I became rich, but first I knew I'd purchase an air conditioner.

On Saturdays, Dad drove me to the roller skating rink at Doling Park. In return for my assistance with the little kids' morning lessons, I skated the rest of the day for free. Although huge fans blew on the skaters, the rink often felt like the inside of an oven. When the owner bought me an icy cola, I tried to find a spot where I could feel the air from the fans while I sipped my luxury.

The afternoon of July 14, my father stormed into the house. The news media had recorded the temperature at a record 113 degrees. "Pack the suitcases. We're going to Illinois."

Mom said, "You know I have to work."

"Tell them it's an emergency. I'm going to die if I don't get out of this heat. Tell them I died. They'll let you off for a funeral."

Mom frowned. "I won't lie. Besides it'll be just as hot in Illinois."

"No it won't. We're going north 400 miles. Never mind. Forget it, I'll go by myself." That tended to be my father's favorite statement when he didn't get his way.

Once a year, we traveled to Illinois to visit relatives. I always rode on the back seat accompanied by a huge ice chest filled with food, cola, and orange crush soda. Dad drove to the last service station in Missouri where he fueled the car while Mom and I unpacked lunch onto a nearby picnic table. We ate our sandwiches and whatever else Mom had prepared, then made a final trip to the restrooms before we headed toward the Illinois line.

I don't know exactly what Mom told her employer, but that night, she had a long phone conversation and then said she didn't have to work the rest of the week. Next, she called my grandmother to announce our upcoming visit.

The following day, at six a.m., Dad and I left to fill our old Ford with nineteen-cents-a-gallon gasoline. Within an hour, we were on our way. The hot wind from the open car windows flushed my face as I wondered how cool it would be on the other side of the Mississippi River.

Three hours later, we arrived at Grandma Stella's large two-story white frame house. As I rushed up the steps, I noticed the air felt hot and sticky. It wasn't any cooler here than at home.

After hugs, we moved into the living room where fans blew hot air at us. As I glanced upward at the ceiling, I smiled, remembering the many times I'd cried when my uncles tied nooses around the necks of my dolls and then hung them from the chandeliers. Now, nearly a teenager, they'd have to find one of my younger cousins to tease.

That evening, we had a supper of roast beef, fresh green beans, homemade bread and mashed potatoes, and then Grandma passed around warm apple pie topped with ice cream. After dishes were washed, I played cards with my uncle until Grandma suggested it might be cooler on the screened-in front porch. We hauled chairs, glasses and a pitcher of homemade lemonade outside. I don't know if it was the slight breeze or the drink, but it did seem more pleasant there.

At bedtime, my parents occupied the guest room on the first floor, and I slept upstairs with Grandma. When Dad grumbled it was hotter in Illinois than in Missouri, my mother said nothing. Later, she told me he had carted a pillow, blanket and her fan to the basement, where he spent most of the night.

The next morning, the smell of bacon woke me. When I rushed downstairs to assist with breakfast preparations, I heard a conversation between my grandmother and my mother.

"Mary Eunice, I'm glad to see you, but why now? It's been over 100 degrees here for days."

Mom sighed. "You know Ed. Not much use arguing with him when he gets an idea in his head."

Soon, our days of visiting relatives, eating Grandma's cooking, and trying to stay cool ended. We packed our suitcases and loaded the ice chest with my grandmother's fried chicken, baked beans and apple pie. No matter what the time, I knew we'd stop at the same service station for a gas refill and lunch served on the picnic table.

Later that day, Dad pulled the Ford into the alley behind our house. After we toted the suitcases and ice chest inside, he left to purchase blocks of ice. The weatherman on the radio reported the temperature had cooled to 97 degrees. The heat continued throughout the rest of July with no rain and only one day with temperatures below 90 degrees.

When I recently wrote a gratitude list, my memories of the summer of 1954 reminded me to include "cool weather" as one of the items, but soon I erased those words. The words "air conditioning" seemed more appropriate.

Rosalie Lombardo

Rose writes in several genres. She is a member of the Society of Children's Book Writers and Illustrators, Sleuth's Ink, and Springfield Writers' Guild. Her works have been published in periodicals nationwide, internationally, and in anthologies. In 2013, she was recipient of The Best of SWG's 20th Annual Literary Contest. She has taught a variety of classes throughout the United States since 1996.

The Sentinel

Rosalie Lombardo

He sits at the front of the castle, peering out from the lowest portion of the casement, still as a statue – yet guarding his fortress. He is motionless except for his eyes, which are in constant movement: scanning, scoping, observing, aware of every infinite sway or rustle of a leaf.

This is his duty. But more than duty, he is guarding all that he loves.

Those who look upon him clearly fall in love with his large chestnut eyes set deep in his firm strong face. His light brown hair striped with pure white strands epitomizing the wisdom that has matured at his temples. A courtly beard adorns his chin. He is a vision of valor.

All comment on his stunning physique and the beauty of his stature. He is ready to sound the alarm and charge at the smallest flicker of a fly.

This is his territory and he is ready to protect it with his life.

He hears a strange sound on the south end of the building. He scurries back there, then freezes again, as in stillness he gazes, ensuring no unwanted guests have entered his domain.

Assuring himself that only a rabbit moved the blades of grass, his muscles relax, his tension releases. Sensing all is well on the south end of the building, he returns to the north end to reclaim his central post. Along the way, he stops by my side to report all is well. I gently stroke his hair. He licks my hand, and then returns to his position keeping us all safe.

Sir Buddy the Great, our sentinel.

The Chair

Rosalie Lombardo

I walked through the front door of Gram's house just in time to see Cousin Joe trying to smuggle my grandmother's chair out the back door.

"Whoa, Joe, where are you going with that? That's my grandmother's chair," I screamed.

"I am taking it home," Joe said with a big smile.

"What do you mean you're taking it home? Stop right there."

"Mamma Costanza (Gram) gave it to me," Joe replied.

"I gave that to her for her seventieth birthday. It's solid oak. Nobody's taking that chair anywhere," I informed him.

"She said I could have it," Joe retorted.

"I don't care what she said," I snapped back. I stomped into the kitchen and yelled, "Mamma Costanza, why are you giving the rocking chair to Joe?"

"I don't sit in it much and, anyway, it is just taking up space," she said.

"But I bought that chair for you."

"I know. It's a rocker," she said.

"I love that chair," I told her.

"It makes me feel old," she finally confessed.

"Well if anybody is taking it out of this house, it's going to be me," I announced, loud and clear. Hearing those words, Joe's face sank as his gaze moved toward Gram's direction.

"I am waiting for the verdict," Joe said sternly. "Mamma Costanza, do I get to take the chair home or not?"

"The chair is coming home with me," I snapped back. "After all, I paid for it."

Gram's face lost all expression and she placed her hand

over her heart as she said, "I am so sorry, Joe, I didn't know she wanted it."

Joe returned the chair to its designated spot in Gram's living room.

My feelings were a little hurt that my Gram did not like the chair. I bought it for her with loving intent and thought she would like it as much as I did. The rocker and old age connection never crossed my mind when I purchased it.

I got over the hurt feelings quickly as I carried that rocker out Gram's back door, drove it to my place, walked it up two flights of stairs, and into my apartment.

After Gram died, that chair became my safe-haven, my meditation place, my counselor, my place of prayer, my imagination corner, my spiritual communication center, my think tank, my relaxation spot, my feedback place, and my creative arena.

Magic happens when I sit in that chair. It has been in my possession for thirty-six years now, and for some reason, I still refer to it as my grandmother's chair.

Patricia Martin

I was born in Minnesota and have lived in seven different states. I currently do jail ministry in Christian County and I am on the board of directors for the Jericho Commission in Springfield.

An Empty Heart

Patricia Martin

Dear Jake,

Today I was going through a box of pictures when I came across the one of you when were just two years old. Remember the one where Grandma GG had taken you to have your picture taken and she dressed you in those red corduroy pants, a white t-shirt, and that gray sweatshirt jacket that she made for you. You had a full head of brown curly hair, just like your papa's, blue eyes and the cutest little smile that would make my heart leap.

The photographer caught you at just the right moment. You were perched on a white wicker chair and he snapped the picture just as your eyes were sparkling and you had that devilish grin on your face. I wish you were smiling like that now.

A picture that will always be in my mind of you, that I will never forget, is your first day of kindergarten. You were so eager to get out of the car and walk up to the schoolyard gate by yourself. You were wearing your new Star Wars backpack, a brand new pair of jeans, and blue tennis shoes. When you got to the gate you turned around and smiled and waved to me. I wanted to jump out of the car and grab you and take you home with me. My heart felt so empty, yet I was so full of love for you. I couldn't wait for the next four hours to pass so I could hear all about your first day of school.

I'll never forget the day you came home from school when you were in the first grade and you proudly announced that, "I want to be a paleontologist when I grow up." I had to ask you what a paleontologist does. "They dig up dinosaur bones grandma," you said as you tossed your lunch box down on the counter. I thought to myself, here's this little boy who is only seven years old and he knows how to spell paleontologist and knows what they do and I've never heard of one before. I was so proud of you at that moment. I was so sure your future would be bright and you would be so successful. I promised myself that I would do all I could to make sure that you could go to college and be all you wanted be. As you grew you continued to amaze us with what you were learning and making us laugh along the way.

One of the funniest memories I still have of you was when you were in third grade. I got a call from the secretary at your school asking me to come and talk to the principal about you. I couldn't imagine what was wrong. I was sitting across the desk from Mr. Ramsey and he began to tell me why I was there, I was shocked at first and then I began to laugh to myself. It seems that you stood in the courtyard of the school, in full view of some of the office staff and urinated on a tree. I told Mr. Ramsey that you had been on a camping trip last weekend outside of Flagstaff with your Aunt Stacy and Uncle Brian and I guessed that you thought it was okay to pee on tree since you'd been outdoors all weekend. We all had a good laugh and you never did that again.

A few years later you decided you wanted to play soccer. My first response was I was worried about how your asthma would be affected by all the running you would have to do. It wasn't long after we moved to Arizona that you began to wheeze and sneeze all the time. I took you to an allergist and after all the skin tests for food and plants, we discovered that you were allergic to just about every desert plant in the area. You began to take allergy shots three times a week but that didn't stop you from playing soccer.

In spite of all the shots, and the daily medications, and the breathing treatments, asthma attacks were still a very real part of your life. Still to this day, some of my most vivid memories of you are when I had to call an ambulance in the middle of the night because you were having an asthma attack. I'll never forget the frightened look on your pale little face when they lifted you into the ambulance. All the way to the hospital I prayed that the oxygen they were giving you would be enough to keep you breathing till we could see a doctor. It seems like ever since you were born there was always something threatening to take you away from me.

A few years went by and you were in ninth grade. You had a good group of friends, your grades were good, you were on the wrestling team, and you were pretty good at it too. You had started lifting weights at school and you were really developing into a strong, good-looking young man. You had good, Christian friends at our church. You completed two years of confirmation classes and had just been confirmed earlier that spring. Your mom and papa and I were so proud of you. I felt confident that we had provided the right path for you. Everything seemed to be going well until one day when you brought a new friend from school home.

His name was Alex, and he wore his pants sagging, an earring in one ear and his overall attitude was one of disrespect and basically he was a smart ass. Alex introduced you to skate boarding and before long you had traded your usual Yu-Gi-OH card game with the neighborhood boys for hanging out at the skate park with Alex.

I would show up at the park and watch you skate after school once in a while, and you were really getting good at it. But I soon found out that it wasn't the skate park atmosphere that I should be concerned about, it was what was happening at Alex's house that began to bring back all those old feelings of dread again.

It didn't take too long before one of your friend's mom told me that I shouldn't let you hang out with Alex because Alex's dad smokes pot and he lets Alex experiment with it too. I was shocked, and when I asked you about whether you were smoking pot too you assured me that you would never smoke pot or cigarettes because of your allergies. All I could do at this point was forbid you from hanging out with Alex, but that strategy didn't work for long.

Coincidentally, that same week there was a woman who was going to be giving a presentation at your high school about illegal drug use and what to look for and how to know if your child is taking drugs. I made sure I went to that presentation. I was eager to learn about drugs and drug paraphernalia because living in a large metropolitan area like the Phoenix valley, and being so close to the Mexican border, there were always reports about drugs being smuggled in from Mexico. Besides, I was determined to keep you as far away from anything or anyone that had anything to do with drugs. And knowing about Alex and his father, I needed to get as much information as I could about the drug culture.

I learned a lot about drugs that night, actually more than I wanted to know. The woman who spoke had first-hand knowledge about drugs; her son was a recovering addict. She told us about the way kids smuggle drugs into their house and how they steal from their parents and we should keep an eye on any valuable items in our homes because kids steal them and pawn them for drug money. I was in shock and I felt as if I had just stepped into some dark world where kids can't be trusted and I have to start spying on my own grandson. Little did I know how dark my world was about to get.

The next day when you went to school, I reluctantly searched your bedroom. I really didn't want to but there were two words that the speaker said the night before that kept echoing in my head: jail and prison. "If your kid is on drugs you have to stop it now before they end up in jail or prison," she said.

Well, I was so happy when I finished going through your dresser drawers and closet and all I found were rocks and sticks and little Star Wars action figures. I also convinced myself, in my naïve frame of mind, that you weren't taking any drugs either. After all, there weren't any valuables missing from our house and you were too young to pawn anything and you didn't have enough money to buy drugs. I was sure that your moodiness was nothing more than puberty or stress from school or just something that boys go through at your age.

A few weeks passed and I got a call from Julie, your best friend Adam's mom. It seems that a pair of brand new paint ball guns showed up at her house and Adam swore that you brought them over. I told Julie that we had not bought paint ball guns for you. I was mad and felt betrayed. I could feel the fear welling up inside me again. The events that came in the next few months turned our normal suburban lives upside down.

We had to move to Springfield, Missouri, to take care of my dad. Dad had been diagnosed with congestive heart failure and the doctors didn't give him too long to live. He was all alone and he had no one to care for him. Reluctantly we moved from Phoenix to Springfield, thinking that we wouldn't be here probably more than about a year and then we would move back to Arizona. But that wasn't exactly how things worked out.

One of the first nights in Springfield, while you, Papa and I were staying at a motel, before we found a house to rent, you suddenly decided to go for a walk. You were fifteen at the time and none of us had ever been to Springfield before. We didn't know where anything was and we had no friends here, but that didn't stop you, nor did it stop my pleading with you not to go out. You looked back at me as you closed the motel door and you just walked out into the hot summer night. I bolted to the door and opened it and called to you and said, "Call me if you need a ride or something." I waited in fear and worry for the next couple of hours until finally my cellphone rang and you wanted me to come and pick you up. To this day I have no idea where you went or what you did.

Walking in the dark turned out to be something that didn't bother you because about a year later, on a cold, damp winter night I got a phone call from you asking if I could come and pick you up. You had been at your girlfriend's house, out in the country and you needed a ride home. I asked where you were and it turned out that you were about fifteen miles south of Springfield, on some country road off the highway. I had trouble finding the road so I called you. You assured me that I had turned onto the right road and I should just keep coming.

It was completely pitch black and the road was filled with sharp twists and turns. I stopped the car for a moment and turned out my headlights, I was terrified, I couldn't see anything. I quickly turned them back on and continued slowly driving this narrow dirt road until you said you could see my headlights coming up the road. Within a few minutes the headlights revealed you standing there by a clump of trees, dressed in your usual all black, waiting for me.

When you got in the car I asked you why you just didn't stay at Stephanie's house and I would pick you up there. You said that you like to walk in the dark it gives you time to think. As we drove home all I could think about was how long gone were the days of my little grandson playing with his action figures and spending the night at a friend's house so the two of you could play army together. I couldn't help it, I started to cry.

Ever since we moved to Springfield our lives turned dark and gray and full of mystery and drama and trouble. I remember thinking during the move to Missouri that maybe living in a smaller town would be good for you that you would be far away from the pot that Alex had introduced to you. Once again I was living in a fantasy world when it came to you. You weren't my little Jake any more. You were seventeen years old and over six feet tall. I had no more control over you, you just came and went as you pleased. I never knew where you were, who you were with, or what you were doing. But today I know exactly where you are and when I can come and visit you.

Every time I get a call from you or when I have to say good-bye to you at the end of our visit, you always turn around and smile and wave to me just like you did on your first day of kindergarten. My heart feels so empty every time I have to leave that prison without you. You will always be my little Jake and I'll always love you and be there for you.

Love always,
Grandma

Wanda Sue Parrott

Wanda Sue is past president of Springfield Writers' Guild and Honorary Life Member. She lives in Monterey, California where she performs with Tap Bananas senior dance troupe. She created the pissonnet and story stanza poetry forms. "Elfinetta's E.T.s" won the Sleuths' Ink Mistress of Mayhem Award in 2007.

Elfinetta's E.T.s

Wanda Sue Parrott

Elfinetta shouted, "Where's Santa Claus?" Lusty squeals responded from a sea of pointed gray faces around holly-festooned toy tables in Santa's North Pole compound.

The sharp-eared imitation elves banged their fists. "Food! Food! Food!"

"Silence!" their surrogate mom said. "If Grandpa and Grandma Claus aren't here soon, we'll have our 2007 holiday feast without them. Crisp tenders in orange sauce with raisins."

Rat-like faces slurped. "Yummm."

"Now sit still. Trust me. I promise food good enough to die for."

Elfinetta rushed toward the kitchen, stopping in the freezer where Mrs. Claus was wriggling on a meat hook. "Sorry, ma'am. This's the President's fault."

Mrs. Claus' eyelids clicked and she belched an oval steam-ring. "Is this an alien invasion?"

"No ma'am." Elfinetta hefted Mrs. Claus to the floor. "When your elves struck for higher wages, the President vetoed their walkout..."

"I know..."

"So no child would be left behind..."

"You mean left without Christmas?"

"Exactly. He sent my gaggle of genetic goofs to replace your elves."

"You mean those things aren't aliens?"

"I'm Doctor Etta Moon, geneticist. I spliced mice cells and human cells. Since he's a right-to-lifer, he vetoed their destruction."

"What did he dub you? He nicknames everyone."

"Dubya dubbed me Elfinetta. He calls them Cheap Labor."

Mrs. Claus nodded. "Well, I'll swan."

"You'll what?"

"It's Hillbilly for *I'll be danged*," Mrs. Claus said.

"You're a hillbilly?"

"Was. I left Possum Holler by eloping with Santa. Snuck aboard his sleigh." Elfinetta frowned. "What's alien about my monster rodents?"

"They look like Grays."

"Wrong. They're terrestrial. Dubya reasons Christmas is more profitable than even Mideast oil."

"Where is my Bubba Claus?"

Elfinetta shoved Mrs. Claus toward the kitchen, where Santa's red suit lay crumpled beside the oven. "He's roasting in M&M-size bits soaked in orange-flavored anti-freeze."

"Judas priest! That's deadly poison!"

"Those creatures reproduce overnight. They're cannibals! I killed your husband to save humanity."

Mrs. Claus shook like a bowl full of jelly. "Wrong!"

"Why do you laugh?"

"You didn't kill Santa Claus!"

"Then who's the fat guy I whacked, then diced up and marinated?"

"Karl Rove."

"No!"

"Yes."

"But Rove's bald. With his wig and whiskers, he looked just like Santa."

"That's why the President assigned him this mission."

Elfinetta gasped. "But, Rove resigned."

"So the public thinks," Mrs. Claus said, peeking in the oven. "He was an undercover agent doubling as my Bubba."

"Why?"

"Because the President reassigned my husband to a secret profit-making mission." Mrs. Claus smiled. "The elves are on furlough and Ambassador Claus is in China, negotiating a cheap deal to outsource their jobs. Now, let me help you."

The women carried the tray of steaming tenders to a sideboard. Elfinetta asked, "What about us?"

"You and me?"

"No. Me and my brood. I begged the President to let me abort the mission."

"And you're doing a good job, dear. Your dinner smells scrumptious." Mrs. Claus offered Elfinetta a chunk of Karl. "You know the saying: *the kitchen is a woman's spiritual domain*. Well, this's *my* kitchen, not yours!" She waved a meat cleaver at Elfinetta, but shrill screeching slurps interrupted.

Elfinetta spotted the surging rat-like rodents filling the hallway, ranting for *food, food food*. "Since dinner didn't come to them, they're coming to dinner!"

Fingers that had nimbly painted eyelashes on porcelain doll faces, and spread glue on little kids' plastic big wheels and toy guns, were now unsheathed weapons that clawed, ripped and tore across the floor and into each other.

Instinctively following the succulent scent of supper, the stronger creatures were devouring the weakest ones in their scramble for survival.

Elfinetta snatched the cleaver from Mrs. Claus and hurled it at the leader, whose once-shiny black eyes were glowing red. It glanced off his shoulder, knocking him to all fours. He spotted Mrs. Claus and drooled, growling: *Grandma, Grandma, Grandma.* His followers echoed the chant.

"Egads!" Elfinetta screamed. "They thought I was serving you for dinner! How do we get out of here?"

Mrs. Claus said, "I'll take the window. You take that side door. Slam it hard so it clicks. That'll trap them inside."

Elfinetta sprinted past the sideboard, knocking the tray to the floor. Elfinetta saluted the mess, then ran outside.

She trailed Mrs. Claus to the corral. The woman in red

said, "I'll take Dancer. You take Prancer. I hope you know how to ride bareback, dear."

***

The president had just settled down for a long winter nap, when out on the lawn there arose such a clatter, he sprang from his bed to see what was the matter; then what to his wondering eyes did appear, but two haggard old women on flying reindeer.

They crashed into the White House Christmas tree. Thinking Karl was back, Dubya waved. "Turd Blossom, you jokester. Merry Christmas."

A Secret Serviceman burst in. "Mister President, those women bear tidings of bad cheer." He dragged the president outside in his undershorts.

"There's mutiny at the North Pole," Elfinetta announced.

"Your cohort is dead," Mrs. Claus smirked.

Elfinetta added, "And we know how to fix it. Demote Santa and pay the real elves minimum wage."

"If you don't," Mrs. Claus interjected, "I—and my new assistant, Doctor Etta Moon—are handing in our resignations..."

"And your legacy will forever be: *the President who killed Christmas.*"

The president went indoors, cell phoned Santa, and said, "Ambassador, your mission is aborted. Air Force One is on its way." He faced Mrs. Claus. "Wh--wh--what happened to Karl?"

"Etta's little E.T. set him."

***

In route to the Santa's Workshop, Doctor Moon gasped, "Oh my! If the real elves get back before we arrive, and they're hungry..."

Mrs. Claus smiled. "Don't worry, dear. They're vegans."

John Pinney

John Pinney is a former professional fighter, carnival worker, and has done stand-up comedy for the past thirty years. He won the Southern Middleweight Boxing Championship and cheated a lot of people out of winning stuffed teddy bears at the carnivals where he worked. Currently, he makes people laugh across the country.

Houdini the Hamster

John Pinney

None of us could understand it. We are a very nice family. People liked us. We are nice people, we have many friends. Not him though. From the very first, he wanted out. He wanted away from us, as far and as fast as he could get there. He would do anything to get away. He was the meanest hamster in the world.

I was driving the kids home from school when something caught the corner of my eye and I pulled sharply to the curb. I told my kids to stay here and that I would be right back. I walked up the stairs to the front lawn of the garage sale. I went immediately to the cage. It was a plastic hab-a-trail for hamsters, gerbils, or guinea pigs. I picked it up, saw that nothing was broken and I asked the longhaired college kid how much the cage was.

"Two dollars, dude," he said, higher than a kite. "That includes the hamster."

"The hamster?" I hadn't even seen the hamster. I looked and he was all covered up with wood curls. I started to say I would buy it, but a woman next to me said. "I'll take that."

I looked at her and said, "I don't know the exact rules of yard sale law, but I am pretty sure if I am holding something, and asking questions about the cost of the item that I have dibs on the object unless I put it down."

She turned on her heel and left. Many times over the years, I thought about how I could have missed all the mess that was heading my way. It had become a competition and I wanted to win, not thinking that maybe by winning I was going to lose in the long run.

I gave the stoner the two dollars and turned to leave.

He hollered at me. "Hey dude."

I turned to look at him and said, "What?"

He said, "Hamsters bite, dude... hard... really hard.

I walked away thinking the hamster was probably trying to eat pot seeds off his fingers.

I put the cage into the trunk and we took off to the house. All three girls started chanting, "Momma's gonna be mad, Momma's gonna be mad." They had a point but I had two hours before she got home.

When I got the cage into the house even the girls were a little excited. Then we found out just how badly the hamster had been treated. There was hamster waste everywhere, there were maggots actually crawling around in the wood curls. The hamster looked like he had never had a bath.

I had the girls all sit on the floor, spreading their legs as far apart as they could. I asked them to touch each other's foot with their foot. Once I had a human cage, I let the hamster on the floor. He ran from girl to girl, they petted him and he seemed to like it. I told them I was going to clean the cage outside and then run to the pet store, if they could watch the hamster. They agreed, and out of the apartment I flew.

I got home in time to take the hamster and give him a much-needed bath. He was a pretty little brown and white hamster with a cute face. I put the tubes I had bought at the pet store around the cage to give the hamster a lot more room to roam. I then put up the running wheel, which he hopped on and started running almost immediately.

My wife walked in and I could tell she wasn't happy I hadn't asked her about buying a hamster, but she has always given me a "Worst" rider. She would look at the stupid things I did (and there are many) and then she would think if it was possible that "IT COULD HAVE BEEN WORSE." She knew how bad I wanted a monkey.

The hamster had to have a name and we figured on "Hammy." A not a hard name to think of and easy off the tongue. I wanted to call him "Gerbil," just to see if it gave him a complex. My wife said no on that request.

Hammy was to live in his cage on one of the living room tables. We said good night to our new family member and went to bed. About two o'clock in the morning my wife punched me in the arm and said, "What is that noise?"

I listened and then figured out. "It's the hamster. He is probably chewing on one of the toys I got him so his teeth won't get too big for his mouth." We lived with that premise for three more days.

The first breakout was on the fourth morning. My wife had gotten up to use the restroom and fix breakfast. As she was sitting in the bathroom a little hamster thought it would be cool to run across her feet. She screamed, a loud scream, a bone-chilling scream. A scream that should make every husband across the planet run to his wife's aid. I just pulled my blanket up over my head.

"JOHN! The hamster is out of his cage."

I got out of bed walked into the bathroom and reached down to pick Hammy up. He nestled into the palm of my hand and then realizing that he was going to be returned to a cage he had just escaped from, he bit me... hard... really hard... on my finger.

My wife later said I screamed like a little girl. I also flung my right hand sideways, which dislodged Hammy and threw him into the door. He was far easier to handle after that. My wife cleaned off my hamster mauling by putting a "Looney Tunes" Band-Aid on my finger. I love Looney Tunes.

Since the hamster had bitten one of us, we now had to have rules. The kids couldn't touch the hamster unless mom and dad were there. The hamster had to stay in his cage unless mom or I were home. Don't make fun of daddy for yelling like a little girl. The hamster also had a new name Houdini, the escape hamster.

We found the hole where Houdini had escaped. He had crawled up into one of the tubes and found a place he could push his back against and reach the other side of the tube with his teeth. He had gnawed and gnawed until he created a hole big enough to crawl through.

My wife suggested putting duct tape around the hole, a lot of duct tape. It worked, it seemed like chewing through hard plastic was far more fun than chewing through about ten wrappings of tape.

It was the next escape that became folk lore in our house. I was again asleep in bed, about two thirty in the morning. My wife punched me in the arm again and said, "Listen. Be quiet and listen."

As I lie in bed I listened, thinking that maybe it takes my ears longer to wake up than my brain because I didn't hear anything. Then I heard it loud and clear. Something was running under the bed through about ten thousand tubes of Christmas wrapping paper, two of my socks I thought I'd lost, and a pair of bedroom slippers that were so ugly my feet wouldn't wear them.

It was Houdini.

I told my wife it was Houdini and just go back to sleep, I'd get him in the morning. It was then that my wife uttered words I never thought I'd hear.

"I CANNOT SLEEP IN A BED WITH A RODENT UNDER IT!"

My wife is a very strong, smart woman. She had had three children using the "natural childbirth" method, no drugs. While I was out of town she had taken my girls to safety during the "Northridge Earthquake," that demolished our apartment. Plus, and I cannot say this strongly enough, she has slept next to me in our bed every married night of our lives, surviving my bad breath, my bad hair days (and they were terrible because I wore a hairpiece) and a bad habit of cracking my fingers in my sleep. Now? At two thirty in the morning, *now* she informs me that the one thing that she cannot sleep through is a rodent under our bed.

I got out of bed, went to the kitchen and got two oven mitts. I put them on, then got a flashlight, and found

Houdini walking around. I put the mitts on, grabbed him, and took him back to the cage. I then put twenty wraps of duct tape over the hole from which he escaped.

I told a good friend about the hamster problem and he said he had the solution. He and his wife had a very large Hab-a-Trail that they gave us. When I combined the two it was awesome. Hammy now had two cages, connected with eight tubes that went around, over and even through the cage. He had a running wheel in each of his cages and now even had two little cabanas he could sleep in. It was the Taj Mahal of cages.

It didn't matter. It was still a cage and he had to live free. Houdini became even more aggressive, trying to bite us even as we were giving him food. He wanted *out*. Nothing else was going to make this hamster happy. He ran through the tubes all day long, not for fun, but to find a place that he could chew through. He was one obsessed hamster.

We took a three-day vacation out of town with the kids. We left Houdini in his cage in the bathtub. He could not get a grip on the tub so we knew he couldn't climb out. We left him plenty of water and food and left the doors of his cage open. What we forgot to do was take the shower curtain out of the tub. It hung just low enough that Houdini ate the hemline of the curtain, and eventually two inches of the curtain.

In the next year or so Houdini escaped at least seventy five to a hundred times. We finally gave up and we would put him back in the cage after his escape. We'd put some tape around the hole and go on with our lives. It got to where when he escaped and we couldn't find him we would put his cage with the doors open on the floor and he would be there in the morning, usually sleeping it off.

Then one morning we saw he was laying half in and half out of the cage. We touched him and he was dead. I think we all felt a little sadness at his passing. The best I could really come up with though was I hope he didn't suffer at all.

We decided to bury him in the back yard. My kids took a cigar box and placed cotton inside for Houdini to lie on. Then they put in a few of his favorite toys. I then lay Houdini in his box and said, "Your human counterpart, Harry Houdini, the greatest escape artist of all time, would have been proud of you." I then took a roll of duct tape and wrapped the entire roll around the box. Houdini wasn't going to get out. Not this time.

Lee Ann Russell

Lee Ann is a past president of Springfield Writers' Guild and Honorary Life Member. She is also an Honorary Life Member of Missouri State Poetry Society, member of Missouri Writers' Guild, Poets & Friends and Poets Roundtable of Arkansas. She is author of *How to Write Poetry* and has myriad awards for poetry, prose and photography and numerous publications in magazines and anthologies.

Concert Grand

Lee Ann Russell

Lana sits with an audience of approximately 2,000 well-dressed, sophisticated patrons. There is no curtain on the stage of the auditorium, only a wooden back wall. House lights dim. Fifty musicians file on stage, men dressed in black tuxedos, women in black jackets and pants or long black dresses. Instruments tune to the concertmaster's violin.

Lana is in on the end of Row U, seat 59, next to her friend, Sue, who shared tickets to the evening's entertainment. Lana crosses and uncrosses her legs, sometimes sitting with one leg tucked sideways on the seat because she cannot comfortably reach the floor. Her view of the conductor is unobstructed, thanks to the zigzag layout of cushioned seats slanting to the stage.

She thinks of someone far away and whispers a silent prayer to no god in particular, but the possibility of an entity greater than herself. She thinks, Please, please, don't let them play "Somewhere in Time." Not now. Not tonight. It hurts too much to remember.

Lana and Sue exchange small talk, opening shreds of vulnerability, both revealing small portions of past, unhappy marriages. Sue confesses how she misses sharing life with someone–companionship, giving, loving. Lana agrees; single life is often lonely.

At precisely 8:00 p.m., a short, petite Asian woman enters from stage right, dressed in low brown heels and grass-green pants suit. She speaks with a Chinese accent, welcomes the audience, then introduces the guest, a Russian pianist who, she says, brought tears to her eyes in a recent concert in Oregon.

The symphony plays Tchaikovsky's *Fantasy Overture Romeo and Juliet* beautifully.

Lana closes her eyes and listens. Violins, basses, cellos, flutes, French horns, bassoons and triangles mold into fluid arrangements with arpeggios, crescendos and lilting rhythms. The mood alters with a solid, thunderous resonance wafting from the main floor through the mezzanine to the petite balcony, filling every softly curved space with reverberations of bass drums and cymbals crashing in harmonious percussion.

Lana has not read the 89-page program, knowing it contains advertisers, sponsors, symphony history and short biographical sketches of the conductor, musicians and guest artist. She intends to read at intermission, when the house lights are on, with time to kill, or fill awkward, quiet times between conversations with Sue. She does not realize that on page 45, in the exact middle of the booklet, Tchaikovsky is listed first on the program, followed by Sergei Rachmaninoff's 1934 *Rhapsody on a Theme of Paganini in A Minor, Op. 43, Variation No. 18.*

The intermission ends and Lana is caught off guard when the conductor gains the musicians' attention, turns, nods to the guest pianist, raises her outstretched hands, and with a downstroke, a faint, familiar tune begins, flowing into a more and more familiar melody. The Russian pianist plays four slow, single notes: high C... D... E... B.... Lana recognizes the tune immediately.

"Somewhere in Time" flows from the stage, rising and falling with unmatched sweetness. She shifts in the seat, closes her eyes and remembers. As the last note fades, Lana brushes a tear from her cheek and wonders if she will ever love again.

The Old Home Place
Cinquain Sequence

Lee Ann Russell

I ache,
ambling along
the path from house to barn,
reminiscing about the child
within.

As I
quietly pass
the crumbling cellar's roof,
vivid images grab my heart
and squeeze.

When young,
I never thought
of staying on the farm,
but precious mem'ries draw me home
again.

Jeanne Sevart

I was born in San Diego, California, and have lived in eleven states. I work at the English Language Institute at Missouri State University. I teach international students.

Waiting for the Right Time

Jeanne Sevart

I waited and waited for you. I tapped my foot and folded my arms and waited again and again and again. If I had a nickel for every minute... I don't understand why you are so elusive. It is frustrating.

This is personal. It is between me and you. I thought perhaps if I lit a candle and made some Darjeeling tea I could cast some kind of spell that would bring you to me.

I thought maybe if I went to the garden you would sweep in like I am Jane Austen and do all the right things. But, alas, no, it didn't happen.

I flipped through thousands of magazines waiting for you. I read book after book about how to make you come to me. I took naps hoping that when I woke up you would be hovering over me like a sweet mist.

I cleaned up the clean kitchen again, and folded my folded socks again, just in case you appeared I would be ready.

What is it you want from me? You want me to beg? Plead? Beseech the heavens? Alright, ok. I...

Wait. No. It will not happen this way. I don't need you. And furthermore, I don't want you. I am running out of time. I have to do this myself. So there!

I start writing. It is then you tap me on the shoulder and appear. Perhaps I should be angry; perhaps I should be mad to the bone. I am not. I am welcoming. I am excited. I am giddy. I have a thousand words in my head.

Hello Inspiration! Where have you been? Why do you show up now?

"I was merely waiting for you to begin."

C.A. Simonson

Candy writes fiction and nonfiction short stories, articles, and books. She has more than 200 publications in anthologies, newspapers, and magazines. Her first novel, *Love's Journey Home*, was published in 2013. She has served Springfield Writers' Guild as treasurer, director at large, and newsletter editor. She lives in Strafford, Missouri.

A Look Back

C.A. Simonson

I look in the mirror
And what do I see?
A strange, funny face
Is staring at me.

So many wrinkles,
Fine lines and crows' feet
Only a bald head
Would make it complete.

I look once again
And oh! To my shame!
It just can't be me,
I'm just not the same.

Where has the time gone?
This face can't be mine
Where once was much hair
Is now just a shine.

This guy I don't know.
An old man I see.
Bet he's related
To a much younger me.

Third place, Humorous Poetry, 2014 Springfield Writers' Guild Prose and Poetry Contest

Far Off Distant Land

C.A. Simonson

Only a teen when an M-16
Was placed in this young man's hand.
A war to fight with all of his might
In some far off distant land.
"I'm ready to go! On with the show!"
The sound of this soldier's cry.
"Able and strong; I want to belong
To a war that's Do or Die."

I saw in his eyes a look of surprise
The day his number was due.
"I'm too scared to try; don't want to die;
Can I please come home to you?"

But once he had signed on dotted line;
This war – his battle to fight.
He'd fight with the best, do nothing less
In setting war's wrongs to right.

He battled and fought; comfort not sought
Far off on hot desert sand.
Grew into a man; that was the plan
In that far off distant land.

Only a teen with an M-16;
A boy who feared giving all.
Became a man; line drawn in the sand;
Steadfast and sure in his call.

No longer afraid, mind had been made;
He knew the choice he must make.
"Do or die" was now his battle cry
Then gave his life for our sake.

Inside Ballerina

C.A. Simonson

Zealous to her love of dance, she pushed ardently through one more pirouette, delicately balancing on one toe. Young, graceful, beautiful, her chiseled body spun weightlessly on the toe of her yellow satin slipper, then knee buckling, she relinquished to the pain of another cramp.

X-rays had revealed a different plan: new life was emerging inside her – a message she embraced, but didn't want to hear; she clutched her belly and thought of Victor. What she would tell him was a problem she didn't want to face; she feared his reaction and his temper, and she was right. Victor was not happy at her news and demanded that she get back to work immediately; they would talk later.

Under pasty makeup and scant clothing, she regretted the fact that her living had to be made another way than her love of dancing. Tears trickled down her cheeks as she headed back to work; things didn't go as planned and she had gotten careless, but she had to eat too. Someday she would dance – and someday she would teach her own little girl to dance – someday.

Right now was a different story and she regretted every ugly day Victor ordered her to take care of his business. Quitting was impossibility, no matter how much she wanted out of this decrepit business.

Putting her emotions and dreams aside, she knew she must obey – do her job, deliver the goods, no looking back, no matter what.

Once she tried to leave and it didn't end pretty – she should have known that watching the other girls.

"No one leaves," Victor screamed as he punched her pretty face raw. "MY girls will never leave me," he smirked wryly, "after all, we are family – right, my pretty?" Like family, she bristled and pasted on a fake smile to cover her wounded heart; she covered her scars then headed to the streets to turn another trick just like before, but now there was another life to consider.

"Kill it," he'd demanded, "just get rid of it; can't have a kid ruin that sleek body of yours."

Jillian was torn – she wanted to dance, but she wanted this baby; she wanted out, but she knew what Victor would do, she wanted to live, but she knew the inevitable choice.

"It's just a blob of tissue," they'd told her, "it will only take a few minutes and you will be done."

Hilton Hospital: stark and sterile, cold and unfriendly; how she longed to be somewhere else. God, how did I get here – and how will I ever get out of this mess, she wondered as she contemplated the outcome of her terrible choice. Fear gripped her heart as she slipped into unconsciousness... will God forgive me? Emotionally drained, Jillian awoke from the anesthetic knowing she had ruined her life. Dreams for a future, the desire for her child and for dance – gone – forever.

Can I ever forgive myself... how can I go back... would life even be possible again? Baby – my baby, she sobbed, my little ballerina will never dance for me; the reality hit hard.

Aborted: her life's dreams and ambitions; Jillian despairingly gulped down the bottle of sedatives and closed her eyes.

First place, Fiction, 2014 Springfield Writers' Guild Prose and Poetry Contest.

Never Failing

C.A. Simonson

Jesus
Christ.
He is the same
yesterday,
today,
and forever.
Therefore, I have
Security.
Hope.
Faith.
I can trust.
He was there before me,
will show me the way today,
and will always be there
when I need Him in the future.
Peace.
Assurance.
Rest.

Based on Hebrews 13:8

Pioneers of Oak Gulch

C.A. Simonson

F ine, white snow whipped against the tent flap that cold, blustery day. The sky was dark and foreboding; but the Deans thought it was nothing more than another snowstorm. Tom Dean searched for a way to prevent the snow's intrusion into their hole in the hill. Their little dugout was dark except for light from their fire burning towards the back of the cave. It worked to keep them dry while plenty of coverings kept them warm. They curled up by their small fire pit and settled in for the night.

Sometime during the night the wind changed. Ominous snow-filled clouds and bitter cold ravaged from the north. By morning, Tom could barely push the door open in order to fetch wood for the fire. The blinding snow masked the woodpile only a few yards from their dwelling. He wrapped his knitted scarf tightly around his face and ventured out to get enough wood to last a few days.

"We'll have to wait this one out, Jane," he said to his wife. "It's a bad one. It's good we have plenty of fruit and vegetables stored up."

"Yes, the vegetables will make a fine soup, and we have plenty of meat to add to it, thanks to you," Jane commented. The baby started coughing, wheezing again. He did not sound good. The temperatures dipped way below zero, and their little dwelling was damp and cold. Jane Dean tucked the covers around her sleeping baby boy, but worried about his incessant cough. The closest doctor was more than 50 miles away, at least a two-day hike, and there was no way they could get to him in this blizzard.

The snow relentlessly piled in front of the door to their dugout for more than four days straight, burying their dwelling beneath a hill of snow. All that could be seen was their stovepipe puffing out small breaths of smoke slightly above ground.

Jane Woodland and Tom Dean married in 1857. When President Lincoln signed a new bill offering free land out west a few years later, they thought this was their chance for a new life. They packed what little they had into their covered wagon and traveled west from Wisconsin. They crossed the South Dakota border a couple weeks later, stopping in an area that looked like the perfect spot for their new home.

On the northern border of South Dakota, they found land with rolling hills, waving with acres of green prairie grass and yellow sunflowers, and a river that bubbled as it skipped over the rocks at the base of the hill lined with oak trees. There was plenty of room to raise cattle and horses and plant a big garden. Lakes were abundant and the land was virgin soil. It was the perfect place to raise a family, and only twenty miles from where Jane's parents, Joseph and Mary Woodland, had settled. They could make the trip in half a day by horse, a whole day if they walked.

The Deans filed a claim on their new-found land called Oak Gulch by the local Sioux. Cattle and horses could wait until later. In fact, a house would have to wait, too. The important thing was that they were together and this land was theirs. They put up a small tent and moved in for the summer. Their first baby arrived in late fall making their joy complete.

Mr. Dean dug a small hole into the hillside to store all the bountiful vegetables from the garden. He salted meat from rabbit, squirrel and deer to make jerky. In the coolness of the hole, he knew the food would keep well for the winter and be safe from predators.

Fall comes early in the Dakotas; sometimes winter came right along with it. As the winds got colder and the months got longer, Tom Dean decided to dig deeper into the hillside, far enough back for his family to live in and be protected from the elements. He fashioned a fire pit on one end, and pushed a pipe up to the top of the hill to allow smoke to escape. He fastened the tent to the front of the cave to provide a barrier against the wind.

"It looks like diamonds," commented Jane when snowflakes began to fall. "Brilliant white diamonds sparkling all across the prairie." Soon the surroundings began to look the same. White everywhere.

Tom found the tent was not working well against the strong north winds. It blew away from the sides of the cave, or it tore, allowing the wind and snow to enter the dug-out. He decided a door would have to be built. He cut out some slabs of sod from the prairie grass to stack around the cave entrance, and then cut down one of the tall oak trees by the river. A small wooden door was erected and set into the sod. It proved to provide much better support and security to their home in the hillside. The rest of the oak was chopped for firewood.

The baby's croupy cough worsened, then turned into pneumonia. He was weakening and his mother knew it, but there was no way to get out of their snowy prison to get the child to the doctor. Even if they could, it might have been too late. The young mother pressed the baby's little body against hers and tried to get him to nurse. The baby shook with cold and fever. He coughed and sputtered so much he couldn't nurse. He would stiffen with pain, and then relax, only to go through the same routine again. After hours of this routine, he just quit fighting; his sick little body became limp in his mama's arms.

"He has quieted down," she told her husband, "I think he has finally gone to sleep." She sighed heavily, and tucked the blankets tightly around both of them. She leaned up against the cold damp dirt wall and cradled the baby in her arms. Jane was so weary with worry and exhaustion, she soon fell asleep too.

The next morning, she awoke with a start. The once-limp baby in her arms was now completely stiff and blue.

He was as cold as the icicles that clung to the door. What would they do now? She sat numbly without saying a word, but her husband saw. He knew.

Jane's father and mother worried. This was the worse blizzard ever, and the coldest winter they had ever experienced. They had not heard from Jane and Tom in over two weeks. They worried about them having enough food or wood for fire. Joe Woodland decided to go check on his daughter and her family and bring them more supplies, even though it would take him almost two days on foot through the deep snow. When he finally arrived, the prairie looked flat and white. No buildings, no tent. Nothing. All he could see was snow for miles on end. They had to be here somewhere.

"Tom? Can you hear me, Jane?" he yelled out. Listening intently, he could hear a slight muffled sound coming from somewhere deep under the snow. Looking everywhere, he noticed a small melted area in the snow where a little wisp of smoke escaped from the ground. He pushed the snow away and found the stovepipe. He was standing on top of their buried home. "Tom! Jane!" he cried out.

"We're down here!" Tom kept calling. "Thank God, you came!"

Anxious, Joe Woodland started pushing snow away with his hands, digging deeper and deeper. Between Joe digging from above, and Tom pushing through from beneath, Tom was finally able to push the door open. The young couple was rescued from their buried cave.

"I'm so glad you found us. We were almost out of wood," Tom choked back his tears. "It was getting too cold. The baby - didn't make it. He died last night." Tom tried to be strong for his wife, but lost all control as his emotions overtook him. Tom broke down and sobbed.

Jane, still clutching the blue baby to her breast, sat stone-still in the shadows. Her father came to her and gently pried her fingers away from the lifeless bundle in her arms. "We need to wash the child, Jane." Reluctantly, she released her grip. Shuddering from the cold and her tears, they washed the little body, and then bundled the baby tightly with a sheet.

Tom, only twenty years of age, but with the strength and fortitude of one much older, would take down the rough-hewn new wooden door from their shelter to build a small casket for their baby. This would be the first burial on their new property, but not today, and not tomorrow. Not even in a couple weeks. They would have to wait several months until spring when the snow melted and the ground was soft enough to dig a hole. In the meantime, the dead baby wrapped in the sheet, would have to reside in a mound of snow on the hill behind the shelter.

That winter had dealt the couple a fierce, cruel blow. They found the blizzard's fury had no remorse, no mercy. Though saddened by great loss, they discovered another child was on the way. Their dug-out would not be sufficient for any more winters such as the one they had just experienced. When the summer arrived, they built a much warmer Soddy and planted a bigger garden. Life on the prairie was hard, but life would go on, and there would be better times ahead.

The Gift

C.A. Simonson

I was about to exit the Special Care unit of the Veterans Home, where the residents with Alzheimer's and other types of dementia lived. It was a locked unit; staff coming and leaving had to know the secret code of the number lock pad to get in or out. I had to be cautious and very quick, for sly patients would follow me to the door to watch my fingers, hoping to decipher the code and hope for escape. They were sure they had to go home.

As part of the social worker's team, I finished playing for the weekly sing-along time with the residents and prepared to go back to my office. As I walked toward the locked doors, a frail, bent-over man with frizzy, thinning, white hair and wild-looking eyes followed close behind. His mumbled words and crazy gibberish made him seem deranged and scary.

Stay away from him, I was warned. *He will try to grab you in places he shouldn't.* I turned to see him coming toward me rather quickly for an octogenarian with arms outstretched and a cock-eyed grin on his face. I quickened my steps, but I was too slow. He caught up with me.

The old man gently grabbed my arm, and turned me so I would face him. He put both hands tenderly on my face, and looked directly in my eyes. *What now?* I wondered, half-fearful. *I had heard stories about this guy. Should I call for a nurse?* Instead, I quieted myself and stood my ground. He didn't look harmful. I smiled at the man and waited. He cleared his throat.

"I remembered the words today," he quietly said, clear and slow. Then a tear slipped from his eye. With that, he smiled back at me, turned around and walked back to his room.

I stood trembling at what just happened. Though he couldn't remember his own name most of the time, the old man was so pleased he could remember the words of the hymns. His words, the first intelligible ones I had ever heard him speak, were a special gift to me that day— a gift I would treasure forever.

Diane Siracusa

Originally from the Chicago suburbs, Diane and her husband
reside in the Missouri Ozarks. Diane taught special
education and raised four children. An animal lover, she has
shared her life with dogs, cats, birds, horses, and donkeys.
She is a color-pencil artist and freelance writer.

A Rich Life

Diane Siracusa

The old man sat at his kitchen table and raised both hands in the air. "I have to tell you a story most people wouldn't believe," he said, "but I swear it really happened!" Ernie lowered his hands and grinned.

"I was out with my 12-gauge and it was foggy. So foggy, you could hardly see anything. Down at the pond I heard ducks. I aimed and shot once into the fog. Then I reloaded and shot again in the direction where I heard the ducks fly up. Well, I tell you, I went over there and I found out I had killed eight Mallard ducks with those two shots!"

Ernie looked at me. He wanted me to believe his story, but I, who knew nothing about duck hunting or shooting-probabilities, remained silent.

Ernie sat straighter in his chair and spoke with more conviction. "I was only *ten* years old and the walk back home was a quarter of a mile. Those eight ducks were heavy and I had to lay 'em down ever' so often and rest."

The sincerity of the old man's voice convinced me, and now I wanted to cheer for the boy who killed eight ducks with two shots and then struggled to carry them all the way home to his widowed mother!

Ernie leaned forward. "Later on, during the war years people could sell game, and cottontail rabbits brought thirty-five cents each."

"It was a real cold winter in '42 and I had eighteen rabbits froze. I asked Mother if she could take me to town to sell them, but she said, 'No, we can't do that.' So after my chores, I put the rabbits in two gunny sacks and tied them on the back of my horse." Ernie said he wore a thin coat and even thinner gloves and he told me he about froze to death, but he needed to sell those rabbits!

"I rode the nine miles to town to sell 'em and afterward I bought a new box of .22 long shells. They cost eighteen cents for a box of fifty rounds."

I stopped writing and asked, "After more than seventy-five years, how do you remember the details of your purchase so clearly?"

Ernie looked at me and said, "A poor farm boy never forgets the price of something he needs or really wants."

I looked at the old man and nodded. We sat in silence until a smile replaced the serious expression on Ernie's face. He laughed, held up his index finger and said he bought one more thing before he rode the horse back home.

"I bought a big bag of candy for five cents. Then, I put everything in my coat. I had about six dollars in my pocket. I was rich!"

Abandoned

Diane Siracusa
Illustration by Diane Siracusa

D ust clouds trailed behind the sedan as it sped down the gravel road. Few families lived this far out of town and the driver knew most folks used the main highway to go anywhere. Yes, this road suited his needs perfectly and its isolation persuaded him to pull over and stop.

The driver opened the door, slid out and stood with his back to the car. A cigarette dangled from his mouth and smoke washed up over his face and stung his eyes. The man took a last, deep drag, flicked the cigarette into the air and watched it fall on the rocks. He carefully surveyed both ends of the road, saw no one and smiled like he had just won something. The smile faded and, with a sense of urgency, he jerked open the back door and reached into the sedan.

The man grabbed something off the floor of the car and dropped it on the road. The something was a dog and the man shoved it with the side of his boot and said, "Go on, you good for nothin'!"

With no one nearby to protest, the dog's owner flung himself back into the car and slammed the door. He laughed as he threw the car into drive and stomped his foot down on the gas pedal! The tires spun against the loose gravel before they finally grabbed the road. As the sedan shot forward, it left behind a mixture of churned-up road dust and exhaust fumes.

Road debris drifted over the dog and instinct made him close his eyes. He coughed dust from his lungs and shook the filthy grit from his fur, but he could not remove the worry he felt when he opened his eyes and stared at the empty road.

Unable to understand the why of what happened to him and desperate to find something familiar, the dog began to pace up and down. He wanted his nose to tell him what to do or where to go, but all he found was the discarded cigarette - it was something and yet it was nothing.

The empty road cared nothing for the unfortunate dog and the sun cared even less; it sent its rays to beat down on him without mercy. Overwhelmed, the old dog began to whine and cry and before long heat-stress and fatigue caused him to stumble. He collapsed into a shivering heap when his legs gave out and folded under him.

The abandoned dog lay on the road with only one thought: He would wait for his man to come back to get him.

Forever

Diane Siracusa

The fragileness of the dog's body made the girl hesitate as she stroked his fur with a gentle hand. This loyal friend who used to chase all seen and unseen enemies, no longer protected the girl – she protected him.

The girl covered her eyes with her hands, but she could not hide from the morning sun. It flooded her room the same way it did all those yesterdays ago when Papa woke her and put the puppy on her bed.

"Happy birthday to the best five-year old in the world!" he said.

Tiny hands clapped for joy and the puppy's happy eyes met hers. The girl reached out and took him in her arms. "Is he really mine?" she asked.

"He's yours forever," said Papa.

She believed him and loved the dog with all her heart.

If the five-year old believed in the forever Papa promised, the girl she grew up to be, knew forever could not be counted on or trusted.

The girl rocked back and forth and the motion mimicked the tick of the clock on her dresser. The clock. It never paused, never took a breath or a time out, but ticked on and on. The girl squeezed her eyes shut and wished for yesterday, yesterday, yesterday!

Yesterday, she could hold hurt at a distance and pretend time would somehow slow down and wait. But today arrived, as she knew it would, and with it came an unbearable ache. Yesterday's hope no longer existed and in its place raw pain had moved in – uninvited and without her consent.

The dog's tongue licked at the girl's tears. She stood up and cradled her friend in the folds of the old blanket. More tears streamed down her face as the girl carried the dog out of the room for the last time.

"I will love you *forever*," she said.

The Trap

Diane Siracusa

Most delicious cheese
Enticingly sets the trap
Small mouse do not come

Marilyn K. Smith

Among Marilyn's writing credits are *Buffalo Reflex Newspaper* (weekly column), *The Ozarks Mountaineer, Springfield! Magazine, Springfield News-Leader* (guest columnist), *Ozark Senior Living* (associate editor), and *Journal of the Ozarks* (contributing editor). Her books include *A History of Highway 65, from the middle of the road,* and *The Window Pane Inn.*

Brian's Surgery

Marilyn K. Smith

"**I**'m normally not afraid to stay by myself, but it was certainly unnerving to hear the front door open, then shut, followed by footsteps on our hardwood foyer floor. The hallway door kept closed during the cold portions of the year, opened, followed by the sound of footsteps coming down the hall. With each creak of the floorboards, my heart pounded faster. It couldn't be Brian. He was in the hospital.

In only seconds, someone crawled into bed with me. A man laid right up against me, with one arm under my body and one over me, caressing me. "It's okay. Don't be afraid. I'm here to comfort you." The man's voice was soft, consoling, reassuring.

An instant later, he was gone. I turned on the lamp, looked over at the clock and it showed 11:37. I got out of bed, and made my way down the hall. The door was shut like it was supposed to be. The front door was locked, and the dead bolt was in place. Nothing or no one had disturbed any of it as far as I could tell. Was I dreaming? If so, it seemed too real.

Sleep did not return easily, but apparently, I did drop off at some point because the alarm jolted me awake. Brian's surgery was scheduled for 8:00, and I needed to get there before they wheeled him away for his surgery.

The door leading into Brian's room was shut when I arrived. I figured they were doing last minute stuff, getting him ready for surgery, so I decided to be patient. But after about ten minutes, my patience wore thin. I asked a nearby nurse, "Can I go in?"

"Oh, Mrs. Hanson, didn't they tell you? Your husband had an episode last night, and he was taken straight to surgery."

"Where can I find him?"

"I don't know," she replied, and we both walked to the nurses' station. She looked on the computer, and then went over and talked to one of the other nurses. A great deal of conversation took place. "Mrs. Hanson, it might be best if you remain here until we can get someone to come talk to you," the nurse said.

"Why, what's wrong? Is my husband okay?"

"It would be better if you talk to someone from that department."

I didn't ask any more questions. When the fellow arrived, he asked Brian's birthdate.

"Two, sixteen, forty-four."

"Ma'am, our records show that a Brian Hanson, born February sixteenth, 1944, passed away last night, at 11:36."

Upon hearing this, my knees gave way and I slumped to the floor. In only minutes, I was placed on a gurney, and taken to a nearby room. "Mrs. Hanson, you need to calm down. Your blood pressure is raging out of control. Breathe slowly, slowly."

After an hour of having my vitals monitored every ten minutes, I was finally told I could go home. "Could someone come after you? We don't believe you should be driving."

"Where is Brian," I asked again. I had asked that question probably twenty times, but no one would tell me anything. "You need to calm down," is all they would say. I certainly wasn't making any headway on this floor, so mustering every ounce of strength I had I walked to the elevator, and punched "Ground." Surely, someone at the front office will know something. When the elevator passed the third floor, the door opened and four police officers got on.

"Is something going on?" I asked.

"Nothing to fret about," the oldest of the four said.

"My husband died last night, and they didn't even call me. What do you make of that?" Not a word was returned.

The police officers headed off to the left, and I turned right and walked to the first hallway to the main offices. "May I help you," the lady at the front desk asked?"

"Yes, I was told that my husband passed away last night, but no one will give me any details. I would like to know where he is."

"His name and date of birth?"

"Brian Hanson, two, sixteen, forty-four."

After punching the information into her computer, a funny look came over her face; an almost sick look. "Please wait here. I'll have Mr. Linder talk to you."

In a short while, a fellow I assumed was Mr. Linder walked up. The look on his face seemed to be that of great concern, also. "Mrs. Hanson, please step into my office." I followed him into a small, cramped room. "Can I get you something to drink?"

"Do you have any idea where my husband is? I don't need a drink; I don't need anything, but my husband!"

"I don't know how to tell you, but we had a shooting in the operating room while they were performing surgery on your husband. The gunman shot the surgical nurse and your husband. Those are all the details I have at this time."

"Where is my husband? I need to go see my husband!"

"He's still up there, but you probably wouldn't be allowed to see him. I'll make some calls, and see what I can arrange."

True to his word, Mr. Linder escorted me to that area. I looked at Brian, and I could have sworn I heard him snoring — loudly snoring. Then I shook his arm, "Wake up, you're snoring! Tammy, wake up, you're snoring!" I jerked awake and looked over at Brian, who was lying beside me in our bed, in our house.

Do you suppose I should be concerned about Brian's surgery scheduled to take place later this morning, at 11:30?

Flu

Marilyn K. Smith

I told my boss that my back aches,
I hurt from head to toe.
I took a pill—that little pill,
does it know where to go?

My stomach churns, I'm really sick,
I took some chalky goop.
I sipped some tea, they say that's good,
then ate some chicken soup.

The flu, they say, is going 'round,
I guess that's what I've got.
I can't come in, you understand,
and yes, I feel real hot.

He'll never know I faked it all,
and fibbed, well quite a bit.
The concert was that very night,
those guys are quite a hit.

The concert was real fab indeed,
those guys could really play.
The hall was full, full to the top,
just standing room, they say.

The trouble with this fun filled night,
on our way out the door.
I ran smack-dab into my boss,
he was hard to ignore.

If you know of a job, please tell,
for I need one real quick.
I promise you, I'll never call,
to say that I am sick.

Second place, Humorous Poetry, 2014 Springfield Writer's Guild Prose and Poetry Contest

If

Marilyn K. Smith

If I could sing, I'd entertain,
in concert halls around the world,
I'd dress so fine, in pearls and lace,
and walk a carpet all unfurled.

My name in lights on a marquee,
declaring me a great big star.
Large crowds would fill the concert halls,
and I'd arrive in a black car.

My nails would get a manicure,
the stylist, she would do my hair,
a voice coach would be on hand,
and his vast knowledge he would share.

At each performance they would stand,
and cheer and clap and want much more,
I'd bow politely, thanking them,
and I'd be thrilled down to my core.

I'd give a party at my place.
The finest wine, and caviar,
would then be served to all my guests.
If I could sing, I'd be that star.

Kali

Marilyn K. Smith

U nhappiness wafted through our house, like the stench of the raccoon that crawled under our front porch and died last year. Janine tried to conceal her sadness, but it permeated the air much the same as the odor of that dead animal. Who could have imagined that a musty smelling, dusty old doll could bring joy back into this house?

When I met Janine, she was the most beautiful, most vibrant young girl I had ever seen. We laughed, sang, cooked all sorts of crazy concoctions, and made love as often as we could steal away time to ourselves. Although her parents would have forbidden us to see each other if they had ever caught on, I realize now they probably knew all along. They were elated, relieved I believe, when we made plans to marry straight out of high school. And without a penny to our names, we were forced to live with Janine's grandma. We worked part-time, while going to college full time. Although both sets of parents wanted a grandchild, we decided a baby would have to wait. We certainly didn't need to complicate our lives any further.

After nearly two years of living with Granny, we decided to get a small efficiency apartment near campus, and that was the best decision we could have made. The privacy allowed us to talk, cook and make love as noisily as we wanted.

Shortly after graduating, I got a job as a newspaper reporter. Janine worked here and there, trying to find her niche, but it wasn't until she began working for her uncle Merle in his store, Treasures You Find Junkin', that she begin to enjoy getting up each morning.

Katherine Isabella Hessie was born about a year after Janine began working for her uncle. Kali was the prettiest baby I had ever seen. She was perfect. That huge smile she flashed when she saw either of us, and those eyes... Kali was our world, our entire world. Then came that horrible morning when Janine went in to see about her, and her little body showed no signs of life. We rushed her to the hospital, and five long hours later, the doctor declared her dead. The autopsy showed that she had a ruptured aneurism in her brain. There wasn't anything anyone could have done.

In an attempt to leave no time to dwell on Kali's death, Janine jumped headlong into her uncle's business. She traveled the area looking for treasures, and even made arrangements to buy entire estates. The majority of her purchases were very profitable.

When her Uncle Merle decided to retire, he gave Janine the option of buying the business. Without consulting me, and with her father's help, she agreed to purchase everything, including the large warehouse. It was quite an undertaking, but I didn't dare cross her. At this fragile stage in our lives, one wrong word might end what little relationship we had left.

My grieving had to be done in private, Janine didn't want to see it. She made it clear that we had to take whatever the Lord dished out—like it or not. There wasn't a day I didn't miss Kali's sweet smile, or how she said "Da Da."

Merle had no computer savvy, but Janine did. She tried to convince him that many of their items could be sold online. He wanted no part of it, probably because he didn't understand how it all worked. But after Janine took over, a third or more of her sales were online. And she was making money—more money than I ever thought possible.

Instead of the success of the business making her happy, it seemed to depress her even further. She became moody and withdrawn—withdrawn to the point of absolute silence for days on end. She talked to her customers, of course, but not to me.

Then something strange happened. She purchased the old Albertson mansion. The magnificent hand carved woodwork alone was worth thousands, Janine said. She hired an Amish crew to dismantle the house, with the stipulation that she got the fireplace mantles, woodwork, old claw-foot bathtub, stained glass windows and flooring. They could have everything else.

While well into the demolition, she received a call from the Amish workers' driver, saying they had found an old doll in a closet in one of the upstairs rooms. It was very fragile, and did she want to come look at it?

Although I rarely visited the shop, I happened to be there when the call came in. She and I drove to the house. The instant the doll was placed into Janine's hands, a look of pure peace came over her face. And in spite of the years of dust and probably spiders, Janine held it to her chest, with its head resting on her shoulder. I had seen her hold Kali this way numerous times.

Every old doll I had ever seen was a bit scary looking, like in the Chucky movies. Their eyes opened and shut, and their fake smiles made me think they were going to turn evil at any minute. I know, I've seen way too many scary movies. But this doll was different. It looked like a real baby. We drove home in absolute silence. Every time I looked over, Janine was caressing the doll to her bosom, and patting its little back.

Months have passed since that day—the day when that little doll was put into Janine's arms. She now smiles for no reason. She will be fixing our evening meal, or simply cleaning the carpet, and a broad smile will come over her face. She even sleeps in my bed, which leads to other things; a pleasure I did without for such a long time. Then one bright, sunny morning, she nearly floated across the kitchen, and announced that we were going to have a baby; a little baby boy!

I was pleased of course, but some of her past behavior worried me. Almost from the instant we brought the doll home, Janine has been buying little girl things; dresses, hair ribbons, and toys that a little girl would want. One day when I came home early, I caught her in Kali's old room carrying on a conversation with the doll.

A baby boy! I knew Janine couldn't be far enough along to know we were having a boy, so how could she be so certain. And if we are having a boy, why had she purchased so many little girl things?

Although reluctant in the past to confront Janine about her behavior, I worked up the courage to bring up the subject. She began to cry—not just cry, but sob uncontrollably. She finally regained her composure and began to talk.

The doll was Kali. The minute it was placed into Janine's arms, it felt soft and warm, like Kali used to feel. Especially when it was put to Janine's bosom, the doll seemed to be alive.

It came back to us—to Janine, to help her forgive God, and to help her forgive herself for not being a better mother, for not being home with her all the time like a "good" mother should have been. I had no idea she felt this way. She wouldn't talk to me, therefore I thought she blamed me somehow, and I guess she did because the doll helped her to forgive me. "He's hurting," the doll kept telling her. "He loved me so."

"God has a baby waiting for you," the doll told Janine. "He is a boy. You and Dad will get such a kick out of him. He will be a handful, but you can handle him."

The doll is now preserved in a glass case, in our bedroom. It will always be a part of our family. Do I believe it was Kali coming back to help us get through the grieving process? I don't know, but if it was, I will be forever grateful.

Marathon Runner

Marilyn K. Smith

Complete exhaustion engulfed me. My body ached and my heart pounded inside my ears. Each beat screamed "Quit, drop to the ground and rest!"

I needed my momma, but she won't be here this year. She won't be at each checkpoint, cheering me on. And she won't be at the finish line, doing her little wacky dance. I can't believe I will actually miss her arms flailing about like an insane person. Until this year, her exaggerated gestures, caused by her excitement of seeing her little girl cross the finish line, made me want to blend into the crowd, and say, "No, I have no idea who that crazy lady is."

"Mom, my legs feel like they are on fire. I have to quit," I shouted, but no one but me heard my cries for help.

"Yes, honey, I know, but you are nearly there–the finish line is almost in sight." Upon hearing my momma's words, instead of concentrating on the route that stretched before me, I turned to see her jogging alongside, keeping pace with me. She hadn't done that for over a year, not since she received her death sentence. Cancer–what a shock. She had never been sick, ever. She was healthy as a horse, and had more energy than all of us put together.

"Mom, I can't go on," I told her, "I'm hurting so."

"Remember, the word can't is not in our vocabulary," and then she proceeded to take the word, tear it into little pieces and throw it into the air, to rain down upon us. "Can, can, can, that's the only word in our dictionary!"

When I saw her do this, I couldn't help but think of the many times she took my mistakes, ones done mostly out of absolute stupidity, and in her imaginary way wadded them up, then said, "We'll just take this and throw it in the trash, won't we."

With the finish line now within my grasp, a new burst of energy drove me onward. Upon crossing the line, I looked around to watch my mother raise her arms in triumph, do her little victory dance and shout, "Yes, yes, yes," for the entire world to hear.

But, the only familiar face in the crowd was my Aunt Jennie. I could tell by the look on her face that what she was about to tell me wasn't good. "Grandma called, your momma went home to be with the Lord about fifteen minutes ago."

"Yes, I know," I told her. I'm sure she wondered how I knew, but right at that minute, I wasn't in the mood to share that last special Mom moment.

Murderous Intent

Marilyn K. Smith

Systematic,
aromatic,
atomizers
can spray attic.

To cover smell
where she will dwell.
No questions asked,
shall be quite swell.

It's almost time,
to do my crime,
no snooping techs,
no smell, no grime.

No one will know,
nothing will show.
I'll cash her checks,
the loot I'll blow.

Toni Somers

Toni is a former studio photographer, guitarist, and teacher. She tried writing mysteries, but was diverted by other muses. Her poetry, fiction, and memoir won local and national awards and were published in *Today's Woman*, *Chicken Soup*, *Life Lessons for Teachers*, *The Binnacle*, and in two anthologies.

The American Lady with the Glasses

Toni Somers

Leola Montgomery lived in a house in the middle of my block of Detroit's little Italy in the late 1930's. With her husband, George, she had lived there before the Irish came, before the Poles came, and before the Italians came. With each change of immigrant group, those residents with names like Montgomery, Sanders, and Beckett lamented, "The neighborhood is going downhill!"

I learned later when I was grown, that phrase was a euphemism meaning people who were different in some way were coming to live there. Those with names like Lucca, Valerio, and Gianetti pronounced those same words in different accents years later when black people bought the little bungalows that stood in a row on my block.

"The neighborhood is going downhill."

Regardless of particular enunciation, the meaning was the same. They're different from us. That happened later, though, after the war when the soldiers came home. So many things changed then. But in the late 1930's, when I was ten, Leola Montgomery lived on a little English-speaking island amid a sea of Italian-speaking paisanos. Her husband had died years before, and she lived alone, visited only on rare occasions by four grown sons with their respective wives. Balding and paunchy sons with wives, either fat and red-faced or thin and gray looking, they seemed quite old to a ten-year-old child of Italian immigrants. I surmised that Leola Montgomery must be exceedingly old indeed.

I never thought of her as Mrs. Montgomery back then, but as the American Lady-With-The-Glasses. That's what my Ma called her. My Pa called her Mee-see-sa Mon-ta-gom-mari. Ma talked a lot more often and more insistently and persistently than Pa, so I abided by her choice of appellation.

"L' Americana con gli occhali," Ma said through pursed lips. "She thinks she's better than us. But I think her underwear is too tight! That's why her face looks like a prune and why she's so mean!"

"Don't talk like that. She's just a lonely old woman." Quiet and gentle Pa spoke only the best about everyone.

We kids were afraid of the American Lady-With-The-Glasses. She spent most of her days sitting on her screened-in porch. It was hard to see her through the screen, especially with the sun in our eyes. We knew she was there though, because we could hear the creaking of her porch glider as she rocked back and forth. We never dawdled on our forays past the yellow frame house with peeling paint. Our feet moved faster as we scampered and scurried to one another's yards to engage in daily games of Cowboys and Indians or to mimic the battles of World War II we saw on newsreel screens at the Saturday ten-cent movie show in our neighborhood theater.

"I think old lady Montgomery is a German spy. That's why she sits on her porch and watches stuff all the time. It's screened in, so nobody can see her real good," was Rosa's opinion.

"Nah. I think she's really a witch, and if she gives you the evil eye, you're in trouble. That's what my cousin, Vinnie, says." Mario was convinced his big cousin, Vinnie, had all the answers.

I kept silent. I was afraid of the American Lady-With-The-Glasses, but I didn't think she was a spy or a witch like Rosa and Mario said. I didn't know what to think. Was she mean like Ma said or lonely like Pa said?

My parents agreed on one thing. We must be polite to the American Lady-With-The-Glasses. My Ma said we should do it to teach her a lesson, to show her we were good, honest people, not "greasy dagos" like some labeled us. Pa urged us to be polite to everyone, especially to people who were lonely or old. He took baskets of Big Boy tomatoes from his garden to the

American-Lady-with-The-Glasses. I went with him to carry the peppers and eggplants. He tipped his cap to Mrs. Montgomery as he stood at the bottom of the steps to her porch.

"Hello, Mee-see-sa Mon-ta-gom-mari. You like some fresh tomatoes and peppers from my garden? I got eggplants today, too."

The American Lady-With-The-Glasses unlatched the door to her screened in porch and beckoned with a nod of her head for my father to mount the steps. She didn't speak or smile, but when she accepted the gift of vegetables from Pa's work-roughened hands, her face didn't look quite so much like a prune. Maybe Ma was wrong about the tight underwear.

When Pa was with me, I was not afraid. He was a slightly built man with a soft-spoken manner, but I knew everyone respected Mees-tra Sam as the piasanos called him. I never could figure that out, but even the American Lady-With-The-Glasses seemed to mellow when she spoke to Pa.

"You're a fine gardener, Mr. Sam. You work hard like my George did. Not like some around here who sing and play their accordions and mandolins all day and keep me awake with their music all night too!" Her mouth tightened and the prune look reappeared.

"That's O.K Mee-see-sa. I be no musician. That's why I got time to grow tomatoes. Soon I bring you acorn squash too."

I descended the porch steps behind my Pa, knowing that my brief look at the gentler side of the American Lady-With-The-Glasses was over until the next vegetable delivery.

After my tenth summer, I did not go with Pa any more to take our garden's bounty to the American Lady-With-The-Glasses. He died in November after the fall harvest. He brought in the last of the green tomatoes and banana peppers for Ma to put in jars with salt and vinegar and garlic. They would enhance many a winter antipasto. In late November, there was a brief warm spell, and the construction crew that Pa was on dug the foundation for the new General George Armstrong Custer Elementary School. Pa was down in the deep empty hole when Pietro Gravelli drove the big cement mixer to the site. Pietro, after a long night of drinking wine and playing his accordion, dumped the load into the wrong end, the one where my Pa was working. My Pa and two other paisanos were buried under the heavy load of wet cement. The bosses told Ma that Pa didn't suffer, and they pressed five twenty-dollar bills into her hand. I don't think my mother believed them, because after they left she cried and called them names in Italian that I knew were bad words. She kept the money though, because we would need it with Pa gone.

We kids cried when we heard our Pa was dead. Ma put on her black dress, cried, wailed, and let the piasanos cook for us for three days. On the fourth day, she rose from her bed of mourning, donned an apron over her black dress and began to cook and worry aloud about how we would survive. The fall harvest had been preserved in jars, and there was sufficient food for the winter. But what would we do after Pa's provisions were exhausted? We did survive. Emmanuela and Antonio, the two biggest kids in the family, dropped out of high school and got jobs. Antonio worked on Pa's old construction crew, and Emmanuela worked at the big Woolworth's on Oakland Avenue. Thirteen-year-old Giuseppe got a paper route, and Isabella and I took care of the littlest ones while Ma did ironing for the rich Americans who lived on Boston Boulevard.

The week before Christmas, the paisanos came carrying a turkey, prosciutto, salami, and strings of fresh salsiccia. The women brought homemade bread, cannoli and biscotti di Natale. They brought oranges and walnuts too. We knew that they would do all these things just as my Ma and Pa had carried food to the Giovannetti family when their father died and to the Piselli home when their mother was in the hospital. Then on Christmas Eve, the front doorbell rang as we were sitting around the big wooden table in the kitchen waiting for Ma to finish cooking.

"Emmanuela! Go see! Who comes to the front door?" Ma said, her face flushed from the steam rising from the boiling pasta.

None of the paisanos came to the front door, only to the back. I trailed behind my big sister wondering who it could be. I could not believe my eyes. Standing on our front porch with snow in her already gray hair and carrying what seemed to me to be the biggest chocolate cake I had ever seen was the American Lady-With-The-Glasses. She had never been known to knock at the door of one of the paisanos' houses. It was truly a Christmas miracle!

"Ma...Ma...it's Mrs. Montgomery, Ma." Emmanuela had recovered some of her composure and summoned Ma.

Ma came from the kitchen, wooden pasta spoon in her hand. She handed it to me and wiped her hands on her apron before extending them to Mrs. Montgomery. The American Lady-With-The-Glasses handed the cake plate to Emmanuela and held out both hands to take my Ma's hands in hers.

"Mr. Sam was a good man...like my George was."

***

In the spring, we watched the little kids while Ma planted what we would always call "Pa's garden". She worked hard to make the rows as straight as he did and to keep the weeds out. We ate cucumbers and radishes, peas and zucchini. Sometimes Ma dipped the zucchini blossoms in egg batter and fried them for me. They were my favorite. Springtime passed, and it was time for the peppers and the tomatoes and the eggplants.

"Will we take tomatoes to the American Lady-With-

The-Glasses?" I asked Ma.

She looked at me for a long moment with lips pursed, and at first I thought I'd said something wrong. Then her face softened and she spoke in the gentle tones of my Pa.

"Si, we will go together. You will carry the peppers and the eggplants, and I will carry the Big Boy tomatoes. But you must remember to show respect. She's an old lady and she's lonely. We will call her Mee-see-sa Mon-ta-go-mari."

Hope Happens

Toni Somers

Hope happens.
Daily she rises with me from my bed.
"You go, girl," she encourages.
"Yeah, right!" I grumble.

Hope persists.
So do aches and anguish and age.
"Age is just a state of mind," she chirps.
"Whadda you know?" I rumble.

Hope perseveres.
So does depression, dejection, despair.
"You can do it!" she proclaims.
"Bug off!" I snarl.

Hope giggles. Hope chuckles. Hope laughs aloud.
"Gimme a break! Don't whine!" she commands.
I try to fend off a smile, but fail.
I try to block joy, but fail.
I try to shun cheer, but fail.

Hope grins, "Nothing like a good debate to clear the sinuses."
"You're damned right," I chortle back.
"I'm here to stay!" Hope declares.
"Me too!" I affirm.

Meeting Minnie Jean

Toni Somers

September 2011, Little Rock, Arkansas

Tears stream down my cheeks. I can't stop the flow. The sight of students from Little Rock's Central High School standing around in close proximity to one another, black and white alike, indifferent to social barriers of the past and without apparent regard for one another's skin color, triggers an emotional outpouring. Gathered in the lobby of the museum across from their school, the students listen to an aging African American woman describe an historic September in 1957. Unaware of how their hanging out together differs from their predecessors' at Central High in days gone by when standing together was not acceptable, they listen attentively to Minnie Jean Brown, but grin and nudge one another when she tells them to stay in school. Her posture is erect and dignified in contrast to the casual physical demeanor of her audience. But her words hold their attention.

Behind them in the museum proper, images of past events roll on inexorably on TV monitors. Ugly faces of housewives in curlers shouting, "Go home where you belong, niggers,", chants of "Two, four, six, eight, we don't want to integrate," from white students lining the walk to Central High, the face of Arkansas Governor Orval Faubus proclaiming he's "protecting" the nine black students and keeping them safe. Instead, he mobilizes the Arkansas National Guard to block their entrance to Central. Those young teenagers, really little more than children, come to be known as the Little Rock Nine. They are turned away from

Central High School, and mob mentality prevails. But a determined President Dwight Eisenhower sends Federal troops–the 101st Airborne–to escort the nine young people up the front steps of Little Rock's Central High. The confrontations begin on September 4, 1957.

Present day students stand in front of the TV monitors, oblivious to the images projected beyond the museum lobby as they listen to Minnie Jean describe how she and eight comrades finally made their way into Central High School on September 23, 1957. My tears flow. I don't need the TV images. I've seen them before, and I will never forget them.

September 1957, Staten Island, New York

We gather in the living room of Nancy Piseri's apartment, a band of young wives of Public Health Service doctors, interns and residents at the nearby PHS hospital. Nancy is the wife of a career PHS physician and is our unofficial leader. The rest of our spouses are short-termers in various stages of medical training. This is our frequent and welcome escape, morning coffee at Nancy's with our toddlers and infants. Their bodies and their toys litter the floor in Nancy's living room. We step over our collective offspring to get a cup of coffee, or to retrieve a stray toddler from attempting to climb the steps or from disappearing into the kitchen or from stalking the Piseris' Siamese cat. Usually a bi-weekly ritual, this September in 1957 we gather almost daily. Without verbalizing it, we recognize history is being made. We watch in fascination as it unfolds.

We are mostly Yanks from assorted northern industrial cities. The events unfolding in what to us seems the faraway land of Little Rock, Arkansas appear foreign to us. So does the vehemence of the opposition to integration. Something we grew up with in Detroit or Toledo or Minneapolis and took for granted as a reality all Americans accepted whether they liked it or not. We stare at the images on the television screen, glancing away now and then to check on our children. Has anyone peed on Nancy's new rug? Has anyone spit up on their stuffed toy? Has anyone caught up with the cat? Reassured, we once again turn our attention to the TV screen as nine clean-scrubbed, immaculately dressed, young people proceed with calm and dignity through a maelstrom of ugliness and evil. We listen to demonstrators spew forth words we're glad our little ones can't understand. We compare the ugly oratory of Faubus with the calm rationality of Eisenhower. We wonder at the courage of parents not unlike ourselves (though less fortunate---we, after all, have married doctors) who send precious children into harm's way for a principle. We are transfixed by these images.

By September 23, calm and reason prevail. President "Ike" leads our nation in choosing the right path. He marshals the authority of the Federal government before, behind and alongside those students as they make their rightful way up the steps of Central High School. Soldiers remain to keep order and to protect the students during that first year. Even those of us who voted for Adlai Stevenson are proud of our Republican President. Even liberal Democrats "like Ike"!

The crisis ends. In early October, we gather again in Nancy's living room to watch the Milwaukee Braves beat the New York Yankees in the 1957 World Series. We celebrate with Milwaukee-born Nancy who decorates her kitchen table with a single red rose in a Schlitz beer can vase. Hank Aaron is the hero of the Series. Somehow, we sense that his achievements and those of the Little Rock Nine have changed our world.

September 2011, Little Rock, Arkansas

The tears have dried on my cheeks by the time Minnie Jean Brown stops speaking. The Central High students disperse and return to class at the historic Little Rock Central High School that now serves all students. The museum guard informs my husband and me we are now free to proceed through the lobby into the museum proper.

Before we do so, I approach Minnie Jean Brown.

"I was a young mother with my first little daughter in 1957. I remember watching television and watching you go up those steps."

Tears flow again, but I struggle out a few more words.

"Thank you for what you did."

Gray-haired Minnie Jean is graceful and gracious as she was so long ago. Outstretched arms offer me a hug. Aging black woman's arms encircle aging white woman's shoulders. Two old women embrace.

Remembering Sidney

Toni Somers

Yawn! Success can be boring. Closing in on my fiftieth birthday, I finally admitted it to myself. I was well educated with a college degree in sociology. I had a successful marriage to a successful physician. I had five beautiful, talented children. I owned a photography studio. I'd been active and effective in local politics. I was comfortable in my community and comfortable in my skin. I should have been content. I'd accomplished things I'd set out to do and more. But success can be boring! Over morning coffee, I verbalized it to my husband.

"You know something, hon? I'm happy with my life. But I'm sorta bored too."

"Hmmm. Uh huh. Is there more coffee? And can you hand me the sports section?"

"Here it is hon."

I poured more coffee.

"I just feel like there's nothing exciting about what I do anymore. Everything's gotten too easy for me. Too routine."

"Uh huh."

Pages rustled.

"I've been thinking of going back to school and getting a degree in art."

"Huh? What on earth for? You're good at what you do. Why art? Why start from scratch?"

"Well, not entirely from scratch. I've always dabbled a little. Now I'd like to do more than just fiddle around with it."

"Whatever you want, I guess. Is there another cinnamon roll?"

Newspaper pages rustle again.

As a youngster I had loved art. I loved to muddle and muck around in clay. Loved to get covered with charcoal and pastel dust. Loved the feel of paint on my hands and cheeks and forehead. When looked in the mirror, I saw an artist. Then in tenth grade I encountered Miss Bowers. I'm certain her intentions for her students were the best. She was conscientious and serious. But she taught art the same way a math teacher might teach quadratic equations. There is only one correct answer to an equation and, in her mind, there was only one right way to draw a flower. Her way was not mine so I quit. Gave up. Threw in the proverbial towel. I would do something else with my life. And I did. But then I approached age fifty, and it hit me.

"Life gets boring when everything's easy. And Miss Bowers was wrong!"

With that realization, I enrolled in college and began work on a Bachelor's degree in art. Boredom ceased the day I became a student in Sidney Larson's painting class.

Sidney taught me more than painting techniques. Early in my art student days he enabled me to express my reasons for being there.

"Orange and blue again! Are those the only damned colors on your palette, Somers?"

Sidney bellowed!

"What are you doing here at your age, anyway? What's the point? You've already got a business, a husband, and grown children? What's the point?"

Why was I here? I asked myself. And I remembered tenth grade high school art class when my creations didn't fit Miss Probst's definition of art.

"I guess I want to prove my high school art teacher was wrong when she judged all art by her standards and tastes and told me my efforts were not acceptable as art," I replied.

Sidney beamed!

"Excellent, Somers! You're right to challenge the opinions of narrow-minded critics! Now show that same rebellious attitude by using more colors than just blue and orange. Enlarge your damned palette and your world!"

Sidney Larson reminded me loudly and often that no matter what colors I started out with, all my paintings ended up orange and blue. Oh, unconsciously I tried to disguise them. Oranges became varied shades of ochre. Blues fluctuated through a spectrum of hues like teal, aquamarine, and indigo. But in truth, I always ended up with orange and blue. Sidney challenged me as he challenged all his students whether they be naïve and tentative innocents from Poplar Bluff, Missouri, hardened toughs from inner city St. Louis, or even, as in my case, local businesswomen approaching the big five-O. Sidney didn't care. Sidney loved us all equally and challenged us all according to our individual needs. I learned as much from Sidney's bellowing at the other students as when he was yelling directly at me.

"Sonya, I saw that same picture in National Geographic! I'm so old I've read 'em all since Geographic was published on stone tablets! Quit plagiarizing and come up with an original composition for once."

"And, Chuck, find a better subject than Salome's dance before Herod! If you think I'm impressed at your painting Bible scenes, think again. Quit looking for excuses to paint beautiful women in skimpy outfits!

"Turn off that damned boom-box, Eric. Nobody can paint with their brains being battered by that noise. If you want music, play Mozart. It's Mozart or nothing. Live with it!"

For two years I started each weekday at 8:oo a.m. and painted until noon while listening to Sidney ranting, raving, cajoling, consoling. He knew what each of us needed and the precise moment at which we needed it.

"Don't let Ida get to you, Somers. She doesn't know any more than you do," Sidney counseled, speaking of the art department's only student older than me. Whether Ida saw me as a competitor for the position of most mature student, or whether she was simply disdainful of my painting, she tormented me regularly. Standing at my right shoulder, Ida critiqued each and every brush stroke. An exceptional painter herself, her ego matched her ability and so did her rudeness.

"Don't let that damned Ida get to you, Somers," Sidney consoled, patting me on the shoulder with an awkward gesture, one he wasn't used to making.

And a moment later,

"Somers, I'll give you twenty dollars if you'll stop smoking those blasted cigarettes! You're going to flick one of those into your turpentine jar one of these days and blow up the whole college!"

"Sidney, you're too stingy to give anyone twenty dollars. Everybody knows that."

My youthful fellow students snickered, pleased that at least someone was permitted to tease Sidney and happy for the "old lady" in their class who go to do it.

Sidney roared his raucous laugh and told me once again,

"Get rid of those damned orange and blue paint tubes, Somers! You're in a rut!"

I remember Sidney who taught me not to listen to narrow-minded critics or to the Ida's of the world. I remember Sidney, who taught me not to plagiarize but to create my own dreams. Sidney who taught me to paint only stories I truly believe. Sidney, who convinced me to quit smoking and kept his promise to pay me twenty bucks. And, most of all, I remember Sidney, who taught me that the colors of life exist in infinite variety, if we only climb out of our ruts to search for them.

We Die in Bits and Pieces

Toni Somers

We die in bits and pieces,
Over time,
Wondering
How and when and where
Life will reach its conclusion.
We die in bits and pieces

We die in bits and pieces
Over time.
Remembering
Bike races and baseball games
Black hair and blushing.
We die in bits and pieces

We die in bits and pieces
Over time
Slowing
Sad

Writer's Curse?

Toni Somers

Why do I write?
To communicate that
Which I perceive to be
A common thread
In the human drama.

I miss things sometimes
A friend's sorrow,
A husband's voice,
A child's cry,
God's whisper.

In searching for generality
I miss the specific.
In searching for eternity
I miss each fleeting moment.
Am I blessed or cursed?

Henry G. Stratmann, MD

Henry is a retired cardiologist and professor of medicine at St. Louis University School of Medicine. Besides his many publications in medical journals, Henry has contributed more than thirty stories and science fact articles to *Analog Science Fiction and Fact*. His books include *Using Medicine in Science Fiction* (2015).

The Invaders

H. G. Stratmann

"**I**'ve brought proof that alien beings have infiltrated our world."

Vincent Davidson, Director of National Intelligence, passed out folders marked "Top Secret" to the other members of the National Security Council all seated around a long table. The President of the United States sat at its head and leafed through the contents of his folder. Then he drummed his fingertips on the tabletop and said, "You believe this 'evidence' backs up your fantastic claim?"

"Yes, Mr. President. These documents prove that thousands of key individuals have been systematically abducted and replaced by extraterrestrial imposters. The scientists we have consulted aren't sure how the aliens managed to take human form. Perhaps they created an age-accelerated body cloned from the 'original' and then transferred an alien's mind into the double's brain. Or they could be what our experts call 'shape-shifters,' able to alter their cellular structure to assume any person's appearance.

"But how the aliens made themselves look human isn't as important as the fact they *have* done it—and what their intentions are."

The Secretary of State rhythmically tapped a pen against her palm. "These lists include high-ranking government officials throughout the world and most members of Congress."

Davidson nodded. "They also name CEOs and other top-level executives of large corporations and financial organizations."

The Vice President chewed on his lower lip until it bled. "Assuming you're right, why do you think these aliens are here?"

Davidson scowled. "They came for the same reason aliens usually do in bad science fiction—to conquer the Earth. What easier way to do that than by surreptitiously assuming the highest positions of power?"

The Secretary of Defense gnawed a fingernail. "But if so many government leaders and businesspeople are really hostile aliens, how do you explain everything that's happened over the past few years?"

Davidson's face darkened. "Actually it was those incredible events that alerted us and other nations' intelligence agencies to the possibility that aliens had taken over. Think of all the world leaders and heads of terrorist groups who suddenly rejected violence. Remember how major companies and banking firms started acting honestly and caring about the consequences of their actions on the rest of society."

He grunted. "Who would have thought three years ago that there would now be peace in the Middle East and throughout the world, a definitive solution to global warming, cheap pollution-free energy, affordable healthcare for everyone, no more world hunger, or all the other social and economic miracles we enjoy now?"

The National Security Advisor picked his nose. "But why would aliens want to improve the world?"

Davidson snorted. "The real question is, why would they want to conquer a planet as messed up as it used to be? Their intelligence must be so far above any human being's that all those problems we found so difficult to solve were easy for them. Now that they have put the world in far better shape than the leaders they replaced were making it, Earth might finally be a worthwhile place for them to rule."

The Secretary of the Treasury loudly passed gas. "It sounds like you have known about this 'threat' for some time. Why are you only informing us now?"

"Until recently my counterparts in other countries and I have just been monitoring the aliens to see what they would do next. We know who they are, and we're poised to 'neutralize' them at any time. In fact, I have a heavily armed team of special agents outside guarding this room, waiting for orders. I'm giving you this information today because we are afraid the aliens have initiated a new plan that will doom the whole human race!"

Davidson lowered his voice. "Remember what happened to that flight the Senate Majority Leader was on two weeks ago? It vanished from radar and couldn't be contacted by radio for over an hour. Then it landed safely, with everyone on board unable to recall what happened during that period—except for the senator. He couldn't remember anything about the last three years, when he was also on a jet that was temporarily 'lost' for the same amount of time."

He sighed. "Now consider what happened after the doctors cleared him to resume his duties. After being so uncharacteristically honest and reasonable for three years, he has reverted to his old habits of cozying up to lobbyists, introducing pork barrel legislation, and stirring up partisan divisions.

"We believe the aliens exchanged their agent for the 'original' senator—and that they plan to do the same with their other duplicates soon!"

The President's digits drummed the table harder. "You say these hypothetical aliens look like humans. Do you know any way to identify them?"

"Yes. Some have nervous habits, like repeatedly striking their fingertips on tabletops or tapping their palms with a pen. Others commit flagrant social faux pas, such as picking their noses or passing gas in public."

The Chief Executive's fingers stopped their incessant tattoo on the table. He and the other Council members glared at Davidson. Finally, the President said, "You also know the Senate Majority Leader was on Air Force One with me and everyone else in this room—except you—when it temporarily 'disappeared' three years ago."

An unearthly expression came to his face. "Yes, your senator was the first and—so far—only human returned. Although we have improved this planet by *your* standards, it still falls well below ours. Despite everything we have done to try civilizing you Earth creatures, your societies are still saturated with mindless greed, hatred, lust, and ignorance. After all our efforts to encourage your kind to act intelligently so it would be worthwhile being your masters, we still experience as much satisfaction from ruling your species as you would reigning over billions of hyperactive chimpanzees. If you let us leave your world in peace, all of your fellow humans will be returned unharmed."

Davidson frowned. "We suspected that's why you're leaving. That's why I called this meeting, to speak on behalf of everyone who knows about you.

"We don't want you to leave Earth or bring our people back!"

The aliens cowered as his voice turned threatening. "It might be better for *you* to end your masquerade—but not for us 'chimps.' Whether you like it or not, we are going to make sure you stay where and 'who' you are..."

The Sinner

H. G. Stratmann

For eons I have walked up this twisting stairway engulfed in blackness. As I numbly lift each leg again and again, I see nothing except the faintly luminescent steps beneath my feet. Alone in this silent ebony void I ponder what I did during my life that condemned me to this fate. I feel like Sisyphus without his stone, perpetually ascending this gently spiraling staircase on a journey without end.

Here in my private hell there is no one to distract me from ruminating on my last thoughts before I died. For what may be eternity I ask myself over and over why Beatrice, my lovely young wife, poisoned me.

As I round a gentle bend in the stairway, for the first time I sense another presence here in the cold smothering darkness. For an instant I glimpse Beatrice's ghostly form as she brushes past me on the steps. The terror frozen on her face makes her look older than I remember. The dark drab prison uniform she wears mocks the exquisite figure I knew so well.

Alone again, I realize that the pitch-black gloom surrounding me is beginning to dissipate and softly brighten like the first subtle shimmer of dawn. A ray of hope gently illumines my soul, telling me that my own misdeeds were not as great as I thought. Somehow I know that my personal purgatory is finally ending and that justice ultimately does prevail.

For I am ascending this celestial stairway—and Beatrice is going down it.

The Warning

H. G. Stratmann

"Y ou must let me speak to him!"

The man pleading desperately was beardless and had strangely bronzed skin. He struggled with the two guards holding his arms until a third one standing behind him yanked viciously on his long jet-black hair.

The richly dressed official to whom he addressed his cries replied coldly, "Why do you want to see him?"

"I have to convince him he shouldn't leave tomorrow!"

The other man held up an oddly shaped dagger. "The guards found this on you. Is this how you planned to 'persuade' him?"

"No... not if he listened to me. If he goes ahead with his plan he'll be inadvertently responsible for the suffering and death of millions—the destruction of whole civilizations and ways of life! Whatever good comes from what he does will be overshadowed by genocide!"

His interrogator sneered. "You talk as if you know the future."

The prisoner hesitated. "I do...in a way you couldn't understand. I know what will happen to my own people and others. Perhaps the horrors I'll describe won't make him change his mind. But in God's name, you must let me try to warn him!"

The official smiled. "So you claim to know the future and to be doing God's work. I will send you to a higher authority on such matters."

He spoke to the guards—and the prisoner went wild. But several well-placed blows from his burly captors made it easy for them to drag away his semiconscious body.

A voice called out from a doorway leading off the

courtyard. "Is anything the matter?"

"Not now. I have taken care of the problem."

"Then follow me. I need to speak with you in private about our final preparations."

The two men entered a cramped dimly lit chamber. The official settled into a chair in front of a small desk. His superior stood hunched behind it, studying the papers and unfurled charts piled on its wooden top. After a moment the latter looked up and said, "What was that disturbance in the courtyard about?"

"We caught a man who claimed to be a 'prophet.' I had him sent to the holy men of the Inquisition for further questioning. They will discover, however painfully for him, whether he practices the black arts or is merely a madman."

"I am sure they will—if the wretch survives their questioning."

As the other man resumed his perusal of the charts the official frowned, considering what he should do next. He had successfully disposed of that idiot in the courtyard—but when would another one appear? The miniature computer implant in his brain had immediately identified that would-be assassin as being of Sioux ancestry. Three of the other five he had stopped in the past month had also been, to use that quaint ancient term, "Native Americans." The remaining two had skin light enough for them to pass as "Moors" despite their distant ancestors originating in western Africa. Those others had been only slightly more difficult to stop despite their carrying much more sophisticated and anachronistic weapons than the latest arrival. But would the next potential killer get close enough to the target to disrupt his own carefully laid plan?

The agent from the Second Age of Time Travel sighed. No wonder the primitives of the First Age—barely a thousand years from now—had quickly destroyed their own so-called civilization and lost the secret of how to travel into the past. Those fools thought they could right every historical wrong using the crudest methods imaginable, without considering how changing the past might produce paradoxes capable of ripping the fabric of Time itself apart.

Fortunately, when the secret of time travel was rediscovered several millennia later, his own contemporaries knew how to erect temporal barriers to avoid altering what was their "present." Unlike their foolish First Age ancestors, he and his comrades possessed the skill and finesse to change history in ways that would merely nudge the River of Time into better tributaries instead of making it overflow its banks in a destructive flood.

Using the augmented computational power of his implant he rapidly ran through countless permutations involving every conceivable parameter. His current plan— the mysterious disappearance of his "superior's" entire expedition a week from now—dramatically increased the probability of a more benign, delayed meeting of cultures a century later. However, although the chance of each one succeeding was small, there were too many ways more late-arriving amateurs from the First Age could interfere and make the resulting future worse instead of better.

The software in his cerebral computer finally concluded that the immediate demise of the target would be nearly as effective as his intended strategy and prevent any potential disasters caused by First Agers. The sharp knife with its steel serrated blade that he had confiscated from the prisoner was still hidden within a long loose sleeve of his tunic. A far cruder weapon than the one from his own time he had intended to use—but at close range, in combination with a genetically enhanced bionic body several times stronger and faster than a contemporary human's, it was sufficiently deadly.

But as the temporal agent started to rise from his seat, the man standing behind the desk reached underneath a chart and extracted a short thin ebony rod. A mental command made its far end emit a teleportation field that enveloped his would-be murderer. The latter, suddenly finding himself in the vacuum of space halfway between the

Earth and Moon, had only seconds of consciousness to ponder what had happened before he died.

Meanwhile the chamber's sole remaining occupant casually replaced the rod under some papers and glanced down again at the navigation charts. But there was no need to study them. The cybernetic processing module replacing most of his organic brain had the information they contained encoded in its database. And he no longer had to pretend to examine them for the benefit of his late associate.

In what would have taken minutes for an unenhanced human but only an instant for him, he mused about the stupidity of Second Agers and their dangerous attempts to "improve" the past. They should have realized that, thousands of years in *their* future, those like him from the final, Third Age of Time Travel would already know their plans and stop them.

Today three wooden ships waited for him in the nearby harbor. Tomorrow, long after replacing the "original" one, the man who future ages knew as "Christopher Columbus" would sail into a history that—for better and worse—*had* to be.

Conetta Taylor, RScP

Conetta once was a professional portrait photographer. Now, she finds entertainment by photographing scenes of nature, architecture, active and still life. As a licensed spiritual counselor, she enjoys writing matters of the heart and spirit. She and her husband Thomas, of thirty-five years, have resided in Nixa, Missouri, since 1979.

The Day I Mowed the Lawn

Conetta Taylor

I n the late 1980s, my husband and I experienced a money crunch. For those who may not understand what that is, here's an example. On a two-week pay scale, there is a slide to billing due dates and the paycheck dates, they slowly move farther apart. Then, every six months you receive three paychecks and that sets everything back to an even schedule. Unless you have fine-tuned budgeting skills, that last month before the third paycheck arrives, makes those monthly payments extremely tight.

My husband has always been forthright in planning for our future. His paycheck, supplying the 401K plan, mutual funds, and IRA's and what was left over made up our budget for living expenses.

We had a successful photography studio home business for several years, but after I made the decision to close the studio, our immediate savings soon began to dwindle and my husband's paycheck was still divided into these non-approachable savings funds.

We were uptight because the night before I figured out exactly how much money we needed. Here's the scenario: It was Wednesday morning and by 4:30 Thursday afternoon, we needed an additional $68 to pay our utility bill. It was already late, and if I didn't pay it the very next day, they could shut off our electricity and water. By 5 p.m. Friday I needed another $96, to pay the bills that were due by then. In fact, every bill we had needed to be paid by the following Tuesday. Payday was Wednesday, exactly one week away. In order to pay all the bills on time, I needed a grand total of $648 the day before payday.

As my husband left for work, he asked me, "What are

you going to do?"

"I'm going to pray and meditate. Then I'll do whatever I feel I am directed to do from there."

He nodded, released a deep breath, kissed me and he left for work.

I... prayed and meditated. I released my concerns and I merged with a feeling that everything really is fine.

What did I feel I was directed to do? One of the things I disliked doing most of all. It did not make sense to me. I did not understand what doing this particular chore had to do with anything that had been on my mind when I went into meditation.

Much to my disfavor, I knew what I was instructed to do. What I was inspired to do. Therefore, I set out to... mow our lawn.

While we had the studio, we had lawn care capably provided by our key photographer, my over ambitious brother-in-law whose hobby was landscaping. After closing the studio, he moved to Oregon and that left the entire lawn in our care.

Do understand, this is not a normal yard. It is over three city lots in size and due to our previous outdoor photo park, it was landscaped with lots of flowerbeds, water gardens, photo prop scenes, and park benches. There were large logs, rocks, and partitions of bamboo, pampas grass, an assortment of fences, a waterfall, a gazebo and lots and lots of trees.

Mowing this lawn was a hard business and I never before found pleasure in mowing it. But I knew that was what I was supposed to do that day. So even though I did not understand the purpose, I followed my intuition.

I just started and was only on my second row when my husband pulled up in the driveway. He was driving through town on business when he saw me mowing our lawn.

Taken by surprise, he asked, "What are you doing? I thought you'd go out and get a job or something!"

He must have been in shock. I tried to explain to him

that even if I did that, I wouldn't get a paycheck any sooner than his would be in next week. No. I had prayed and meditated and I knew I was to be mowing our lawn, no matter that it didn't make any sense to me either.

He only stayed maybe three minutes, but his last statement was firm and had something to do with "getting a job" and "learning to live in the real world."

It made me think, even as I continued to mow our lawn. When I consciously prayed to release my concerns, something physically changed. I had actually released the worry that I had been feeling earlier. I believed everything would be fine. My husband, on the other hand, went off to work, taking his concerns with him.

As I continued to mow the lawn, I prayed for him, to feel calm the way I did.

It did not change the outward fact that I still needed money to meet the deadlines for these bills, but praying changed the urgency. It changed the feeling of being desperately out of control into a feeling of direction. Even if I didn't understand it, I could trust God was in control.

As it turned out I *was* on course.

During the fourth row of mowing- another car pulled into my driveway. It was a previous photography customer. She had placed an order for an enlargement, but never picked it up. She explained that she had experienced a money crunch and couldn't afford to get it last year. But, she couldn't get the portrait off her mind and today she decided to come over and see if I still had it. She paid me her balance in cash.

As she drove away, I stood there holding in my hand the balance paid of exactly $68! I took that, to the city hall and paid my utility bill, in full. Within twenty minutes I was willingly mowing my lawn again.

Then another car pulled up. Without hesitation I immediately went to see who it was.

I did not recognize the man's face at all. He explained, a long time ago he had us do some pictures of him in his clown costume and make-up, since then he had gotten distracted with his *real* job. With enthusiasm he said, "Today, I was driving through town and happened to see you mowing the lawn and thought I'd stop to see if you still have those proofs and if I can possibly buy them." I smiled, and nodded as I gratefully walked inside with this clown. His very presence thoughtfully reminded me to keep my sense of humor, even in tough times.

I paid two more bills. All the bills that needed to be paid by Friday 5 p.m. were now paid. It was still Wednesday and it wasn't even noon yet!

When I returned home I checked my mailbox. I was grateful to find a check in the mail. I decided I'd run to the bank a little later, but for now, I just *really wanted* to get back to mowing the lawn!

I had been mowing for maybe an hour in a state of total gratitude for all that was unfolding. I had prayed, meditated and followed my intuition, my knowingness, and I was so rewarded. Worry would not have gotten me any further along. In fact, it would have sent me in another direction altogether.

Another car pulled up. A young couple got out and waved to me. Happily, I once again turned off the lawn mower. They explained, "You guys did our wedding pictures a couple of years ago. We want to apologize for not getting back with you. But right after the wedding we moved to Iowa and we're down this week visiting. We were planning to call and come by before we left the area, but we were driving by and we just happened to see you in the yard and we already feel pretty guilty about taking so long to get back with you. We love our pictures and we want to pay you what is yours, so if it's okay with you, here is a check for all the proofs." I smiled, and that wasn't even everybody.

With all my visitors, it took me nearly two full days to get my lawn cut. By Friday morning I had already paid all of the bills that were currently due. All $648 of them! In two days, I received more than $700.

Because I was open and receptive and obedient to doing what I knew was true for me to be doing at that time. I didn't have to understand any of the outer circumstances. I only had to understand where I put my faith. In the stillness, I chose to put my faith in God, not in fear.

What is the natural tendency when we have a need or when we are suffering in some form or fashion? Is it not to think about, contemplate or pray for the need? Why then are we so surprised to find ourselves deeper and deeper into the problem? It is where we are focused. The need, rather than the desired end result, has become our main concern. The only meaning that life can have to us is the meaning that it has in and through us.

Paul wrote a letter, known as the Book of Philippians. This is a letter of confidence, although he was facing considerable personal difficulties and challenges, his main concern was for unity in faith. That we should not be worried or anxious. Rather, we should rejoice and be thankful. We should express our thanks to God for the answer, not focus on our problems.

Paul acknowledged a letter and a gift that he had received. He was assuring his friends that even though he and they had been experiencing fierce conflicts and struggle, he was grateful and did not need their pity.

According to Paul, "Let our understanding be pure and just and admirable. If anything is excellent or praiseworthy, think about *these* things." Remember the scripture to pray without ceasing? Whatever we are thinking of and how we choose to think about it, *that* is our real prayer.

Happiness can be experienced in everyday human life, but scripture declares that true joy results from understanding. We do indeed live, and move, and have our being with God. Choose to feel the feeling of peace for whomever we are praying. Make the choice to focus on the laws of Truth, what is right and pure, what is the highest and best for all concerned.

By praying with conscious awareness, we move into a deeper sense of a bigger picture. We release concern and feel gratitude for being a part of the process. Realization of being an active participant unfolds with a new, enlightened understanding of just how connected we all really are.

Ralph Waldo Emerson said, "All I have seen teaches me to trust the Creator for all I have not seen."

That money crunch I was telling you about certainly was not the first challenge in my life, neither has it been my last. Moreover, that day of deciding to mow my lawn firmed the foundation for me to know that I know. To plan ahead for the inevitable and be prepared for the unexpected is common sense. Learning to trust the process of a higher purpose at work not only becomes easier with practice, it can be joyful. I always look forward to the unveiling of the next pure and precious blessing that I have yet to see. Memories of mowing the lawn that day continue to serve me well.

Thomas Taylor

Thom is a psychological illusionist who has entertained audiences since 1970. He combines storytelling, audience participation, and humor creating live on-stage situation comedies to the enjoyment of his patrons. Whether you experience him as Thomas Taylor, Thom Taylor or as Nicholas Nicklebie Inskyov, your experience will be remembered for years.

Dueling Banjos

Thomas Taylor

We finally got home, but before we did, got chewed out by a teenager, backed into a pole, blew a tire and almost got robbed on the side of the road, and or wacked by two guys in an old, beat-up, rusted, black pickup, claiming to be Triple-A tire changers.

Interesting to note, these guys had no markings on their person or truck, did not ask us for our Triple-A card, show us their ID or license, did not have us sign anything proving who we were, nor was the truck even a tow truck. Furthermore, it was void of any CB antennae, which additionally perked my alarm. As they approached our van to inquire as to our need of their assistance I could hear the sound of a banjo and guitar emanating from their four-wheel drive, mud-hole racing competition, hillbilly squeeze-box truck console..

Listening more intently, the second instrument was in fact not a guitar but a banjo. This gave me the idea no one here was pickin' and grinnin', especially now not me or my wife. Now I don't know if the actual music was coming from the console of their collateralized heap or from my imagination, but the tune of "Dueling Banjos" was becoming more distinct in my mind. It was the first time ever in all my traveling years I unlocked my hidden mobile gun safe, fearing that after the tire was changed my wife and I would be done in, in broad daylight on the side of a busy freeway somewhere near the legendary town Li'l Abner was domiciled. I was interrupted by two grease-faced, tattered-torn-clothed, tobacco-chew-spitting dudes offering to "put on my spare."

Praying we one, even had a spare; two, it was full of air;

and three, it was a full-sized tire, we somehow allowed the procedure to begin. The procedure started with a simple floor jack shoved under our van in the wrong place where it could easily punch a hole in the floor or crimp a brake line as opposed to simply raising the wheel to change it. Stopping this tragedy from happening, I realized they were not with the "good hands" people and maybe not even a "good neighbor."

Next, the rear hatch was raised for access to the spare tire hoist-lift in which we had to remove some of the treasures we acquired on our trip. Thankfully, the hoist worked on the way down but unfortunately not back up. Consequently, we stuffed the blown-out tire not under the van where it was designed to go but inside the van cramming it in with all the precious pretties. As these, not-employed-by-NASCAR, duo-grease-monkey, Indy-quick-change tire artists completed their work and got into their truck, I quickly whipped out a five-dollar bill as a tip. Not so much as a reward but as an offering to God thanking God my beloved and I were still alive. As one of them took the five he asked, "What's that for?"

I explained it was a tip like you would give a waiter, but they had done a lot more than serve grits and chitlins. As he shoved the Federal Reserve fiat note with Lincoln's image on the face into his pocket, I realized I was in the part of the country where the name Lincoln might still be shootin' words. He, in full southern hospitality, thanked me, pointing out the spare was pretty low and to get some air in it at the next truck stop, which reminded me this pit-stop crew wasn't even equipped with a pressure tank.

As my wife fumbled to stuff her unused Triple-A card, driver license and cell phone back into her purse, I hurriedly encouraged her to leave without delay before those two characters from the likes of Dogpatch USA changed their mind, or our spare went flat. Upon which an elderly friend called my cell phone and told us a story, asking if we thought he just got scammed out of more than a thousand dollars. Yes, he had. By virtue of his timing, it confirmed to us that we did narrowly escape a scam.

Next, I got chewed out by a teenager–maybe twenty-something–out-of-wedlock mom for pointing out it's dangerous to leave two babies and a toddler all alone outside in a twin jogging stroller in front of a busy convenience store on the Fourth of July weekend, on a forty-five percent decline aiming downhill toward the bustling freeway. In an uneducated, countrified southern-drawl defense, I was told, "Them brakes was on!" I pointed out the stroller could be bumped and roll through this crowded truck stop parking lot down onto freeway traffic. In a tongue-lashing civil defense, she instructed me she had the right to live her life any way she chooses. I rebutted her by agreeing with her, with the exception that I was not concerned with her life but the lives of the three left -alone innocent babies exposed to heat prostration, unrelieved hyperthermia, dehydration, sun burn, mosquito bites, being hit by a car or semi-truck, not to mention kidnapping and murder!

I further instructed her in the most liberal fascist way that they weren't her kids anyway but wards of the state, that she was just an inconsequential breeder and that is why it apparently does "take a village to raise a child!" in the most Clintonian way. She stomped off down the dirt road at a speed that made power walking look like a stroll in the park. I could see smoke steaming off of her in the distance, not completely sure if it was the release of anger she had for me pointing out the obvious, or the cigarettes she just bought at the most inconvenient truck stop store I ever came upon. Upon crossing the congested lot back to our van parked near the distant air hose, my wife mentioned a most peculiar scene she just witnessed while awaiting my return. That of a teenage girl pushing a stroller full of babies at a most unusual high stomping pace, all the while flailing her arms and arguing with herself in a crazed, wild manner.

Jan A. Way

Jan had forty-three years in law when he retired after seventeen years as a district judge in Wyandotte County, Kansas. He has written several thousand senryu impressionistic poems after beginning to write in 2010. Since July 2014, he has switched to traditional poetry.

Amish Night Glow

Jan A. Way

In the night, clip clopping,
The Amish buggy,
A giant orange triangle
Reflecting on the back.

Road apples steaming
In the cool night,
Headlights catching
Wisps of vapor.

Horse's nostrils blowing
Without a whip.
A black box moving,
Sowing fertilizer.

Lights probe and strobe,
Blinding the left eyes,
At eighty miles per hour
Gone into civilization,

Between me and thee.

One-Legged Throne

Jan A. Way

A four-legged manger
A three-legged milk stool
Two-legged people
Stood and walked about

Golgotha
Mount Calvary
A one legged throne
Holds up two feet

Above the ground
Above the snakes
Preparing to go
Air walking

Shattered Wine

Jan A. Way

Two glasses of fine wine;
He would delight her,
With his gift and visit.

Hearing her in the downstairs
Parlor, he poured two goblets,
Whisper stepped to surprise her
Shiny eyes. He stopped.

Inside the door, two lovers
Deep in a vintage kiss
Jumped apart.
A stem snapped, cut his hand.

Goblets crashed, the angel's portion
Lost. Red blood dripped, fermented,
Absorbed by a white rug,
Except for the aftertaste.

Imogene Altis Woods

Imogene says her writing focuses on people, places, or things, plus memories. The people she writes about are usually relatives or people found in doing genealogy. Her book, *The Ordinary Infantry Men: Heroes Then, Heroes Again*, was for the men she communicated with about WWII. It contains their stories, hers, and her KIA father's.

August 30, 2013

A Visit to Bass Pro Museum

Imogene Altis Woods

Guns can be an abomination because they have the capacity to kill. To see their beauty and to appreciate the intricacy, one must visit the new gun museum at Bass Pro.

I'm no hunter; I don't shoot a gun and usually have no interest in them. However I do have an interest in history and as a historian, I was caught up in the exhibit as much as a hunter or gun owner might. We came away in awe of what had been done at Bass Pro to house the museum for sporting guns and their history.

Johnny Morris, with his elaborate Bass Pro Shops, has shown us that he appreciates nature, and within his store has transported us to scenes that some people never have experienced–animals, waterfall, fish, waterways, etc. Whatever he, or they (however), can dream, one seems to find it somewhere in the store on Campbell. Similar decor can be found anywhere he chooses to build.

Nevertheless, when it was announced that Bass Pro would be housing the National Rifle Association Museum in their store, we paid little attention. A collection of guns–yawn, yawn.

We frequented the store while they were building and puzzled at their narrow mezzanine-type structure. Nothing impressive. Looked small. Must not be very big collection. It was when the expansive stairway to the new addition was being built that we scratched our head in puzzlement. Terribly big and expansive! Then it started reminding us of mansions of the south where we'd toured. But they finished and opened without us.

This week we finally decided to make a visit. The newspaper reporter gave it a big thumbs-up. It shouldn't take long–in spite of the good reviews. Were we in for a surprise! More than one in fact. We've now gone through maybe a fourth of their offerings. And plan to return for our next "edition"–part three, in our case.

It reeks of the new smells and shiny plate glass but there was more than that–there was a feeling of elegance– the metals of the barrels were found in rails, etc. with their dull but polished finery. The woodwork, done in a smooth mahogany color, was intricate polished fine wood similar to that found in the stocks of the finer guns. The ceiling tiles took us back in time to those of yesteryears with their slight echo. The polished floors were perfection. Even before the guns, pictures, murals, exhibits had been moved in, there had to be a feeling of luxury. Impressive! For a gun museum? Unusual, surely. Bright lights allowed one to take in all the details.

After mounting that expansive sweeping stairway that tapered to an entry door above, we started on the left side only and found ourselves immersed in the history of weapons. Behind each gun arrangement was a sepia mural, usually with people, showing us the time period of that particular selection of guns. The guns, arranged sometimes in clusters, sometimes mounted on clear gun racks, sometimes alone, had clear notations of what we were seeing and usually either their place in history or the mechanics of the device. Along with our country's history, we were introduced to the development of the workings of the gun or the significance of that particular model. We read every word and soaked in the fact that guns had played a large part in our country's history. Without them, it would not have been the same. One had to come away with an appreciation of what they had sometimes caused positively.

Each section was climate-controlled and individually lit. Some guns were property of the NRA–the donor was named. Some guns were on loan only–again with a name. Credit was given to the type and model of each artifact.

Reproductions of famous paintings pertaining to the west graced the empty spaces in the exhibit cabinet. All had signs indicating they would be replaced this fall with the original, which is now being refurbished. What could be the value of some of these as originals? Some of the paintings were on-loan only.

Between the sections were found smaller, individual cubicles containing life-size dioramas. It was here that one could be truly amazed at the depth of planning that had gone into this exhibition. Not only were the mannequins life-size but their garments appeared to have been hand-made of the same original-type construction and materials. With the one containing the Indian and his buckskin, one could see the roughness from the skin as it had been tempered into fabric–the manner of setting in the sleeve, the "button-on" legging, etc. transported us back in time. Brush, weeds, etc. added to the realism. Another diorama was Lewis & Clark with his hand-made garments, even the collarless blousy off-white shirt. Still another diorama showed a "modern?" well-equipped hunting lodge. This probably took up four feet by four feet of space.

The total space that we had covered in our ninety minutes of history alone covered in length maybe fifty feet. We had barely touched the museum contents and the soles of our feet were yelling for rest. A trip around the corner to Hemingway's for lunch would help to relieve the burning.

After eating, refreshed by our lunch, we went into the museum through the Archery section, not stopping to look. We found ourselves on a higher level than previously. In front of us stood an eight-foot (I'm guessing at size) black bear standing on his hind legs–mounted of course. He was impressive, towering over even our tallest men.

A smaller room to our right would be our destination for today's part two. We noted it was devoted to former president Teddy Roosevelt. There were personal artifacts and hunting pictures of Teddy. An extremely large timetable showed the important events in his life. He was a big-game hunter (elephants, etc.)–how could he miss those humongous beasts. A life-size diorama of Africa gave us the feel of the tall brown-weeded area. As a tribute to the big-game hunter were smaller, stuffed game recognized as still available in Africa. Also shown was his letter to the NRA complimenting them and containing his dues for lifetime membership.

On his presidential side, the focus was on his formation of national parks .A large wall map highlighted all the parks that he had been instrumental in forming–I didn't count the number, which was significant for their times, but their numbers have also increased drastically since then.

Off to the side, with no seeming significance, was a set of cased pistols Teddy had given to Cabot Lodge. They were beautiful and expensive as well as rare now. This gave us another side of this president. However no history or significance was given to the ebony black oversized chair setting in one corner. It was very unique and sturdy looking. A 400-pound man might be able to sit on it.

I thought I knew a little about Teddy Roosevelt, but this room's exhibit showed me that I knew practically nothing. I decided a book of his life would be nice to obtain. Ironically, in a newspaper a couple of days later, I found reference to an upcoming biography about Teddy to be published by a noted prize-winning author. Maybe I'll just wait on that one.

We had seen this small room and one side only of the entry exhibits. We're looking forward to at least two more days, maybe three. We're trusting they will be on the same exciting caliber as what we had seen. The worth of the entire exhibit has been estimated by one at more than $25 million. Clearly, we are most fortunate to have this exhibition where we can see it. I was so engrossed in the readings and analyzing that I didn't notice how others were reacting. The strolling docents, members of NRA, could probably have enlightened me on this matter. We look forward to phase three–maybe next week–this would probably be the famous guns of the past. We understand that the originals are there for us to view.

December 1943

Imogene Altis Woods

We're moving. To another state. We have been living in Oklahoma but now we're moving back to Missouri. I was born there but I don't remember much about living in Missouri.

Riding in the car gets real tiresome. I have my books with me—three of them. One of them I can't read most of the words in it because we haven't had those at school yet. I just look at the pictures in it. A cousin in Blackwell gave that one to me. The other two are my Dick and Jane books. I'm six now so I can read. The car is noisy and bumpy but if I hold my finger under the words I can keep my place. Grownups are strange. Always before they would ask me to read aloud and would act real proud; but not now. When I read aloud, Mom says to read to myself.

I don't understand why they act so strange now. Mom cries a lot and always has red eyes. Daddy is just quiet. He's always quiet but more so now. Mommy says we're going to live in Springfield and Daddy will be living somewhere else—Army, I think she said. I don't know anything about where Army is but I guess not in Springfield.

"Mom, I need to pee." She said there wasn't a good place now so just hold it and read my book. I was tired of reading.

So I quit reading and just sat there staring at the inside of the car and thought. I sure hope Springfield has teachers who aren't so crabby. My teacher gave me a spanking before we'd been in school two months. She said I was humming. She sure didn't know me or she would have known that I couldn't hum. Even if I could, I'd be too afraid to be heard. Boy, was Daddy and Mommy mad. Daddy went to the teacher and told her something. I don't know what he said to her. One day we had a new teacher. Mommy said the teacher had a nervous breakdown. I don't know what that is, but it got us a new teacher. The teacher seemed okay but so did the first one for a while.

We had a flat tire. Daddy said there was air in the tire and the tire had a hole in it so all the air got out. The car wouldn't go then. One side of the car was lower than the other side. When I watched Daddy patch the tire, I noticed the smell. I've smelled it before. It's not unpleasant, just different. We always have patches with us so I guess people have these problems all time.

The weather seems to be getting colder. It's nearly Christmas. We celebrated Christmas early this year in Oklahoma. Daddy and a friend took us kids for a ride in the car looking in the sky for Santa Claus. He was supposed to come in on a sleigh driven by reindeer. We never did see him. Daddy thought he saw him once but it turned out to be something else. When we got back to the friends' house, Santa had already been there and left some gifts. I guess we were looking in the wrong direction. That was our last Oklahoma Christmas, Mom and Dad said.

I sure wish Mom had not packed my leggings as my legs are so cold now. She had just made me a new coat and a pair of leggings, but it was warm when we left so she packed away the leggings. At least I have the coat. Boys have it lucky as they wear long pants so their legs don't get cold. At home, I would sit with me legs under me and spread my dress over them. In the car there isn't room to sit like that. My dress is pretty short and it's a long ways down to my anklet tops to try to cover.

Mom says we'll be staying with Grandma and Grandpa in Springfield and that I'll have someone to play with all time. She's my age and she's three weeks younger than me. Mom says she's my aunt. I thought aunts were always older, more like Mom's age. Guess I was wrong.

I had another aunt but Mom says she's in heaven now;

her name was Alice. We went to a town called Mountain Grove sometime past. Grandma and Grandpa lived there then. She said Alice would be there but every time she mentioned Alice, she always cried. Somebody asked Mom if she wanted him to lift me up to see inside the puzzling big, long box with the pretty pink material hanging out. I was too short to see inside it. Mom shook her head no. I had been chasing the pretty yellow long-haired cat that ran under the big box. It wouldn't let me catch it. The cat knew that it could dart under the skirt of the box and I couldn't get it. Every time I came close to the box, Mom told me to go somewhere else to play. I just decided then, I didn't want anything to do with the box. I never did see Aunt Alice, and I didn't see what was in the big box in my grandparent's house that so many people came to look in. Oh, well, I had the cat to chase and pet if I could catch it, and I had somebody to play with. So I had a good time.

That was one of the times that Mom didn't curl my hair. She didn't today either. She calls my hair Shirley Temple curls. Somehow she uses rags and rolls my hair around the rags and my curls then bounce when I just up and down. It's a fun feeling when I do that.

I had a friend in Blackwell who had Shirley Temple paper dolls. They were special, and I didn't have that kind. Mine were just the usual. One day as I walked home from her house, a big dust storm came up. I couldn't even see where I was walking. I got scared then and started crying because I was lost. And I lost some of my paper dolls then. Mom cut them out for me as I was having trouble with scissors. Every time I tried to write or to cut, Mom would place the pencil or scissors in my other hand. I have a big knot on my middle finger that sometimes bleeds and I suck on it when it gets hard. Wish I could use my left hand instead.

There's not much to do in the car. My doll that I've had so many years is in the back of the car, packed away I suppose. That leaves me nothing to do. I get sleepy when I ride. I wonder what happens if Daddy gets sleepy as Mom doesn't drive. Will the car drive itself? Or do we get in the ditch? I sure hope he doesn't get sleepy.

"How much longer 'til we get there?" Be patient is the answer from Mom. Hmmm. That's no answer. "I need to stop to pee." There's no place here, unless it's by the road, she said and besides, you remember our car is old and when it stops, it's hard to get it started again. And you remember that we only have so much gas allotted to us . Be a good girl and we'll see if they have your favorite soda—orange or strawberry--when we get to the service station. You know how you like to watch the bubbles when the gas comes down.

"... Oh... oh... oh... no!" Just the mention of liquid was too much. Too late now.

The Friendship Quilt

Imogene Altis Woods

I stared with mixed feelings at the name written on the raffle ticket I had drawn. A feeling of glad familiarity with a name that I knew, but a shiver that said something wasn't right. Somebody in the audience should have been the winner because they had worked so hard selling tickets and hoping one of their contacts would win. A temptation to put the ticket back in swept over me but that would have been not only illegal but also disloyal to my new friend Jana.

Jana contacted me sometime after Mom's death when finding Mom's obituary on the internet. She had bid on a friendship quilt on E-Bay and obtained the quilt. The quilt, made during the 1930s, was put together with various blocks, each made by different woman with the block maker's name embroidered on their block. My mom's name, Hazel Altis, was not a common name and easy to trace. Could it have been my mother, she asked? I didn't know.

So she and I both started searching for any indication that it might have been a community where Mom had lived. We knew it was Texas County, so being familiar with genealogy, I soon located the area. Yes, it was possible as far as area and as far as quilting, absolutely, as I had about twenty-nine quilts that I owned made by her. But knowing Mom with her shyness, I wasn't so sure that she would be involved in a community project. The other names on the quilt were the only clues. Further search proved that, unless she had lived in a different community than I knew about, the quilt block was not done by my mother. There had apparently been another Hazel Altis. Jana and I kept in contact. She moved to Oklahoma close to Fort Sill and did some searching there for WWII records that might have mentioned my dad being stationed there for training. At Christmas or if something interesting came up we corresponded by e-mail. A friendship quilt brought together two strangers in different parts of the country.

About the same time a beautiful quilt was put on display at the Civil War Round Table meeting, and members were encouraged to sell raffle tickets as a money-making project. Not wanting to sell the tickets, we bought some, hoping that we wouldn't win because we didn't need another quilt; we'd just have them draw another name. Curiosity made me ask about the quilt maker. Since a member of Piecemakers had acted as liaison between the donor organization and CWRT, I asked if they might like more quilts. I didn't quilt and had enough hobbies already so didn't want to learn to quilt; besides we had more than enough quilts. Thirteen quilt tops were donated to Ozark Piecemakers Quilt Guild.

The next year, CWRT brought out the new quilt for raffle; it sure looked familiar. Yes, it was one of Mom's quilt tops and it was beautifully hand quilted. This time I felt obligated to take a packet of raffle tickets to sell. After procrastinating for a while, I realized that I was not a sales person.

It would be so much easier to simply purchase the tickets myself and put other people's names on the tickets. I chose people who were either relatives of Mom, those who inquired about Mom's health during her illness with us, or who showed an interest in her afterward. I drafted a letter and sent to each person telling them of the situation and that their name had been entered in the raffle drawing. I took my packet and money back to the next meeting and felt good that it was finally a done deed.

It wasn't until the drawing, when I had been asked to reach into the container of ticket stubs, that I had feelings of remorse and wondered whether I had done the right thing. I had this feeling of dishonesty–I hadn't actually sold the tickets. Granted, the drawing was legitimate and honest.

Maybe if someone else had done the drawing, I would have felt less concern about the whole situation. But, again, the deed was done. The quilt was sent to Oklahoma.

In retrospect, I see how my mom's interest in quilting had been an instrument in causing events to happen. Her interest gave Jana two quilts, both linked to my mom, Hazel Altis. Mom's interest in quilting had created products that were eventually donated to a good cause. And a quilt had brought together two people that previously were unknown to each other, making for a friendship between them. Two quilts could now be called Friendship Quilts–each in its own way.

www.ingramcontent.com/pod-product-compliance
Lightning Source LLC
Chambersburg PA
CBHW071240170626
46809CB00001B/20